God in the Teeth of Suffering

Tackling the Toughest Obstacle to Faith in God

God in the Teeth of Suffering

Tackling the Toughest Obstacle to Faith in God

C. Jerriton Brewin

2016

God in the Teeth of Suffering: Tackling the Toughest Obstacle to Faith in God— published by the Rev. Dr. Ashish Amos of the Indian Society for Promoting Christian Knowledge (ISPCK), Post Box 1585, Kashmere Gate, Delhi-110006.

ISBN: 978-81-8465-588-9

e-pub ISBN: 987-81-8465-592-6

Laser typeset by

ISPCK, Post Box 1585, 1654, Madarsa Road, Kashmere Gate, Delhi-110006 • *Tel:* 23866323

e-mail: ashish@ispck.org.in • ella@ispck.org.in
website: www.ispck.org.in

Dedicated

to

My Mother

Contents

III

The Christian Response to the Problem of Evil

Acknowledgements

I would like to thank my parents and my brother for their constant support in writing this book. I thank my friend in Christ, John Joshua, for the encouragement and interest in bringing out this book. I specially thank Rev. Gibson Johndas for providing the initial steps that made the publication of this book possible. I thank my grandfather, Rev. Simson Sigamony, for the constant motivation and healthy critiques of the book. I thank Rev. Thomas Thangaraj, author of *The Crucified Guru*, for writing the Foreword for the book. I also thank all my friends who were well-wishers who supported me. My sincere thanks to my publisher, ISPCK, for giving my book wings to fly. Above all, I thank the Lord for crafting every stage of this long and difficult process of publishing this book.

Foreword

Let me begin by congratulating Dr Jerriton Brewin for his bold and thoughtful engagement with the most complex theological question of all times, namely, how we tackle the presence of evil in a world created by a loving God. This book is the result of thoroughgoing research, careful analysis, and creative proposal. Brewin begins his project with some of the philosophical issues connected to the linking of the presence of evil and the existence of God. Then he moves to look at the way Buddhism, Islam, and Hinduism have addressed the problem of evil. Finally, he offers his own theological proposal, having looked at the way theodicy has been addressed in the history of Christianity and in the Bible itself.

Two things stand out for me while reading this book. First, here is a young medical doctor, who is not a professionally trained theologian, addressing the problem of evil with utmost seriousness and clarity. It is really impressive to find the interweaving of medical experience and biblical knowledge in a creative way to propose a new way of understanding the question of theodicy. Second, Brewin is able to move out of dry logical and scientific arguments to an imaginative presentation of God as an artist engaged in painting a picture of the world, one brush stroke at a time, while moving towards a full and perfect picture. His excellent use of garden imagery is very helpful in understanding his tentative but firm solution to the problem of evil. Of course, not all theologians and laity would agree with the conclusions of Brewin since it is based on a particular type of biblical realism. But what *God in the Teeth of Suffering* does is to propel our thinking about biblical theodicy into a fresh set of questions and even more fresh ways of answering those questions.

I commend this book with great enthusiasm to all who wish to explore the problem of evil. Let me wish Brewin God's blessings on his witness to the abiding love of God in the midst of suffering and evil.

Rev. Dr. M. Thomas Thangaraj,
Retired Presbyter, Church of South India,
Professor Emeritus of World Christianity,
Candler School of Theology,
Emory University, Atlanta, GA, USA.

Preface

eing a student of medicine, it has become my routine to see people suffer, and suffer a lot. As a Christian, this led me to ask the inevitable question: God, when you're there, why? I had locked up this question in myself and never really began any search for answers. One day, one of my Christian high school friends met with an accident and had to amputate his foot. Some years after the incident, he slowly began to question his religious convictions about God. In his search for answers, he had come across a video created by an atheist who had brought up the problem posed by evil and suffering for those who believe in God. God is there – all knowing and all powerful – and yet he is simply sitting there, allowing evil and suffering to continue in this world. If there really is a God, then shouldn't we expect this world to be without pain and suffering? My friend sent me the video to watch and respond. Having watched the video, I wrote a small article on the issue of God and suffering and shared it in a social networking site. But deep down I was unsatisfied with the little expertise I had in addressing this important problem which every believer in God has to face. As I began reflecting more deeply on the problem of suffering, one day when my father and I were driving down the road in our car, he happened to talk about an old friend of his who had been a fervent Christian worship leader during his college days but who eventually lost his faith upon reflecting deeply on the problem of suffering by concluding that if there really is a God, then he wouldn't be allowing all the crimes and misery that fall upon people every day. Later, doubts and questions emerged inside my own family circle and I felt the need to say something about it as clear and satisfying as possible. So I began to search extensively for good answers to the problem of evil and suffering, which led me to read several books and articles and listen to lectures and forums by some of the world's leading philosophers, scientists and theologians on the question of God and suffering. Many of them had great things to say that were highly satisfying, both intellectually and emotionally, but ultimately I found that none of the books takes into account the full scope of the available information on the issue of God and suffering and provide a coherent, composite and a rich response to the question of God and suffering. Some books talk on a highly intellectual level and is circulated mostly within the academic circle of philosophers and theologians alone. Others are too simplistic which leave us with more questions than answers. Some do not draw out the full implications of a particular thesis, leaving us to wonder how and why the thesis is related to the problem of suffering. Some are frustratingly incomplete, talking about only one aspect of the problem of evil, either philosophical, pastoral or theological. And some do not get the facts right. In this book, I have tried my best to overcome these limitations by offering something that is both *accessible* to the wider general public and *comprehensive* in taking up and addressing many aspects related to the problem of suffering. I have, in the first part of my book, crystallized the theses of several first-rank academic philosophers and put them together in a format that is, to the best of my knowledge, easily understandable and readily usable. In the second part of the book, I have outlined three major religions and their undertaking of the problem of suffering. And in the third part of my book, I have synthesized several strands of biblical theology as defended by leading biblical scholars, while criticizing others, and breaking traditional barriers, I have proposed a new way of looking at the problem of evil and suffering by using the metaphor of a garden. Although I may not by academically qualified to write on this subject, I am confident that I have dealt with the 'problem of evil' in a way that will leave academics surprised. I have taken the pain and hard work to write this book after years of deep reflection and wrestling with the problems myself. I hope and pray that this book will help readers better think about the problem which evil and suffering pose on existence of God and find new ways of thoughtfully dealing with the problem and eventually come out with an unshakable faith in the Christian God even in the teeth of all suffering.

Glossary

Agnostic – A person who suspends judgment. In relating to God, he neither affirms that God exists nor affirms that God does not exist. He makes no judgment concerning the existence of God by saying that he doesn't know whether God exists or not.

Argument – In philosophy and critical thinking, an argument is a set of propositions (or premises) that will lead to a logical conclusion. It is not used to designate a quarrel, dispute or a fight.

Atheist – A person who affirms that God does not exist.

CORNEA – Condition of Reasonable Epistemic Access is a technical term coined by philosopher Stephen Wykstra as a response to philosopher William Rowe's evidential argument from evil.

Determinism – It is the idea that every event, including every human decision and action, is determined by antecedent factors. In simple terms, it is the opposite of free will.

Dhyana-yoga – It is the yoga of meditation wherein a person sits and assumes a characteristic posture by which he can concentrate his senses on anything he wants.

Eschatology – *Eschaton*, meaning the end, and *logos*, meaning the word about (or the study of) the end, is that discipline that concerns itself with the study of the final events of individuals, of world history and the universe. Religious eschatology is the study of the fate of the dead and the fate of the world as described in various religions.

Evil[1] – An event may be categorized as evil if it involves any of the following:

1. some harm (whether it be minor or great) being done to the physical and/or psychological wellbeing of a sentient creature;

2. the unjust treatment of some sentient creature;

3. loss of opportunity resulting from premature death;

4. anything that prevents an individual from leading a fulfilling and virtuous life;

5. a person doing that which is morally wrong;

6. the "privation of good."

Explanatory power – It is the ability of a hypothesis or theory to effectively explain the subject matter it pertains to.

Explanatory scope – It refers to how many things a hypothesis or theory explains.

Good[2] – An event may be categorized as good if it involves any of the following:

1. some improvement (whether it be minor or great) in the physical and/or psychological well-being of a sentient creature;

2. the just treatment of some sentient creature;

3. anything that advances the degree of fulfillment and virtue in an individual's life;

4. a person doing that which is morally right;

5. the optimal functioning of some person or thing, so that it does not lack the full measure of being and goodness that ought to belong to it.

Guna – Gunas are both the qualities of the material world and the characters of each individual. There are three gunas: sattva, rajas and tamas. They exist in all beings, including human beings, in various degrees of concentration and combination, and they determine the nature of beings, their actions, behaviour and attitude.

Karma – It refers to any deed or action. Good karma is rewarded with good life in the next birth and bad karma is rewarded with a bad life in the next birth.

Karma-yoga – It refers to any deed or action done without any selfish motivation for personal gain.

Logical entailment – It means to involve something as a necessary or inevitable part or consequence. For example, being a bachelor necessarily entails that you are unmarried.

Logical impossibility – Whatever cannot be imagined or coherently thought without generating a contradiction is said to be logically impossible. Examples would include a square circle or a married bachelor. One cannot imagine a square in the shape of a circle and one cannot imagine a bachelor (a man who is not and has never been married) who is married.

Logical possibility – Whatever can be imagined or coherently thought without a contradiction is said to be logically possible. It is logically possible, for example, for pigs to fly, though it is *actually impossible* because they do not have wings. For something to be actually possible, it must correspond to reality. But something that is logically possible doesn't have to. It is not actually possible for anything or anybody to go faster than the speed of light. But logically speaking, it is possible even for a tortoise to run faster than the speed of light because we can imagine it without a contradiction.

Moksha – It means liberation from the cycle of rebirth that causes suffering.

Monism – *Monos*, meaning single, is the view that reality is a unified whole and that all existing things, divine and non-divine, can be described by a single reality.

Monotheism – Mono, meaning one, and theos, meaning God, is the view that only one God exists.

Moral evil[3] – This is evil that results from the misuse of free will on the part of some moral agent in such a way that the agent thereby becomes morally blameworthy for the resultant evil. Moral evil therefore includes specific acts of intentional wrongdoing such as lying and murdering, as well as defects in character such as dishonesty and greed.

Morally sufficient reason – "[A] morally sufficient reason is a circumstance or condition which, when known, renders *blame* (though, of course, not *responsibility*) for the action inappropriate."[4] An example would include a doctor cutting the patient's body with a scalpel blade during surgery – thereby causing hurt – and not being blamed for his action because of the greater good of enhancing the long-term quality of life for his patient.

Natural evil[5] – In contrast to moral evil, natural evil is evil that results from the operation of natural processes, in which case no human being can be held morally accountable for the resultant evil. Classic examples of natural evil are natural disasters such as cyclones and earthquakes that result in enormous suffering and loss of life, illnesses such as leukemia and Alzheimer's, and disabilities such as blindness and deafness.

Necessary truth – A statement is said to be necessarily true if it retains its truth value in all logically possible circumstances. There is no situation where the statement becomes false. For example, $2+2=4$ is necessary truth that remains true in all logically possible circumstances. If something is not necessarily true, then there is a logical possibility for it to be false.

Objective moral truths – To say that there are objective moral truths is to affirm that, in a given circumstance, there are moral actions that are either morally right or morally wrong that are independent of human opinion. A moral action is anything – good or evil – done by one human being to another human being.

Omnibenevolence – It is the quality of being maximally loving. When used for God, it means that God loves his creatures to the greatest extent possible. It could also mean 'perfect goodness' or 'moral perfection' and can be used interchangeably with the word 'all-loving.'

Omnipotence – It is the quality of having unlimited or maximal power. When used for God, it means that God has the power to do anything that is logically possible and that which is consistent with his nature. It can be used interchangeably with the word 'all-powerful.'

Omniscient – It is the property of having complete or maximal knowledge. When used for God, it means that God knows everything there is to know – past, present and future. It can be used interchangeably with the word 'all-knowing.'

Ontology – *On*, meaning existence or being, and *logy*, meaning the word about (or the study of) existence, is the study of the nature of being, becoming, existence, or reality.

Panentheism – *Pan*, meaning God, *en* meaning in, and *theos*, meaning God, is the view that the everything in the universe is a part of God.

Pantheism – *Pan*, meaning everything, and *theos*, meaning God, is the view that the universe is identical to the divinity.

Polytheism – *Poly*, meaning many, and *theos*, meaning God, is the view that there are many gods that exist.

Theist – a person who affirms that God exists

Theodicy – A theodicy is an attempt to justify the ways of God to humans. It tries to spell out the reasons that a good God might have for allowing terrible evils in the world that would serve to vindicate God's goodness and justice.

Theology – *Theos*, meaning God, and *logos*, meaning the word about (or the study of) God, is a discipline undertaken to understand how different religions conceive of God/gods and the properties and characteristics attributed to that God/gods.

Endnotes

[1] Nick Trakakis, The Evidential Problem of Evil in The Internet Encyclopedia of Philosophy (http://www.iep.utm.edu/evil-evi/) [Last accessed on 02/04/2014].

[2] *Ibid.*

[3] *Ibid.*

[4] Nelson Pike, "Hume on Evil," The Philosophical Review 72, No. 2 (1963) reprinted in Nelson Pike, ed., God and Evil, p. 88. Emphasis original.

[5] Nick Trakakis, The Evidential Problem of Evil in The Internet Encyclopedia of Philosophy (http://www.iep.utm.edu/evil-evi/) [Last accessed on 02/04/2014].

Introduction

We live in a world that is saturated with evil and suffering. From large-scale disasters such as earthquakes and tsunamis to small-scale tragedies such as murder, rape and virulent diseases, the world is suffused with pain and tears from the hearts and eyes of everyday sufferers. Humankind, in trying to find their own place in this rough and turbulent world, often look up to God to find hope and peace amidst pain and suffering. But the more they look up to God for help in times of crisis, the more they see God far away, uncaring or worse – not existing. And so the very search for God in the midst of suffering has become a reason to abandon finding him altogether. If there really is a God out there, then he should be looking after us instead of us looking out for him. 'Look at this young child dying of cancer. How can I believe in a God who allows *this* to happen – and that too on an everyday basis? What sort of a God do you want me to believe in? A sadistic and a malevolent God who wants innocent people to suffer and enjoys it? I'd rather believe that he doesn't exist, thank you very much.' The problem of evil and suffering is perhaps the greatest obstacle for anybody to come to faith in an all-loving and an all-wise God. It is also perhaps the single most common reason why people abandon belief in God entirely. It is like a large Ferris wheel that has gone out of control and is clocking at an overwhelming velocity such that people are being thrown out of its compartment seats and nobody can get in to sit in its compartments. What was once a delight for children and adults alike has become a source of great danger because the one who controls this giant wheel has either become untrustworthy or has gone missing.

But the questions that we ask about God and his reasons for allowing pain and suffering to infect our lives are not only intellectual, mind-framed questions, but are also the cries of the heart. We are not like legal lawyers questioning God in the dock in the abstract sense. We are the sufferers. And we convulse in pain as we ask God the questions. And deep down inside, we actually want God to exist and remove all our misery and pain. For who else can solve the problem other than the God who created the problem in the first place?

The issue is made more complicated by the fact that there are many religions in the world that seek to inform us of who God is and why he allows evil and suffering to exist in this world. Which religion is telling the truth about God and his ways? Or is every religion a lie? Such vexing questions are not incentives for abandoning the quest for answers downright, but rather they are intriguing questions that should lead us to undertake a vigorous search for answers to the toughest questions of life and death. Indeed, I presume that to be reason why you, the reader, has caught hold of this book. We need answers and answers we will get.

This book is divided into three parts. Part One begins with the outline of the ways in which the problem of evil can be posed to question the existence of God. Some people have argued that God and evil are logically impossible to exist together. If one exists, the other simply cannot exist. If there is a God, then it is impossible for evil to exist. If there is evil and suffering, then it is impossible for God to exist. This argument is perhaps the most common one out there in the street. Even those who had never really reflected on the relationship between the existence of God and suffering will easily draw the conclusion that evil and suffering disprove the existence of God. We will see how the argument actually works in its logical format and explore the successful ways in which the problem has been solved (yes, solved!). Others have said that the existence of evil and suffering, although they might not disprove God's existence, will nevertheless render the existence of God highly improbable to the extent that we are no longer justified in believing in God. This is a more nuanced version of the problem and several responses have been given which we will explore. Then, as an unexpected move, we will overturn the tables by arguing that evil and suffering, far from disproving the existence of God or rendering his existence improbable, actually serve to *prove* the existence of God! The very fact that we call certain things as evils – as things that are aberrations from what is normal – is in fact evidence that there is a God who grounds all goodness. This is because in a world without God, categories such as good and evil, right and wrong will have no moral significance whatsoever. This is a powerful argument *for* God *from* evil which help us to stand firm in our faith in God in spite of all the evils in our world. The problem of evil also encounters us on an emotional level and we shall discuss about it under Part Three of this book.

The second part of the book undertakes the quest to explore the ways in which the dominant religions of the world (other than Christianity) treat the problem of evil and suffering and their relation to God. The religions we shall explore are Buddhism, Hinduism and Islam. I will address the inadequacies inherent in each of these religions in their dealings with the problem of suffering. I should emphasize at this point that my analysis of these religions does not carry with it any sense of ridicule or hatred. It will be an honest and polite analysis of the implications that come out of their theological statements about God and the world.

The book will then steer towards considering the Christian approach to the problem of suffering in Part Three. Although I am a Christian, I may disappoint a lot of Christians who hold to traditional doctrines of Christianity with the vigorous scholarship I shall bring to the forefront in exploring the biblical responses to the problem of evil. I begin by listing out the many reasons that the Bible offers to explain why God allows evil and suffering in our world by interacting with the work of a Bible scholar. And then, using the metaphor of eyeglasses, I will step back and talk about the single large story that the Bible as a whole has to say and provide a thorough textual analysis of relevant biblical passages that will serve to criticize the competing popular story of going to Heaven as the ultimate dream and destiny of human beings. I will demonstrate how the crucifixion and the resurrection of Jesus take on a new and more relevant significance to the problem of evil when understood in its proper biblical context. And continuing with the metaphor of the eyeglasses, and drawing on a wealth of scholarship, I will offer three revisions of the popular doctrines of God, the world and man. All these preliminary steps will equip us with the right spectacles to see the monumental answer which Christianity offers to the problem of evil and suffering. Here I will propose a new way of seeing the problem of suffering by offering, what I have called, the *Garden Theodicy* by using the metaphor of a garden. I will then explain how we are to live as Christians in this world by drawing on the arguments I had previously made and defended. Finally, I will show how the Christian response to the problem of suffering satisfies the cries of the heart with its warm embrace like no other, while still being rooted in historical reality. The book will end with a call to faith for all those who haven't known or believed in Jesus Christ with the promise of eternal life to all who believe.

Technical terms used in this book have been defined and explained under the glossary section of the book. Hence I would encourage readers to turn to that section whenever they encounter a word in the book which they do not understand. References to citations have been listed in endnotes. I hope and pray that this book will enable the readers to revive their faith in God and sustain belief even in the midst of all suffering.

I
Resolving the Tension between God and Evil

1
Versions of the Problem:
Questions from the Mind and the Heart

When a child falls to the ground while playing, injures herself, and begins to cry, would it do her any good if she was immediately taken to a classroom and taught a lesson on the science of pain? Probably not. What she needs is for the parent to come and embrace her and tell her, "Daddy is here. Everything will be alright." Are adults any different? Whenever we ourselves are in a state of pain and misery, we do not want someone who will rationalize our situation by telling us why we are in such a miserable situation. We want someone who will simply be with us and listen to our story and offer practical advice on how to manage and overcome our situation. When someone who is diagnosed with a terminal end-stage cancer cries out in the privacy of his room saying, "Why did this happen to me?", he is not really asking the question '*why?*'. He doesn't want to know how genetic mutations within body cells can result in an uncontrolled multiplication of those cells. Rather, it is an expression of the anguish that comes from the heart. But if the same question of '*why*' is asked by a medical doctor to his students, then the doctor *wants* his students to talk about gene mutations and cellular replications. Thus the '*why*' question comes from two different sources - one from the heart of emotions and the other from the mind of intellect. This is true of the problem of evil as well. When people ask why God allows suffering and death to happen in this world, some want intellectual answers that can silence them while others want emotional answers that can comfort them. And so the problem of evil and suffering can be divided as follows:

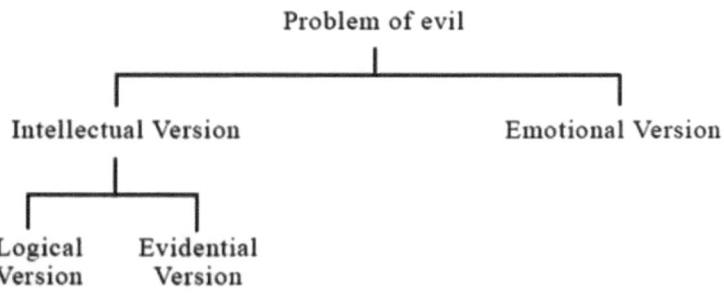

The intellectual version questions the *existence* of God. The emotional version questions the *integrity* of God. People who ask the intellectual question want to show their *disbelief* in God. People who ask the emotional question want to show their *dislike* for God. The intellectual question requires philosophical reasoning. The emotional question requires pastoral counseling. A person who is undergoing tremendous suffering will not be satisfied no matter how effectively we may prove that his suffering doesn't logically disprove the existence of an all-powerful and an all-loving God. Indeed, he may find the logical answers to be dry, uncaring, brutal and out of connection with the actual problems of his life. Likewise a person who, out of his rational thinking about God and evil, comes to conclude that there is no God, will not be satisfied by emotional answers that tell him to trust in God even when nothing makes sense to him. He needs to be led down the roads of logical reasoning to be shown why belief in God can be sustained in spite of all the suffering and evil in this world. But often people find themselves in between the two polarizing ends. They want both logical and emotional answers to the problem of evil. An honest sufferer may, at first, want emotional answers for his suffering. But after he has coped up with his suffering, he may need logical answers that will sustain his faith in God even as he continues to face his sufferings. Likewise the rational thinkers do not just want a mathematical formula that will show the compatibility of

God and evil on paper. They also want the comforting embrace of the God they cannot disprove. Nevertheless, for any person who ponders on the '*why?*' question, it is always important to start with the distinction between the intellectual and the emotional ways of posing the problem so that the person himself can better understand the question which he is asking and thereby be satisfied with the appropriate answers. The next two chapters of the book will be a formulation of and responses to the intellectual version of the problem of evil.

2
The Logical Problem:
Can God and Evil Co-exist?

Is he (God) willing to prevent evil, but not able? Then he is impotent.
Is he able, but not willing? Then he is malevolent. Is he both able and
willing? Whence then is evil?

Epicurus, 300 B.C.[1]

Have you ever thought of drawing a square in the form of a circle? Nonsense, you might say. How can one possibly draw a square circle? If it's a square, then it's not a circle. If it's a circle, then it's not a square. The idea of a square circle is simply a contradiction in terms, isn't it? So too has it been said about God and evil: If God exists, then it is logically impossible for evil to exist and if evil exists, then it is logically impossible for God to exist. But think with me here: is it really the case that God and evil are like the square circle? Imagine a man having his morning cup of tea in his home. And as he turns on the television to watch the morning news, he sees that an earthquake claimed the lives of many in another state of his country just the other day. And as he is watching the news, he hears his door bell ring. He gets up to open the door and is astonished to see the cops with handcuffs to arrest him. They tell him that he is being arrested because of the earthquake that he had just witnessed in the television. Now of course the second half of this story seems absurd because the man is neither responsible for causing the earthquake, nor is he responsible for not preventing the earthquake. This is because he is not omniscient to know in advance that there would be an earthquake, not omnipotent to be able to cause or prevent the earthquake and is not omnibenevolent (though we may presume that he is a loving man) to be willing to prevent the earthquake. We can now see the three crucial qualities ascribed to God that would in turn bring out the contradiction between God and evil: omnipotence, omniscience and omnibenevolence. As Epicurus saw it, if God is both able and willing to prevent evil, why then does evil still exist? If God is all-knowing, then he will anticipate in advance whether evil will happen or not. If he is all-loving, he would be willing to prevent evil. If he is all-powerful, he could act on his will and be able to prevent evil.

In its most simple yet powerful form, the logical version of the problem of evil can be formulated as follows: the following five points cannot all be true at the same time:

1. God exists.
2. God is all knowing
3. God is all loving.
4. God is all powerful.
5. Evil exists.

If God exists (1) and if he is omniscient (2) and omnibenevolent (3) and yet evil exists (5), then he is not omnipotent (4). If God exists (1) and he is omniscient (2) and omnipotent (4) and yet evil exists (5), then he is not omnibenevolent (3). If God exists (1) and if he is omnibenevolent (3) and omnipotent (4) and yet evil exists (5), then he is not omniscient (2). If God is thought to be omniscient (2), omnibenevolent (3) and omnipotent (4), but evil exists (5), then there is no such God (1).

Put in simple terms, if God exists and if he is all-knowing and all-loving and there is evil, then he doesn't get what he wants. So he's not all powerful – he is impotent. If God exists and if he is all-knowing and all-powerful and yet there is evil, then he wants evil. So he's not all-loving – he is malevolent. If God exists and if he is all-loving and all-powerful but if evil exists, then he didn't anticipate evil – he is ignorant. But if evil exists and if God is thought to be all-knowing, all-loving and all-powerful, then there is no such God. So the theist, it has been argued, has to either accept that God is malevolent, ignorant or impotent or he has to give up the concept of an omnibenevolent, omniscient and omnipotent God in the light of the evils that happen in our world. It is the latter challenge which we are concerned with. As the philosopher Anthony Flew puts it,

> The issue is whether to assert at the same time that there is an infinitely good God, second that he is an all-powerful Creator, and third that there are evils in his universe, is to contradict yourself.[2]

Our task in the following pages, under the logical version of the problem of evil, will be to show that God (who is all-knowing, all-loving and all-powerful) and evil are not like that of the square circle. Let us recall that the logical version of the problem of evil claimed that God and evil are logically impossible to co-exist. If one exists, then the other cannot exist. Such an incompatibility between God and evil has been argued in two forms. First, it has been argued that God and *any* evil are logically impossible to co-exist. Second, that God and *some* evils are logically impossible to co-exist.

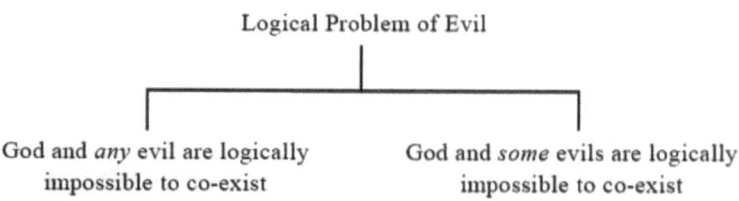

Logical Problem of Evil

| God and *any* evil are logically impossible to co-exist | God and *some* evils are logically impossible to co-exist |

Let's explore the first challenge together: God and *any* evil are logically impossible to co-exist. Here the arguer will point to any evil in the world – be it poverty, injustice, murder or disease – and say that it disproves the existence of God. When we unravel this claim and lay it down in a standard argumentative form, we will be able to clearly see how the apparent contradiction between God and evil emerge:

Premise 1: God is thought to be omnipotent, omniscient and omnibenevolent.

Premise 2: If God is omnipotent, then he can create a world without evil.

Premise 3: If God is omniscient, then he will know what evil will happen in the world and he will have the knowledge of how to eliminate them if they occurred.

Premise 4: If God is omnibenevolent, then he will want to create a world without evil.

Premise 5: So if an omnipotent, omniscient and omnibenevolent God exists, then evil cannot exist in the world.

Premise 6: However, this world is filled with evil and suffering.

Conclusion: Therefore an omnipotent, omniscient and omnibenevolent God does not exist.

In the above argument, if the conclusion needs to be true, then premises 1-6 have to be true as well. Moreover, the strength of the conclusion will depend on the strength of the premises. Let us consider a simple example of an argument to better understand these two statements.

Premise 1: Christie is a girl.

Premise 2: Christie is 16 years old.

Conclusion: Therefore Christie is a teenage girl.

In this argument, if premises 1-2 are true, then the conclusion is true as well. But suppose somebody comes in and questions the first premise by asking, "What if Christie is a boy?" The only evidence of knowing whether Christie is a girl or a boy is by looking at the name. And suppose somebody says that Christie is a common name that can be used for both genders. Now the conclusion weakens. The argument will have to be rewritten as follows:

Premise 1: Christie is *probably* a girl.

Premise 2: Christie is 16 years old.

Conclusion: Therefore Christie is *probably* a teenage girl.

Now suppose the second premise is attacked as well. Suppose someone says, "What if there are two people with the same name and one is a teenager and the other an adult?" There is no way of knowing which Christie is being referred to as 16 years old. The argument will therefore have to be rewritten again as follows:

Premise 1: Christie is *probably* a girl.

Premise 2: Christie is *probably* 16 years old.

Conclusion: Therefore Christie is *probably* a teenage girl.

The whole argument has been rendered invalid by simply finding loopholes in the two premises. The 'what if' questions don't have to be true. Maybe Christie is a girl and she is aged 16. Maybe she is not. And that's the point. By stating that it is *possible* for Christie to be an adult male, and even without any evidence to support the possibility, the argument has been weakened: it is possible for Christie to *not* be a teenage girl.[3]

Similar loopholes have been discovered in the logical argument from evil such that this form of the argument is no longer defended in the academic circles today. Before we proceed with the response, it is important that we understand some basic terms. When we say that something is possible to happen, we usually mean that something can or could happen in this world. If it's possible to rain tomorrow, we mean that it could rain tomorrow. If it's possible to drink a cup of coffee, we mean that we can drink a cup of coffee. And something that is impossible is usually thought to be something that cannot or could not happen in this world. It is impossible for a man to run at the speed of light. It is impossible for a pig to fly in the sky. This is the common way we think about possibility or impossibility. In philosophical discussions, this can be called *actual* possibility or impossibility. However, there is a much broader sense in which these terms can be used and are known as *logical* possibility or impossibility. Whatever can be imagined or coherently thought without a contradiction is said to be logically possible. It is logically possible, for example, for pigs to fly, though it is *actually impossible* because they do not have wings. For something to be actually possible, it must correspond to reality. But something that is logically possible doesn't have to. It is not actually possible for anything or anybody to go faster than the speed of light. But logically speaking, it is possible even for a tortoise to run faster than the speed of light because we can imagine it without a contradiction. Likewise, whatever cannot be imagined or coherently thought without generating a contradiction is said to be logically impossible. Examples would include a square circle or a married bachelor. One cannot imagine a square in the shape of a circle and one cannot imagine a bachelor (a man who is not and has never been married) who is married. Everything that is actually possible is also logically possible. But not everything that is logically possible is actually possible. Everything that is logically impossible is also actually impossible. But not everything that is actually impossible is logically impossible. The diagram below shows the relationship between the logically possible, the actually possible and the actual.

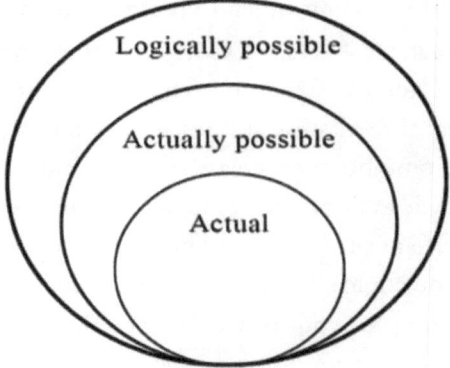

Logical possibility is the broadest of them all. Actual possibility is a portion within the broad logical possibility and the actual is a portion within the actual possibility. A few examples might help us better understand these terms. For me to climb stairs is both logically possible and also actually possible. There is no contradiction involved in imagining myself climbing the stairway and it is also actually possible for me, in the real world, to climb the stairway. But I am not *actually* climbing the stairs right now. Hence the proposition that I can climb the stairway is both logically and actually possible but not actual. That my heart is beating right now is logically possible, actually possible and also actual. That the moon is made up of green cheese is logically possible but not actually possible or actual.

The logical argument from evil claims that it is logically impossible for God and evil to exist together. Hence a critique of the argument will succeed if it can be shown that it is *logically possible* for God and evil to co-exist.

The philosopher Alvin Plantinga is widely praised for having provided the logical possibility for the co-existence of God and evil. In 1974, Plantinga's book came out titled, *God, Freedom and Evil,* which has single-handedly changed the discourse of scholarly debates on God and evil. Plantinga offers what he calls the 'Free Will Defence' as the solution to the logical version of the problem of evil. His contention is to question the second premise of the logical argument by introducing the well known concept of the freedom of the human will. Premise 2 states,

If God is omnipotent, then he can create a world without evil.
Plantinga says in essence, "What if God wanted to create a world where human beings are given the freedom of the will to choose between good and bad? And what if God chooses not to interfere with their actions?" Can God, with his omnipotence, create such a world without introducing the possibility of evil? Let's carry out a small thought experiment. Imagine standing with a knife in your hand and before an apple placed on a table. Now if you want you could slice the apple or if you want you could refrain from doing so. It is up to you to decide since there is nobody near you to prevent you from carrying out your decision. The fate of the apple is squarely in your hands. What if God has created human beings as such – with the freedom of the will to think good and evil thoughts and the freedom of the will to perform good and evil actions? Can God then guarantee that you will never slice the apple into two or slit the throat of a person? Of course not. Thus Plantinga writes,

> Now God can create free creatures, but He can't cause or determine them to do only what is right. For if He does so, then they aren't significantly free after all; they do not do what is right freely. To create creatures capable of moral good, therefore, He must create creatures capable of moral evil; and He can't give these creatures the freedom to perform evil and at the same time prevent them from doing so.[4]

By suggesting that it is logically possible for God to have created human beings with human free will and that it logically possible for God to have chosen not to interfere with their free actions, Plantinga argues that it is *logically impossible* for God to make human beings freely choose to do only what is right. In a world where people are free to choose what they want to do, and without divine intervention to stop their wrongdoings, God cannot guarantee that people will always choose to freely do the right thing. Another thought experiment would help. Imagine that your friend is now holding the knife and is standing in front of the table with the apple on top of it. He freely chooses to slice the apple with his knife. You are standing behind him and you are not allowed to talk to him or touch him. Now can you *make* your friend *freely* choose to refrain from slicing the apple? If you *make* him choose, then he no longer *freely* chooses. If he *freely* chooses, then you did not *make* him choose. It is logically impossible to make someone freely choose to do something. Even infinite power cannot make logically impossible things come true. And so even if God is omnipotent, if he chooses to create free creatures whose actions go unchecked – which is logically possible, then it is logically impossible for God to make these creatures freely perform only good actions. Hence God cannot guarantee a world where there will be no evil. He cannot actualize a world where these free creatures never commit even a single crime and thereby never introduce any evil in the world. Hence the second premise in the logical argument from evil is weakened. But what if someone insists that God, if he is omnipotent, must be able to do logically impossible things? What if the arguer says that God must be able to maintain a world where there is no evil even if he has given humans the freedom of the will? But even if God's power includes the ability to do what is logically impossible, then again the logical argument from evil is dissolved. Consider how below:

Premise 1: God and evil are logically impossible to co-exist (the arguer's claim).

Premise 2: God can do what is logically impossible (the arguer's claim).

Conclusion: Therefore God and evil can co-exist.

How easy was that?! By insisting that God should be able to do what is logically impossible, the arguer would have solved the problem he himself had raised! So by now the arguer would have drawn back from his claim that God should be able to do what is logically impossible. Omnipotence does not include the ability to do what is logically impossible.

This, then, is the Free Will Defence: by introducing the logical possibility of human freedom (that is, the freedom to think and perform the good and the bad), the logical possibility of evil is introduced in the world without jeopardizing God's omnipotence. Hence the second premise that if God is omnipotent, he can create a world without evil is not necessarily true. We have provided a *logically possible* scenario where this premise is false. Hence the conclusion that an omnipotent, omniscient and omnibenevolent God does not exist is not necessarily true either: it is *logically possible* for such a God to exist even if evil exists. Hence the logical form of the argument which contended that God and *any* evil are logically impossible to co-exist is rendered invalid. But what about the other form of the logical argument which states that God and *some* evils in the world are logically incompatible with God's existence?

The arguer might say, "Well, maybe moral evils which occur as a result of the abuse of human free will are compatible with God's existence. But there are certain forms and varieties of evil that are incompatible with the existence of an all-powerful and an all-loving God." It has been claimed that certain forms of evil such as its unjust and widespread distribution in the world, the quality of being horrendous or gratuitous and its variety such as natural evils are logically inconsistent with the existence of God. Let us take the claim that God and natural evils are logically impossible to co-exist. Natural evils such as tsunamis and earthquakes that claim the lives of thousands of innocent people would not exist if there was an all-powerful and all-loving God. Since they do exist in this world, there is no God who exists as omnipotent and omnibenevolent. The logical argument is thus framed as follows:

Premise 1: God is thought to be omnipotent, omniscient and omnibenevolent.

Premise 2: If God is omnipotent, then he can create a world without natural evil.

Premise 3: If God is omniscient, then he will know what natural evil will happen in the world and he will have the knowledge of how to eliminate them if they occurred.

Premise 4: If God is omnibenevolent, then he will want to create a world without natural evil.

Premise 5: So if an omnipotent, omniscient and omnibenevolent God exists, then natural evil cannot exist in the world.

Premise 6: However, this world is filled with natural evil like tsunamis and earthquakes.

Conclusion: Therefore an omnipotent, omniscient and omnibenevolent God does not exist.

Plantinga attacks the second premise of this form of the logical argument with a similar 'logically possible' claim. The essence of his claim is this: what if natural evils are caused by the free will of demonic creatures? He writes,

> Satan, so the traditional doctrine goes, is a mighty nonhuman spirit who, along with many other angels, was created long before God created man. Unlike most of his colleagues, Satan rebelled against God and has since been wreaking whatever havoc he can. The result is natural evil. So the natural evil we find is due to free actions of nonhuman spirits."[5]

Plantinga doesn't claim this to be actual or even actually possible. He only insists that it should be logically possible. Plantinga writes,

> The Free Will Defender, of course, does not assert that this is [actually] *true*; he says only that it is [logically] *possible*...He points to the [logical] possibility that natural evil is due to the actions of significantly free but nonhuman persons.[6]

This point should be stressed because people often dismiss this appeal to demons as ridiculous. Who, with a rational mind, would believe that natural disasters are caused by demonic creatures? But recall what we are doing: we are attacking a logical argument from evil which states that it is logically impossible for God and natural evil to co-exist. As a response, all we have to do is show a logical possibility for their co-existence. Paul Draper, an agnostic philosopher and a proponent of the evidential argument from evil, says thus:

> The appeal to demons may seem fanciful or even desperate, but one must keep in mind that Plantinga is responding to the logical argument from evil. If one's goal is only to prove logical compatibility, then it is legitimate to appeal to any [logically] possible state of affairs, no matter how unlikely [to be true].[7]

Plantinga has thus found a loophole in premise 2 again: even if God is omnipotent, if he chooses to create demonic creatures with free will whose actions he will not interfere with – which is logically possible, then it is logically impossible for God to make these creatures freely perform only good actions. At some point of time, at least one of the demonic creatures will use its free will to stir the natural order of things and introduce a natural disaster. Hence God cannot guarantee a world where there will be no natural evil.

Maybe God and natural evils can co-exist. But, the arguer might say, there are certain forms of evil, which are unacceptable to us, that render God's existence impossible. The exceeding amount, the ubiquitous perfusion, the unjust distribution and the appalling nature of evil, it has been claimed, are logically incompatible with the existence of God. The arguer might say that there is *so much* evil in the world and so God and *this much* evil are logically impossible to co-exist. Otherwise he might point to the unjust distribution of evil in the world and say that it is not compatible with God's existence. Many times it is the weak who are bullied by the strong; the poor who are left in the streets by the rich; the good who suffer from terminal diseases and die at a tender age. This unjust distribution of suffering and death, it has been argued, is incompatible with the existence of God. And finally, certain forms of evil like the horrendous nature of evil or the pointlessness of suffering in life is brought as evidence against the existence of God. The arguer might say, "Well, maybe evils like catching a cold or falling from a tree is compatible with the existence of God. But a psychopath torturing a little child and mutilating the child's limbs for fun – *this* kind of pointless and horrendous evil is logically impossible to happen if a good God were to exist." The argument can be formulated as follows:

Premise 1: God is thought to be omnipotent, omniscient and omnibenevolent.

Premise 2: If God is omnipotent, then he can create a world without the unacceptable forms of evil.

Premise 3: If God is omniscient, then he will know what unacceptable forms of evil will happen in the world and he will have the knowledge of how to eliminate them if they occurred.

Premise 4: If God is omnibenevolent, then he will want to create a world without the unacceptable forms of evil.

Premise 5: So if an omnipotent, omniscient and omnibenevolent God exists, then the unacceptable forms of evil cannot exist in the world.

Premise 6: However, this world is filled with unacceptable forms of evil like innocent suffering, universal ageing and dying, brutal torture and murder of people and so on.

Conclusion: Therefore an omnipotent, omniscient and omnibenevolent God does not exist.

In this formulation of the argument, the premise to scrutinize is the fourth one. Is it necessarily true that an all-loving God will never, in any circumstance, allow the apparently unacceptable forms of evil to happen in this world? We all can think of at least some evils that can be justified to be allowed. A parent disciplining his or her child, a dentist operating on a patient and a teacher punishing his or her pupil are all evils that are acceptable to us and which we would allow. We can also think of some evils that are necessary in order to obtain particular goods. For example, the development of courage in the midst of pain or adversity is only possible if pain or adversity is present. One cannot develop this fortitude without actually suffering. Since we can think of real goods that necessitate and justify suffering, couldn't there be real goods, which we cannot think of, that would necessitate and justify the evils in the world? Couldn't it be the case that the omnibenevolent God has morally sufficient reasons for allowing all those forms of evils that seem unacceptable to us? Since it is logically possible for God to have outweighing good reasons for allowing all the horrific and apparently unjust and widespread evils in the world, the fourth premise of the logical argument from evil cannot be maintained as necessary truth. Even an omnibenevolent God might be forced to allow evil in the world in order to obtain a compensating greater good. Paul Draper, the agnostic philosopher who doesn't believe in God, has this to say:

> (1) there may exist goods far more valuable than any we can imagine, (2) these goods may logically imply the existence or risk of horrific evils, and (3) these goods may (if there is life after death) include among their beneficiaries the victims of horrific evils.[8]

Draper does not think that there are *actual* goods that outweigh the evils in the world or that they are even *actually possible*. He remains agnostic. But he agrees that it is *logically possible* for them to exist. For the logical argument to succeed, says Draper,

> it is necessary to show that, for some known fact about evil, it is logically impossible for God to have a good moral reason to permit that fact to obtain. This, however, is precisely what most philosophers nowadays believe cannot be shown.[9]

Hence he shares the conclusion of the vast majority of philosophers in stating that the logical argument from evil has been defeated.

> I do not see how it is possible to construct a convincing logical argument from evil against theism...[10]

Atheist philosopher William Rowe, a leading proponent of the evidential argument from evil, says this about the logical argument:

> Some philosophers have contended that the existence of evil is *logically inconsistent* with the existence of the theistic God. No one, I think, has succeeded in establishing such an extravagant claim...[T]here is a fairly compelling argument for the view that the existence of evil is logically consistent with the existence of the theistic God.[11]

Philosopher Stewart Goetz writes,

[The logical version of] the problem of evil can be likened to the skeletal remains of dinosaurs that are housed in the back room of a museum and occasionally brought out for reexamination and public viewing.[12]

Likewise philosopher William Alston reports,

It is now acknowledged on almost all sides that the logical argument [from evil] is bankrupt.[13]

So does evil disprove the existence of God? Philosophers universally agree that it doesn't. This news has to reach the ears of people who aren't philosophically trained to think about the relationship between God and evil. Very often we encounter instances of evil either in our lives or in the lives of others such that we are intuitively driven to the conclusion that there is no God who is all-knowing, all-powerful and all-loving. We need to be informed that belief in such a God can be rationally maintained even in face of the worst possible instance of evil.

Before we end this chapter, a residual objection to our analysis of the logical argument from evil remains. Since we have shown that premises 2 and 4 are not necessary truths, the conclusion is not necessarily true either. In other words, we have shown that it is logically possible for God and evil to co-exist. But someone might say, "Well, I will agree that it is *logically possible* for God and evil to co-exist. But I don't think that it is *actually possible* or *actual* for them to co-exist." But this is merely a statement and not an argument. What argument can be given, with its own set of premises and conclusion, to show that the co-existence of God and evil are not actual or even actually possible? The arguer might say that God having morally sufficient reasons for allowing worst cases of evils is logically possible but not actually possible or actual (premise 4). But what supporting evidence can he give to argue for the truth of this statement? In order to disprove God's omnibenevolence (premise 4), he has to gain direct access into the mind of God and then be able to show that God, in reality, has no good reasons for allowing the forms and variety of evil in the world – a task which is actually impossible. You can now see how hopeless it is for someone to argue that God does not exist because evil exists. Nobody has ever succeeded in arguing for its truth and nobody ever will, which is why atheistic and agnostic philosophers have embraced the evidential argument from evil instead of the logical argument. And it is to this argument we turn to in the next chapter.

Endnotes

[1] David Hume, *Dialogues Concerning Natural Religion*, Part X.

[2] Antony Flew, *God and Philosophy* (London: Hutchinson, 1966), p. 48. Since God's omnipotence and omnibenevolence are sufficient to formulate the logical version of the problem, God's omniscience is often omitted. Hence we see philosopher Flew make the point that believing in an all-powerful and all-good God while at the same time acknowledging that there is evil in the world is to contradict oneself.

[3] I actually have a senior male working in our hospital whose name is Christie.

[4] Alvin Plantinga, *God, Freedom and Evil* (Harper & Row, NY, 2002), p30. First published by Harper and Row, 1974. Present edition 1977 by Wm. B. Eerdmans Publishing Co., Grand Rapids, Michigan 49503.

[5] Plantinga, God, Freedom and Evil, p 58.

[6] *Ibid.* Emphasis original. Brackets mine.

[7] Paul Draper, *The Problem of Evil* in *The Oxford Handbook of Philosophical Theology*, edited by Thomas P. Flint and Michael C. Rea (Oxford University Press, NY, 2009), p 335, Kindle location 8309-8311. Brackets mine.

[8] *Ibid.,* p 336, Kindle Location 8346-8348. Brackets original.

[9] *Ibid.,* p 335, Kindle Location 8317-8318.

[10] *Ibid.,* p 337, Kindle Location 8351-8351.

[11] William Rowe, "The Problem of Evil and Some Varieties of Atheism" in *American Philosophical Quarterly* 16 [1979]; reprinted in Chad Meister, *The Philosophy of Religion Reader* [London: Routledge, 2008], 523-35. Citation on page 534, note I.

[12] StewartGoetz, "The Argument from Evil" in *The Blackwell Companion to Natural Theology,* edited by William Lane Craig and J.P. Moreland (Blackwell Publishing Ltd, Chichester, West Sussex, UK, 2009), p 449. Brackets mine.

[13] William Alston, "The Inductive Argument from Evil and the Human Cognitive Condition" in *The Evidential Argument from Evil,* edited by Daniel Howard-Snyder (Indiana University Press, Bloomington, IN, USA, 1996) p 97. Brackets mine.

3
The Evidential Problem:
Evil as Evidence against God

Imagine a woman hastily getting down from a car parked at the side of a highway and running away, leaving an eight year old girl weeping alone inside the car. Two people who witness the scene from afar are deeply disturbed and begin to discuss among themselves. "What an uncaring mother she must be," says one person to the other, "why on earth would she abandon her child like this?" The other person thinks for a moment and says, "Maybe she isn't uncaring. Maybe there are good reasons why she left her child and ran away." "What good reasons do you think she might have for doing this? Whatever be the reason, couldn't she just carry her child with her?" asks the first person. "What if the mother heard the shocking news that her husband had met with an accident in a nearby spot and she is rushing to go help him after safely parking the car in the side of the highway?" reasons the second person. "I guess that seems reasonable to believe," says the first person, "but I still think she should have carried her child with her. After all, she is the mother of the child." "How do you know that?" asks the second person. "What if she isn't the girl's mother? Perhaps she is a servant working for them." "Well," says the first person upon pondering, "that seems reasonable to believe too. Let's wait and see whether the woman comes back for the child." They wait for a couple of hours to see what happens. But instead of seeing the woman come back, they see a man come and console the child and drive her away. "Who on earth was that?!" asks the first person. "Could it be her father? A thief? A policeman without his uniform?" The second person thinks along those lines as well and says, "I don't know either. But we have little evidence to make any judgment regarding the man. I guess it's better if we admit our lack of evidence and not speculate on who the man was." As they were talking, a third person walks by them and asks them what they were discussing about. When he heard that they were talking about the woman who left her child alone – an apparently evil act, he says that he knows the woman. "She is indeed the child's mother," he says, "and I know her personally to say that she loves her child so much." "Well then, that seems to confirm some of our speculations about the woman," says the second person to the first. "Indeed it does," says the first person. Then looking at the third person, he says, "But why hasn't she told you the reason why she ran away like that?" "Why would she?" asks the third person. "Why should I expect her to inform me the reasons for everything she does? Just because she hasn't told me the reasons for abandoning the child, that doesn't mean she has no morally justifiable reason for the same." And so the conversation ended and the first two people leave the spot convinced that a loving and caring mother does indeed exist for the child, even though they were not able to know why the mother had left her child alone and had run away.

In a similar manner, the evils in the world have been used as evidence to suspect the existence of an all-loving and an all-powerful God. Although the evils in the world do not render God's existence impossible (the logical version), they do make his existence improbable or unreasonable to believe. The evidential version of the problem of evil has been argued in two forms: the extra-mental version and the intra-mental version.

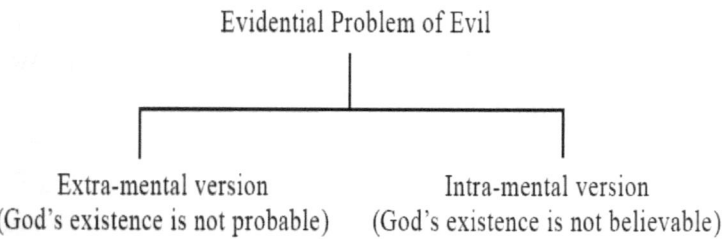

Evidential Problem of Evil

Extra-mental version   Intra-mental version
(God's existence is not probable)   (God's existence is not believable)

In the extra-mental argument, evil serves as evidence to drastically decrease the probability of God's existence. In the intra-mental argument, evil serves as evidence to warrant disbelief in God. Sometimes the two versions are combined to argue that evil decreases the probability of God's existence to the extent that we are justified in believing that God does not exist. In all these versions of the argument, however, the proponent will agree that God could actually exist in reality. His intention is only to show that God's existence is improbable or unwarranted to believe.

There are two popular versions of the intra-mental evidential argument from evil – one argued by atheist philosopher William Rowe and the other argued by agnostic philosopher Paul Draper. Rowe's evidential argument takes the following form:

Premise 1: There exist instances of intense suffering which an omnipotent, omniscient being could have prevented without thereby losing some greater good or permitting some evil equally bad or worse.

Premise 2: An omniscient, wholly good being would prevent the occurrence of any intense suffering it could, unless it could not do so without thereby losing some greater good or permitting some evil equally bad or worse.

Conclusion: There does not exist an omnipotent, omniscient, wholly good being.[1]

The first premise of the argument is, for Rowe, the controversial premise. In essence, it claims that there exist evils in the world that are unnecessary and purposeless for God to carry out his plans for the world. Such evils are gratuitous in the sense that God could achieve the same results he wants to achieve in the world even without allowing such evils to occur. Imagine, for example, a doctor who operates on his patient in order to cure a particular disease. We would consider that doctor to be morally good even though he had used blades and scissors on his patient. This evil was needed in order to obtain a greater good, namely, the restoration of the patient's health. But suppose the disease could have been cured without any surgical operation by just taking a pill. Then the doctor would be deemed either ignorant for being unaware of the proper treatment or selfish for trying to earn more money by performing an unnecessary operation. In another example, consider a doctor inoculating live polio viruses into a baby's arm through a needle. This evil is needed in order to trigger the baby's immune system so that the same type of virus does not affect the health of the child in the future. Hence this evil is done with the aim of preventing an even greater evil. But if the polio virus infection could be prevented without the pain of immunization, then the immunization wouldn't have been necessary. It is these types of gratuitous evils – that is, evils that God could have prevented without thereby losing some greater good or permitting some evil equally bad or worse – that are in conflict with an all-knowing, all-powerful and an all-loving God. But Rowe admits that nobody can prove that premise one is actually true. He only claims that we have rational grounds for *believing* that premise one is true.[2] He writes that his conclusion only means that "it is reasonable for us to believe that the theistic God does not exist."[3]

Rowe provides two examples of apparently gratuitous evils in order to argue his case. In his first example, he describes the brutal rape and murder of a five year old girl. In his second example, he describes a fawn slowly suffocating to death as it is trapped inside a forest fire. Rowe claims that since we cannot think of any good outcome that will justify the occurrences of these two evils, we are not warranted in believing that there are good outcomes that will justify the occurrences of these evils. Hence these two evils can be believed to be gratuitous. We will explore three responses to Rowe's first premise:

1. The CORNEA critique

2. The Agnostic Thesis

3. Theodicy

Philosopher Stephen Wykstra developed the CORNEA critique to argue against Rowe's first premise.[4] According to the CORNEA, one is entitled to reasonably believe that there are no good outcomes that will justify the occurrence of a particular evil only if it is reasonable to believe that the good outcomes would be known to us if they really did exist. Suppose, for example, a doctor looks closely at the needle of a syringe and says, "I can't see any bacteria in this needle. Therefore there are no bacteria in this needle." What will our reaction be? We would say, "Sorry doc, but bacteria are not seeable." Even if bacteria existed in the needle, we *shouldn't* expect to be able to see them with our naked eyes. So the doctor is not warranted in believing that there are no bacteria in the needle just because he can't see any. But suppose someone enters an empty room, sees no chair in it and concludes, "I see no chair in this room. Therefore there are no chairs in this room." His conclusion would be warranted because if any chair existed in the room, he *should* expect to be able to see it. In other words, one is warranted to move from 'I see no X' to 'there is no X,' only if one should expect X to be visible if it were to exist. Rowe says in essence, "I can think of no goods that will justify the sufferings of the girl and the fawn. Therefore there are no goods that will justify the sufferings of the girl and the fawn." But, Wykstra asks, should you expect to be able to discern or cognize the goods if they existed? If God has adequate reasons for allowing evils in the world, what makes you think that you should be the first person to be able to know what those goods are? Since we are dealing with an omniscient God who knows the end from the beginning, there is no reason to think that God would communicate his reasons for permitting evils in the world to temporally limited creatures like us. Hence, Rowe is not warranted to believe that there are unnecessary and purposeless evils in the world (premise 1).

The second response to Rowe's first premise is the Agnostic Thesis argued by philosopher William Alston.[5] He provides two groups of analogies to show why Rowe is wrong about premise one. First, he argues by analogy that God's knowledge is infinitely greater than ours. Imagine the scientist Albert Einstein writing complicated equations on a board and us, as laypeople, standing to witness what he writes. "Therefore," concludes Einstein, "$E=mc^2$". "Wait a minute!" we exclaim, "How did you draw that conclusion from that complicated set of numbers and symbols above?" We then say to him, "I see no reason for your conclusion. Therefore you have no reasons for your conclusion." Are we right to make such a judgment? Certainly not. Our inability to discern the reasons why Einstein draws his conclusion is expected given our lack of expertise on the subject. Likewise, argues Alston, we stand as laypeople before an omniscient God. God's reasons for permitting an instance of evil may be so complicated that it may transcend the boundaries of human cognition. Rowe is warranted to conclude that God has no morally sufficient reasons for permitting the evils in the world only if God's extent of knowledge is on level plane with ours. But it clearly isn't. Hence we are not warranted to believe that God lacks morally sufficient reasons for permitting evils in the world just because we can't discern any.

Second, Alston argues that Rowe is trying to deny something which he has no adequate knowledge of. In order for Rowe to believe that there are no greater goods that would necessitate the occurrence of the evils in the world, he has to have some knowledge about the goods that he wants to deny. If I want to deny that there are alien creatures in the universe, I have to first know what I mean by alien creatures and then survey the vast universe to make sure I do not find any such creatures. Only then will I be warranted to believe that there are no alien creatures in the universe. But Rowe is stepping foot into an unknown territory, like the vast universe, where he has no insight about the greater goods which he seeks to deny. According to the Bible, God's compensating and justifying goods for permitting the evils in the world are beyond what man could possibly think of (1 Corinthians 2:9). Since Rowe has no cognitive grip of the goods he wants to deny and since he cannot survey the vast options that God might have for justifiably allowing the evils in the world, he is not warranted in believing that God has no reasons for permitting the evils in the world. Given that we are dealing with an omniscient mind such as God's mind, we have to admit our own lack of omniscience and remain agnostic about the reasons for allowing evil. The appropriate response to the evils in the world would be to say, "I don't know whether God has or lacks morally sufficient reasons for the evils which he allows."

The third response to Rowe's first premise of the evidential argument is to try to provide reasonable justifications for particular evils in the world. This is the role of theodicies. A theodicy is an attempt to justify the ways of God to man. It is like the two people who were trying to justify why the mother had left her child inside the car and ran away. A theodicy should appeal to the human cognition and make us say, "If God has *this* reason for allowing this evil to happen, then I will accept that God will still remain just and loving in spite of allowing that evil to happen." A theodicy should offer reasonable (though not necessarily true) explanations as to why God has allowed evils to happen in the world. As such, it should meet the following three conditions:[6]

1. The Necessary Condition: The good secured by the permission of evil, E, would not have been secured without permitting either E or some other evils morally equivalent to or worse than E.

2. The Outweighing Condition: The good secured by the permission of the evil is sufficiently outweighing.

3. The Rights Condition: It is within the rights of the one permitting the evil to permit it at all.

Consider Rowe's case of the rape and murder of the five year old girl named Sue. What reasons could God have that could justify Sue's suffering and death? Perhaps the well known compensating good for Sue's suffering would be to go to paradise and remain in the presence of God forever. To be rewarded with infinite joy in the paradise of God could easily compensate for any amount of suffering gone through in this world. Rowe himself concedes this point. He writes,

> [T]his good [of experiencing infinite joy in the eternal presence of God] may justly be held to outweigh almost any horrendous evil that may befall Sue in her earthly life[7]

So what problem does Rowe have with the theodicy of paradise? His problem is that paradise *compensates* but doesn't *justify* Sue's suffering. The Paradise Theodicy fulfils the Outweighing Condition but not the Necessary Condition and the Rights Condition. Imagine, for example, your friend breaking your car with iron rods without your permission. You are shocked to see what has happened to your car and you go and confront your friend. Your friend then agrees to pay you ten times the price of your car. That would certainly compensate for your loss. But that doesn't explain why your friend had to break your car in the first place. Why not give the amount to you without breaking your car? What necessary reason was there to break your car before paying you ten times the money and who gave your friend the rights to break your car? Likewise, although Sue would receive adequate compensation in paradise, she could have been taken to paradise without going through hell on earth. Her suffering on earth was unnecessary in order to go to paradise. And what rights does

God have to allow Sue to suffer like this? In response, we shall explore two theodicies that would both necessitate and justify Sue's suffering: the free will theodicy and the soul-making theodicy. According to the free will theodicy[8], God has given human beings the freedom to think and to perform the good and the bad. Such freedom is required for moral behavior to exist. Morally good actions such as love, friendship, charity, courage, sacrifice and tolerance would have meaning only when they are freely chosen. During my high school days, one of my teachers told us a story about a king who wanted to wed his beautiful daughter to the bravest man alive. The King called for a competition and invited everyone to participate in the challenge. What was the challenge? The challenge was to swim across a river filled with man-eating crocodiles. So a huge crowd of participants were standing on one side of the river bank but none of them dared to jump inside the river. The day almost ended and the King was about to call off the competition in disappointment. Then all of a sudden he heard a splash in the river. A man had jumped in the river and was swimming with all his might until at last he managed to reach the other side of the river, unharmed by the crocodiles. The King was overjoyed to see the man standing tall after having overcome the crocodiles. He was about to embrace and congratulate the man for his courage and determination to marry his daughter but was held back by the fact that the man, instead of happily facing the King and his daughter, turned back, angrily looked over the other side of the river where the participants were standing and shouted, "Who pushed me?!" In reflecting upon the story, one cannot help but wonder whether or not the man is worthy of wedding the king's daughter. I think not. This is because he had no other choice. He was pushed inside the river. His act was not voluntary. But suppose if someone had jumped into the river voluntarily, without any compulsion. Would we then praise him for what he did? We certainly would because he would have freely chosen to take the risk of losing his life. In order for God to create a world where morally good actions are possible, he has to create a world where human beings are given the free will to choose between morally good and bad actions. Christian apologist Ravi Zacharias invites us to think of four possible worlds which God could have created:

[T]here are only four possible worlds that scholars have talked about. The first is that there be no creation versus this world. Would it not have been better for God to have created no world rather than to have created this one where good and evil are possibilities? The second is to have created a world where only good would have been chosen, a kind of robotic world. The third option would have been a world where there was no such thing as good and evil, an amoral world. The fourth is this world that we live in, where good and evil exist along with the possibility of choosing either.[9]

Let us explore each of the four possible worlds. First, where there is no beginning. Nobody is there and nothing is there, except God. There is nothing to imagine in this possible scenario. But we will have this for our comparison with the other three possible worlds. Second, a world where only good is possible. In this world, all human beings are pre-programmed by God to always to the right thing. There is no freedom of the will to refrain from doing the right thing. I have heard parents say to their children, usually because of their children's annoying disobedience, that it would have been better if they had an obedient robot instead. Do they really mean that? Has a robot ever been praised for doing something extraordinary or have the praises gone past the robot to its inventor? If, for example, Mother Teresa had been pre-programmed by God to serve humanity so that she couldn't have done otherwise, would we be praising her for what she has done? Would not her actions be morally insignificant because she would have had no other choice other than to do good? The bottom line is that in a robotic world, human ethics would be a meaningless term. The third world is a world where there is no creature at all. Imagine an empty universe where God created only a single basketball or a wall clock floating in space – an amoral world. Then, at last, imagine our world – a world where moral actions are both possible and significant because of human free will. God, in determining the best of the four worlds, chose this world where moral goodness is possible. But it comes with a price – even for God. And he will pay it with blood and tears.[10] Some objections might be raised against the free will theodicy. First it might be said that God could allow free choices to be made but not free actions. In the case of Sue, God could have allowed the man to freely think evil thoughts but could have done something to prevent him from raping the girl. When the man was about to enter the house, God could have caused the door to magically slam his face or the ground to magically turn into water and drown him. By this way God could preserve the free will to think but remove our free will to act. But can the free will to think really be preserved when the freedom to act is removed? Philosopher Michael Murray writes,

> I intend to pull the trigger to shoot you but suddenly find that my finger is paralyzed, or...I intend to steal the car but when I rear back to throw the brick at the car window to gain entry, I suddenly fall asleep...Were the world so configured, I would not be able to bring about any evil beyond my evil choices. Unfortunately, the result of such an arrangement is that, before long, I would not be able to make evil choices either. The reason for this is that my experience will make it clear to me that doing evil is no fact impossible.[11]

I no longer think about flying with my hands or eating the moon, as I used to think when I was a child, because I have learnt by experience that such tasks are impossible. Likewise, argues Murray, if all evil actions will be prevented, then people will no longer think evil thoughts. Their freedom to think evil thoughts will be removed and hence their good thoughts and good deeds will have no moral significance. But, one might insist, why not prevent major evils alone? Stealing a car might be permitted by God in order to preserve the freedom of creatures. But permitting the horrendous rape and murder of a five year old girl just to preserve the free will of her rapist seems repugnant. Why can't God prevent major evils without losing an overall balance of free will? The one who asks this question should first be able to define what a major and horrendous evil is, provide inclusion and exclusion criteria, show how much of the evils in the world fall under its inclusion criteria and then demonstrate how an overall balance of free will can still be maintained if all the perpetuators of major and horrendous evils were robbed of their freedom to perform their evil actions. Besides being subjective, this task seems almost impossible and it could very well be the case that a very large proportion of the evils in the world fall under the criteria of major and horrendous evils such that the removal of human freedom in these cases would destroy the overall balance of free will. In fact, as philosopher Bruce Reichenbach argues, our present world situation could just be that point where God is actively involved in removing all the major and horrendous evils without losing the overall balance of free will:

> [I]t is at least possible that the present state of affairs represents that point, that God already intervenes to prevent the worst evils to the maximal extent consistent with human freedom, preserving the world as a theater for moral action and development, and his purposes for the world and human beings.[12]

Another possible objection to the free will theodicy concerns its existence in paradise. Paradise is envisaged as a place where God and man get along with each other and where evil is no more. But will human freedom still prevail in paradise? If yes, then how can paradise be a place where no human commits any crime? If no, will not our love and kindness towards God and others be robotic in the sense that we would be lacking the freedom of the will to be able to freely love God and others? Consider the possibility of free will in paradise. Will that entail that paradise could not be a sin-free place? Not so. It could be that in paradise, doing the right thing would be as easy as adding up 2+2: we would *freely* and *always* get it right. While the freedom to do evil would remain, the people who stand in the direct presence of God and witness the sheer glory, beauty and the goodness of God such they *would not* sin because doing good would be as easy as doing a simple math. But then why didn't God directly create us in such a state? Why is life on earth necessary?

Philosopher John Hick proposed the soul-making theodicy to explain why God has created the world with evil.

> [Moral evil is] an inevitable result of God's creation of man as an immature creature, at the beginning of a long process of moral and spiritual development.[13]

Hick sees even natural evil as helping the individual in soul making:

> [T]he harsh features of the world, which we call natural evil, are integral to its being an environment in which a morally and spiritually immature creature can begin to grow towards his perfection.[14]

According to Hick, the purpose in life is not happiness but moral and spiritual development. God has made our world a place of soul-making where there can be moral and spiritual growth. The development of moral characters such as love, courage, honesty, nobility, generosity, tolerance, endurance and so forth require that we face obstacles, tasks, setbacks, problems and dangers. As Alston points out, referring to Hick's soul-making theodicy,

> [B]y confronting difficulties, hardships, frustrations, perils, and even suffering and only by doing this, we have a chance to develop such qualities of character as patience, courage, and compassion, qualities we would otherwise have no opportunity to develop.[15]

It could well be that only in a world that is infiltrated with moral and natural evil will the maximum number of people freely come to a saving relationship with God and exhibit love for others which, for all we know, might be God's prime purpose for human beings. In the case of Sue's suffering and death by the hands of her rapist, it could be that following the girl's death, her mother is taken good care by her relatives who otherwise would have left her alone. Perhaps it could be the case that the mother herself turns a new leaf, coming out of her alcoholic addiction, and therefore taking good care of her other children who would have otherwise been poorly taken care of. Hearing the incident, the government could strengthen rape laws leading to a substantial decrease in crime rates. The little girl's death could pave the way for people to be more engaged in social justice. Her brutal death could be the only way in which callous hearts are led to repentance. Many criminals themselves, who are in prison, may look at the incident in horror and repent of their ways as they turn to God. Maybe that only through such a terrible incident would the girl's mother move away to a place where her other children might in turn come to the knowledge of God and inspire many people to fight for justice and peace in the world through the story of their sister. But, as a first objection, it might be said that this soul-making is of benefit to *others* and not the victim. It seems unfair for God to use the rape and murder of a Sue so that other people can be benefitted from it. As a second objection, it might be argued God could find other ways of soul-conversion for people. Since he is omnipotent, he could show visions or illusions of people suffering and thereby help them grow morally and spiritually. He doesn't have to allow the actual death of an innocent girl just in order to achieve something which he could have achieved by other means. As a third objection, it could be said that God could have created us with ready-made virtues such that we do not need to develop them over time that would involve so much suffering for ourselves and for others. As a fourth objection, it could be said that the soul-making theodicy has a high failure rate. Many people, when confronted with suffering, rather than coming closer to God, choose instead to rebel against God and people. As a fifth and last objection, it could be said that the soul-making theodicy has a narrow scope of explanation. It doesn't explain suffering and death in the animal world. We will look at each of the five objections more closely. First is the claim that the soul-making theodicy, in the case of Sue, doesn't apply to the victim but only for others. Is that fair enough? Consider the state permitting to quarantine a patient with a highly infectious disease and is perhaps denying proper treatment for the patient for the benefit of other citizens who might contract the disease.[16] Such an act of evil is justified since:

1. The state government is in a position of lawful authority over the patient.

2. The state government is responsible for the welfare of the citizens.

3. The good to be gained by allowing the patient to suffer overweighs the suffering of the patient.

4. There is no other way of protecting the citizens from the infectious disease.

Likewise, in the case of Sue, even though the benefit of her suffering is for other people, God is justified in permitting her suffering if he has lawful authority over every human life, is responsible for the good of the entirety of his creation, and if Sue's suffering is necessary for obtaining certain outweighing goods for his creation. Concerning the second objection, which appeals to God's omnipotence in order to find other ways of soul-making without having to allow innocent suffering, God could certainly appear directly to us, or he could send dreams and illusions that will motivate us to change our immoral lives and draw closer to him. While this seems possible, it doesn't sound plausible. God's intention might be that people should *freely* come to develop moral character and spirituality. Hence God cannot directly appear to people and motivate us to come to him. As Hick points out,

> God must set man at a distance from Himself, from which he can then voluntarily come to God...the reality and presence of God must not be borne in upon men in the coercive way in which their natural environment forces itself upon their attention. The world must be to man, to some extent at least, *etsi deus non daretur,* 'as if there were no God'. God must be a hidden deity, veiled by His creation. He must be knowable, but only by a mode of knowledge that involves a free personal response on man's part...[17]

What about dreams? If God could show visions and make people dream about suffering and evil, will that motivate people to freely develop character, sympathy and so forth? Will that really bring together broken families or impact state-level policies? It could be that on comparison, it is only when evil is present in reality will the maximum number of people grow morally and spiritually. The arguer cannot simply appeal to God's omnipotence and say, "God should be able to find other ways." He has to demonstrate that there are indeed other ways for God to be able to inculcate moral and spiritual characters in man that are at least equally (if not more) efficacious compared to our present situation. It is best, I think, to remain agnostic about the possibility of God having other ways for soul-making that wouldn't involve human suffering. What about illusions? God could give us illusions such that we come to believe that we have hurt ourselves or other people and thereby grow morally and spiritually. The problem with this suggestion is that, apart from making God work deceitfully in our lives, it would disconnect us from the real world. If a man intends to murder someone, and receives the illusions that he successfully murdered the person, then his eyes have to be veiled when the victim actually walks in front of him. Eventually, so much of what is real in the world has to be covered up by God in order to keep the illusion going. The person would become utterly disconnected from the real world such that the very purpose of providing illusions would be defeated without proper interaction with the world.[18] As to the third objection, which claims that God could have created us with ready-made moral characters and spirituality, Hick appeals to the principle that,

[Virtues] which have been formed within the agent as a hard won deposit of her own decisions in situations of challenge and temptation, are intrinsically more valuable than virtues created within her ready made and without any effort on her own part.[19]

If God wanted to create people having the most valuable kind of moral character and spirituality, he would have to create them as imperfect creatures who, with their freedom of the will, would develop moral and spiritual characteristics through trials and temptations. The fourth objection to the soul-making theodicy is the appeal to its high failure rate. Often times the evils that befall us cripple us, both morally and spiritually, rather than make us grow. People who are over stressed suffer from emotional breakdown and other psychiatric problems. People often give up in times of trials and temptations rather than face them and overcome them. The success rate of the soul-making theodicy is, therefore, too low. To this objection, Alston responds,

When dealing with free creatures God must, because of self-imposed limitations, use means that have some considerable likelihood of success, not means that cannot fail.[20]

Since God is working with human beings who are free to act on their will, God cannot guarantee that trials and difficulties that people go through will always (or even most of the time) work positively in his free creatures. If God does not have any other logically possible way of making human beings *freely* grow in their spiritual and moral dimensions, then God would be justified in allowing difficulties, hardships and sufferings in our lives *even though* the success rate would be low. The last objection to the soul-making theodicy concerns its narrowness: it does not explain animal suffering. Here a distinction between explanatory power and explanatory scope has to be made. Suppose a doctor sees a patient limping into his hospital room and notices that his right great toe is bleeding and assumes that he might have dashed his foot against a concrete object. That assumption has a good explanatory power: it easily explains why the person has a bleeding toe. Let's call it the injury hypothesis. But suppose the doctor also notices that the patient looks emaciated. The injury hypothesis doesn't have the scope to explain why the patient is emaciated. Hence the injury hypothesis has poor explanatory scope but good explanatory power. Poor explanatory scope is not a reason to reject a hypothesis. Likewise, although the soul-making theodicy may not explain *all* types of suffering, it does explain why God allows *some* of the sufferings fairly well. Sufferings that are beyond the scope of the soul-making theodicy can be explained by other theodicies. So what theodicy can be offered for animal suffering?

In dealing with animal suffering, we have to first ask whether or not animals suffer the same way humans do. What if the fawn entrapped in the forest, as described by Rowe, does not suffer the same way we suffer? Rene Descartes (1596-1650) is notoriously famous for arguing that animals are automata that might act as if they are conscious, but really are not so. Hence he argued that animal pain and suffering has no moral significance whatsoever. He and his followers, known as Cartesians, were notorious for torturing animals. Although Descartes and the Cartesians took a radical position on animal pain and suffering, which seem questionable, philosophers have come up with much more modest theodicies that are more scientifically grounded. Cartesian theodicies can be construed in several ways and more recently, several neo-Cartesian theodicies have been developed. I will discuss one form of the neo-Cartesian theodicy in what follows.

In his book, *Nature Red in Tooth and Claw*,[21] Murray discusses three types of consciousness which living beings have: creature consciousness, access consciousness and phenomenal consciousness. Compared to inanimate objects such as rocks, living beings move and have control of their body movements. The creature, as a whole, can be said to be conscious in this sense (creature consciousness). The second type of consciousness pertains to the awareness of external environment. Murray gives the following example for access consciousness:

> Insofar as a housefly can accurately represent a state of affairs external to itself, it has access to its surroundings and is consciously aware of what is nearby.[22]

The third type of consciousness, known as phenomenal consciousness, is the "subjective or phenomenal character of experience, the particular way it is like to have certain sorts of experiences, or the qualitative aspect of sensory awareness."[23] In this type of consciousness, the sort of awareness to external stimuli will differ from one creature to another. When, for example, a fawn is trapped in a forest fire and its legs are broken such that it can't escape, the kind of awareness that the fawn would experience would be qualitatively different from the awareness which human beings would have if we are to be caught up in that same situation. It could also be the case that lower animals[24] such as insects and worms have no phenomenal consciousness at all. As Murray points out,

> [A] creature can be in a state of access consciousness without being in a state of phenomenal consciousness.[25]

He gives the following two interesting examples:

> Patients who have sustained damage to their primary visual cortex may retain the ability to detect, discriminate, and localize visual stimuli presented in the areas of their visual field in which they report that they are subjectively blind. Such 'blindsighted' patients report that they are no longer able to see, and yet they are capable of giving correct motor responses to changes in their environment that could only be detected through the visual modalities. In a natural sense, they are conscious of what they think they do not see (they have some access to the external information), while in another sense they are blissfully unaware, for they are not phenomenally conscious of this access. Patients with corresponding damage to the auditory cortex similarly report being unable to hear, while nonetheless showing a capacity to detect, localize, and exhibit appropriate autonomic reactions to sound. As with blindsighted patients, it is natural to regard these patients as deaf when we consider phenomenal consciousness, while acknowledging that they have mental states which manifest auditory access consciousness.[26]

In such a case, in one sense, the person will be unable to hear, for example, the annoying sounds of machinery or see, for example, the disturbing scenes in the external world, and yet, paradoxically, in another sense, they will be able to hear and respond to the sound or see and react to the sight.

In yet other real life cases, Murray says that patients who have had the front portion of their brain removed no longer experience the same quality of pain that we would experience:

> Individuals who have undergone a prefrontal lobotomy, for example, sometimes report an awareness of familiar pains but paradoxically insist that they no longer find the pain to be undesirable or unpleasant. They

claim the pain 'feels' the same, even though it no longer bothers them. As a result, creatures of this sort have first-order pain states, and second-order awareness of them. But because they lack the capacity to regard those states as undesirable, such creatures do not *suffer* because of their pain.[27]

These patients lack the cognitive power of recognising the qualitative aspect of pain. What Murray concludes from these cases is not that it is *really* the case that animals lack phenomenal consciousness or that they don't experience the same kind of pain that human beings experience, but only that it *could* be the case:

> [I]t is obvious that many animals are neuroanatomically and neurophysiologically quite different from us. It is possible that these differences make a qualitative difference when it comes to the case of animal pain and suffering.[28]

We know very little about animal consciousness and pain. If it turns out that the animals do not suffer in the same way humans do, then the problem of animal pain begins to fade away.

We have, so far, explored three responses to the first premise of Rowe's intra-mental evidential argument from evil that render his argument invalid. There is, of course, another version of the intra-mental argument proposed by Paul Draper.[29] Draper's version of the evidential argument is to compare theism (T) with an alternative hypothesis which he thinks best explains the existence of evil. Draper calls this alternative hypothesis, the Hypothesis of Indifference (HI), which claims that this world is not created by an omnipotent and an omniscient God. He then observes (O) ordinary experiences of pain and pleasure in the human and animal world and argues that we would be less surprised to observe O if we assume HI to be true than if we assume theism (T) to be true. So our observation of pain and pleasure (O) is a reason to prefer HI to T. His observation (O1 and O2) is that much of the pain and pleasure in the world serve the purpose of survival and reproduction. If, for example, one touches a hot pan, one would immediately withdraw one's hand as a mode of survival. Such an observation, argues Draper, is surprising if God exists (T) than it would have been if God did not exist (HI) because an omnipotent God could have found alternatives to pain for survival. Draper also observes (O3) that many forms of pain and pleasure do not serve the purpose of survival and reproduction. For example, someone drowning in a flood is not going to serve the purpose of survival and reproduction for that person. This too, argues Draper, is surprising if God exists (T) because God, being omnipotent and omnibenevolent, would not allow such a gratuitous form of pain. But gratuitous pain is to be expected if God does not exist (HI). Moreover, according to Draper, since on the assumption that God exists (T), pain and pleasure would have intrinsic moral values (pain being intrinsically bad and pleasure being intrinsically good), an omnibenevolent God would minimise pain and maximize pleasure. But that's not what we observe in this world. Hence the pattern of distribution of pain and pleasure makes HI more probable than T. Draper's argument takes this complicated form:[30]

1. We know that *e* obtains.

2. *e*'s obtaining is antecedently many times more probable given some alternative hypothesis h to theism than it is given theism. So,

3. *e*'s obtaining is strong evidence favouring h over theism (i.e. our knowledge that e obtains increases the ratio of the probability of h to the probability of theism many-fold).

4. *h* is at least as plausible as theism (i.e. h is at least as probable as theism independent of all evidence for and against theism and h, or at least we have no good reason to believe otherwise). So,

5. Other evidence held equal, theism is very probably false.

Draper, in thus construing his argument, attempts to show two things. First, he attempts to show that the observed pain and pleasure (O) is much less probable on theism (T) than on the hypothesis of indifference (HI) and second, this fact poses a serious problem for believers in God. For the sake of simplicity, I will not engage with Draper's first contention. Let us grant that the observed pain and pleasure in the world makes HI more probable than T.[31] Should we, therefore, reject theism? Do pain and pleasure pose a serious problem for theists? Consider his three paraphrased propositions:

1. T – This world is created by an all-powerful and an all-loving God.

2. O – There exists pain and pleasure in the world that are both

biologically useful and gratuitous and not distributed according to moral behaviour.

3. HI – This world is not created by an all-powerful and an all-loving God.

(1) is something theists believe. (2) is something theists can see. (3) is a serious alternative to (1). Draper claims that (2) is highly probable on (3) compared to (1). Hence (1) is evidentially challenged by the high probability of (2) on (3). This fact is, therefore, a reason to reject (1). But should we abandon belief in (1) just because that belief is evidentially challenged by a more probable hypothesis? Plantinga argues that we needn't.[32] He gives some analogies to Draper's argument, one of which is as follows:

1. I am within four feet of a dog.

2. I hear no doggie sounds such as barking, growling, panting, or jingling of tags, and

3. I am not within earshot of any dogs.

Let (1) be what I believe and (2) be my observation. Suppose somebody comes and tells me (3). I now make a judgment based on probability: the fact that I do not hear any doggie sounds is more probable on the assumption that I am not within earshot of any dogs than on the assumption that I am within four feet of a dog. Should I, therefore, reject my belief that I am four feet of a dog? Suppose my evidence for (1) is my eyesight: I can *see* a dog within four feet. In such a case, even though (1) is evidentially challenged for me by (2) on (3), I can continue to believe in (1) because I have another source of warrant for believing in (1), which happens to be my eyesight. Similarly, even if pain and pleasure act evidentially to question my belief in God, my warrant for believing in God's existence can derive from other sources that can counterbalance the evidential challenge posed by Draper's argument. In fact, Draper's conclusion of his argument says, "Other evidence held equal, theism is very probably false." In other words, Draper claims that when other evidences for God's existence are left out of the equation, theism is very probably false. But why do we need to leave out other evidences for God? There are propositional as well as non-propositional evidences for God that philosophers of recent years have defended.[33]

On April 8, 1966, TIME, one of the America's popular magazines, asked the question, *Is God Dead?*' in its cover page. Only two years later, on December 26, 1969, the magazine's cover was worded, '*Is God Coming Back to Life?*' A new generation of philosophers began providing intellectually satisfying and scientifically sound arguments for the existence of God. Back in the past, it was the 'religious' people who were defending the existence of God. From 1970s, it became the turn of the philosophers. On April 7, 1980, TIME ran another story titled, '*Modernizing the Case for God.*' TIME reports,

> God? Wasn't he chased out of heaven by Marx, banished to the unconscious by Freud and announced by Nietzsche to be deceased? Did not Darwin drive him out of the empirical world? Well, not entirely. In a quiet revolution in thought and argument that hardly anyone could have foreseen only two decades ago, God is making a comeback. Most intriguingly, this is happening not among theologians or ordinary believers, but in the crisp intellectual circles of academic philosophers, where the consensus had long banished the Almighty from fruitful discourse.[34]

When we consider all the evidences for God's existence and lay them alongside Draper's evidential argument from evil, then the problem of evil isn't really a problem for theists. Thus even if Draper's evidential argument succeeds, it doesn't reach far enough to warrant disbelief in God. I can rationally continue to believe in God even if evil and suffering pose a threat to my belief in God's existence.

Extra-mental evidential arguments from evil are rare in philosophical debates and often include evidences that were used in the intra-mental version. Arguers of the extra-mental version of the evidential problem would say that since there are probably gratuitous evils in the world, there is probably no God. The reason for saying that there are probably purposeless evils in our world is that of our failure to see any purpose in an instance of evil: since I can't think of any good reason why God would allow X to suffer, there is probably no good reason that God might have to let X suffer. We have already explored why such a conclusion is fatally flawed. Besides that, making such probability judgments is beyond our cognitive capacities. William Lane Craig writes,

[A]ssessments of probability with regard to evil can be very difficult and even impossible. Certainly many evils seem pointless and unnecessary to us—but we are simply not in a position to judge. The brutal murder of an innocent man or a child's dying of leukemia could send a ripple effect through history so that God's morally sufficient reason for permitting it might not emerge until centuries later or perhaps in another country.[35]

Given the complex ways in which every single event in history is intertwined with each other, we are not in a good position to confidently say that a given instance of evil probably has no God-justifying reason and therefore renders God's existence improbable. Craig gives the following illustration from the movie *Sliding Doors* (1998):

In this film a young woman's life is dramatically affected by whether or not she manages to catch a subway train before the doors slide shut. The film shows that in one case her subsequent life is prosperous and wildly successful, whereas in the other case it is filled with suffering and disappointment. All because of the seemingly trivial incident of catching/ missing a subway train! But that's not all. At the film's end we discover to our surprise that the course of her life which is filled with hardship actually turns out to be the better life, while the seemingly happy life ends prematurely in tragedy.[36]

Whether or not the woman manages to enter the subway train is in turn dependent on whether or not a little girl playing with her doll hinders the way for the woman. Whether or not the little girl playing with her doll is in turn dependent on whether or not her father pulls her back at the right moment as the woman rushes down the stairs to catch the train. Whether or not her father pulls her back at the right moment could in turn be dependent on whether or not the father had a quarrel with his wife that day and hence the delay in reaching the station. Whether or not the father had a quarrel with his wife that day could in turn be dependent on whether or not he had gone to pick her up from her work at the right time, which in turn could be dependent on whether or the fuel in his car was empty. This chain of interconnected events could go on extending into the past, to different people's lives and situations, such that it would be almost impossible to predict the outcome of any event. Who could have predicted that a man's car running out of fuel one day would result in the success of an unknown woman's life many years later?

We cannot put an instance of evil, say the murder of an innocent man, in a small clean box and analyse it within that box. God's justifying reasons for allowing it could very well extend beyond the box and hence we are in no position to say, with regard to a particular evil or its totality, that God, if he exists, would probably not be having any morally sufficient reason for allowing it. We lack the necessary data required to make such probability judgments because we are limited in time and space. Only an omniscient mind, that would know the end of history from its beginning, would be warranted in making such probability judgments.

Returning back to the analogical story in the beginning of this chapter, one of the two friends who witnessed the woman leaving behind a weeping child in a parked car and ran away, couldn't think of a good reason why the woman, assuming she was the mother, abandoned the child like that. So he concluded that the child has no kind and caring mother. But his friend pointed out that there are live possibilities (theodicies) to be considered before arriving at such a conclusion. Then they see a man come out of nowhere and console the child and drive her away. Who was that? Rather than speculating something which we have no evidence for, it is better to suspend judgment (Agnostic Thesis) about the matter. Then a third person who knows the woman came up and testified to the loving nature of the mother. But they shouldn't expect the mother to tell them about her family matters and why she left her child like that (CORNEA critique). In the end, we conclude that evidential arguments from evil, despite their apparent attractiveness, fall short in making a case against God. In the next chapter, we will explore how evil and suffering can be used as evidence *for* the existence of God!

Endnotes

[1] William L. Rowe, "The Problem of Evil and Some Varieties of Atheism," in *American Philosophical Quarterly* 16 (1979): 335-41. Citation on page 336.

[2] *Ibid.*, p 337.

[3] *Ibid.*, p 338.

[4] Stephen John Wykstra, "The Humean Obstacle to Evidential Arguments from Suffering: On Avoiding the Evils of 'Appearance' in *International Journal of Philosophy of Religion* 16 (1984), pp. 73-93.

[5] William P. Alston, "The Inductive Argument from Evil and the Human Cognitive Condition" in *Philosophical Perspectives* 5 (1991), pp. 29-67.

[6] Michael J. Murray, "Theodicy" (Chapter 16) in *The Oxford Handbook of Philosophical Theology* (Oxford Handbooks in Religion and Theology), edited by Thomas P. Flint and Michael C. Rea (Oxford University Press, NY: 2009), p 356, Kindle Location 8812-8816.

[7] William Rowe, "The Evidential Argument from Evil: A Second Look" in *The Evidential Argument from Evil*, edited by Daniel Howard-Snyder (Indiana University Press, Bloomington, IN, USA, 1996) p 277. Brackets mine.

[8] Recall that in the logical problem of evil, the concept of free fill was used as a *defence*. But in the evidential problem of evil, free will is used as a *theodicy*. As a defence, it only had to be logically possible. But as a theodicy, the free will has to be reasonable to believe. Hence several objections to the free will shall be dealt with below.

[9] Ravi Zacharias, Cries of the Heart: Bringing God Near When He Feels So Far (Thomas Nelson, Nashville, TN, 2002), p 216.

[10] I am, of course, hinting the sacrifice of Jesus Christ on the cross which we will explore more fully under Christianity.

[11] Michael J. Murray, "Theodicy" (Chapter 16) in *The Oxford Handbook of Philosophical Theology* (Oxford Handbooks in Religion and Theology), edited by Thomas P. Flint and Michael C. Rea (Oxford University Press, NY: 2009), p 364, Kindle Location 9004-9008.

[12] Bruce R. Reichenbach, *Evil and a Good God*, fourth printing (Fordham University Press, NY, 2001), p 84. First published in 1982 by Fordham University Press.

[13] John Hick, *Evil and the God of Love* (Palgrave Macmillan, Great Britain, UK, Reissue edition, 2010), p 369.

[14] *Ibid.*

[15] William P. Alston, "The Inductive Argument from Evil and the Human Cognitive Condition" in *The Evidential Argument from Evil*, edited by Daniel Howard-Snyder (Indiana University Press, Bloomington, IN, USA, 1996) p 105.

[16] Michael J. Murray, "Theodicy" (Chapter 16) in *The Oxford Handbook of Philosophical Theology* (Oxford Handbooks in Religion and Theology), edited by Thomas P. Flint and Michael C. Rea (Oxford University Press, NY: 2009), p 359, Kindle Location 8906-8908.

[17] John Hick, *Evil and the God of Love* (Palgrave Macmillan, Great Britain, UK, Reissue edition, 2010), p 281.

[18] Michael J. Murray, "Theodicy" (Chapter 16) in *The Oxford Handbook of Philosophical Theology* (Oxford Handbooks in Religion and Theology), edited by

Thomas P. Flint and Michael C. Rea (Oxford University Press, NY: 2009), p 365, Kindle Location 9029-9032.

[19] John Hick, Evil and the God of Love (San Francisco: Harper and Row, 1977), 255-56; Hick, "An Irenaean Theodicy," reprinted in Mesle, John Hick's Theodicy, xxii.

[20] William P. Alston, "The Inductive Argument from Evil and the Human Cognitive Condition" in *The Evidential Argument from Evil*, edited by Daniel Howard-Snyder (Indiana University Press, Bloomington, IN, USA, 1996) p 105.

[21] Michael Murray, *Nature Red in Tooth and Claw: Theism and the Problem of Animal Suffering* (Oxford University Press, NY, 2008)

[22] *Ibid.*, p 52.

[23] *Ibid.*, p 53.

[24] I use the word 'animal' to mean all non-human creatures ranging from bacteria to chimpanzees.

[25] *Ibid.*, p 53.

[26] *Ibid.*, p 53.

[27] *Ibid.*, p 56-57. Emphasis original.

[28] *Ibid.*, p 42.

[29] Paul Draper in "Pain and Pleasure: An Evidential Problem for Theists," *Noûs* Vol. 23, No. 3 (Jun., 1989), pp. 331-350.

[30] Paul Draper, "The Problem of Evil" (Chapter 15) in *The Oxford Handbook of Philosophical Theology* (Oxford Handbooks in Religion and Theology), edited by Thomas P. Flint and Michael C. Rea (Oxford University Press, NY: 2009), p 339. Kindle location 8412-8419. Brackets and emphasis original.

[31] For some critiques of Draper's argument, see Gregory E. Gannssle, "God and Evil," in *The Rationality of Theism*, ed. Paul Copan and Paul K. Moser (Routledge, 2003), pp. 259-277. See "Draper's Evidential Argument," pp. 265-274, Richard Otte, "Probability and Draper's Evidential Argument From Evil," in *Christian Faith and the Problem of Evil*, ed. Peter van Inwagen (Eerdman's Publishing Co, 2004), Christopher Bernard, "Induction, Abduction, and the Argument From Evil," in *God Matters: Readings in the Philosophy of Religion*, ed. Raymond Martin and Christopher Bernard (Longman Publishers, 2003), pp. 323-338. See pp. 334-336, Richard Otte, "Evidential Arguments From Evil," *International Journal for Philosophy of Religion* 48 (2000), 1-10, Loren Meierding, *God, Relationships, and Evil* (Writers Club Press, 2000). See Chapter 17, "The Indifference Hypothesis," pp. 399-423, Alvin Plantinga, "On Being Evidentially Challenged," in *The Evidential Argument from Evil*, ed. Daniel Howard-Snyder (Indiana University Press, 1996), pp. 244-261, William Alston, "Theism as Theory and the Problem of Evil," *Topoi* 14.2 (1995), 135-148. See Section V, pp. 145-147, Daniel Howard-Snyder, "Theism, the Hypothesis of

Indifference, and the Biological Role of Pain and Pleasure," in *Faith and Philosophy* 11 (1994), 452-466 and Peter van Inwagen, "The Problem of Evil, the Problem of Air, and the Problem of Silence," in *Philosophical Perspectives, 5, Philosophy of Religion,* 1991, ed. James E. Tomberlin (Ridgeview Publishing Co., 1991).

[32] Alvin Plaintinga in *Warranted Christian Belief* (Oxford University Press, NY, 2000), pp 381-90.

[33] For non-propositional evidence, see Plantinga's "Is Belief in God Properly Basic?" in *Noûs,* Vol. 15, No. 1, 1981 A. P. A. Western Division Meetings (Mar., 1981), pp. 41-51. For propositional evidence, see William Lane Craig's *Reasonable Faith: Christian Faith and Apologetics,* 3rd edition (Wheaton, IL: Crossway, 2008). There are, of course, many other philosophers who have defended God's existence. But since Plantinga and Craig are names that may have become familiar to readers by now, and since they are among the first-class philosophers of today, and their works easily accessible, I have mentioned their works that contain the arguments for God's existence.

[34] "Modernizing the Case for God," *Time* (April 7, 1980), 65–66.

[35] William Lane Craig, *Hard Questions, Real Answers* (Crossway Books, Wheaton, IL, 2003), p 93.

[36] *Ibid.,* pp 92-93.

4
Turning the Tables:
Evil as Evidence for God

If there is *no* God, then why is there evil in our world? On December 16, 2012, a horrendous crime took place in India's capital city that soon generated widespread national and international coverage. A 23 year old medical student from the state of Uttar Pradesh was brutally assaulted, raped and eventually died in spite of being given the best medical care. A single event can encapsulate and articulate an entire universe of experience. The Nirbhaya case is one such event that shocked the world. Thousands of men and women took to the streets in protest as the news spread all over our country. The initial emotions were all on the rapists – six of them. People expressed their anger in all sorts of ways because of the abominable act done by the rapists. But after the news of Nirbhaya's death reached public ears, anger turned into sorrow. The whole nation wept for the girl and the fight for justice reached new heights. One of the convicts was a juvenile at the time of committing the crime and hence was sentenced to only three years of confinement in a rehabilitation center, prompting further outrage from the public. Today, Nirbhaya – the fearless one – has become an emblem of bravery throughout the country. Nevertheless the crime committed against the woman remains an instance of horrendous evil – a moral abomination – in the hearts and souls of people who know in their bones that such actions are wrong and ought not to be tolerated. But if there is no God, what basis do we have for condemning evils such as these as morally wrong?

I have heard many people say that we don't need God to tell us what is right and what is wrong. We can judge an action right or wrong without reference to God. We can clearly see that cases of child abuse, rape and murder are wrong and we don't need God or religion to tell us that. The well-known writer, George Eliot, was one among the many atheists to promote this view. According to Eliot[1], morality does not require a religious foundation. In fact, for her, religion only dilutes morality as the people tend to be more focused on leaving earth and going to heaven and thereby it reduces moral motivation to love our fellow human beings. To this, Friedrich Nietzsche, the famous atheist philosopher who proclaimed the death of God, poured scorn on Eliot and others like her for rejecting God and yet holding on to moral facts.

> They are rid of the Christian God and now believe all the more firmly that they must cling to Christian morality.[2]

Nietzsche's conclusions were firm: if there is no God, then "There are altogether no moral facts."[3] Eliot argued that moral truths are objective and real. Nietzsche argued that if there is no God, then morality is an illusion. When the convictions of these two atheists are brought together, a powerful argument for God's existence is formed:

Premise 1: If God does not exist, then objective moral truths do not exist.

Premise 2: But objective moral truths exist.

Conclusion: Therefore God exists.

Consider the first premise of the argument. What we mean by objective moral truths (as opposed to subjective moral truths) is that, in a given circumstance, moral actions are either morally right or morally wrong that are *independent* of personal opinion. To understand the difference between subjective truths and objective truth, consider a 1000 rupee currency note as we have it today. We consider the currency valuable because it can be used to buy something we want to have. But does the currency itself have any value or is its value dependent on the social circumstances within which it is used? Suppose the government decides to use only coins for selling and purchasing. Would we then consider the currency valuable? Or suppose, hypothetically, our currency was given to a man who lived 3000 years back in world history. Would it be valuable in the same way it is today? We can now begin to see that the currency has no intrinsic worth in itself. It is the relevant social setting that imparts value to something which is of no value in and of itself. The statement, 'this currency is valuable', has no objective truth in it. The truth of that statement is relative to the socio-cultural setting in which it is used such that if the socio-cultural setting is removed, the statement loses its truth. By way of contrast, consider the revolution of the earth around the sun. We now have conclusive scientific evidence that the earth revolves around the sun. But the ancient world thought that it was the sun that revolved around the earth. But although the people in the ancient world thought that way, in reality, it is the earth that revolves around the sun. Thus the statement, 'the earth revolves around the sun', is a true statement that transcends socio-cultural factors and people's opinion. Even if the entire human race is removed from the earth, the earth would still be revolving around the sun. In other words, the statement 'the earth revolves around the sun' is independent of human mind and culture and is objective. This is in contrast to the value of the currency which, as we saw, is clearly dependent on the human mind and culture and is subjective. And so when we say that there are *objective* moral truths that exist in our world (second premise), we are affirming something similar to the earth revolving around the sun. The statement 'rape is morally wrong' is objective and true regardless of human opinion and culture because it transcends them and is independent of them. If Adolf Hitler had won World War *II* and had brainwashed the entire world into believing that his murdering of six million Jews was something morally good, the murder would still be morally wrong even if there would have been no human being on earth to stand up and judge the action to be morally wrong. But why do we say that the moral wrongness of rape and murder is objective and real? I think it is because it violates something that is intrinsic to every person on earth. We often speak of each person's right to life, dignity and worth. But are they all intrinsic in each person or are they relational and dependent on something else? For example, consider a human being who is also a husband. That the man is a human being is something that is intrinsic to him. But that he is a husband is something that is dependent on his wife.

The husband remains a husband as long as he is related to his wife. But his humanness is not related to anything other than himself. It belongs intrinsically to him.[4]

Now do the rights, dignity and value of each human being belong intrinsically to each of us or are they merely social constructs that are designed by the constitution of each country and then imposed on us who, in reality, have no rights, dignity and value? In the latter case, human rights, dignity and value are related to and are dependent on the constitution that gives us something that doesn't belong to us. If human rights, dignity and value are not truly possessed by each person but are merely convenient labels given to us to maintain the social fabric of our country, then the moral distinction between man and animal would be lost, and the man who rapes and murders a woman would be doing nothing more than the equivalent of a female spider killing its male mate after copulating with it (sexual cannibalism). Actions like rape, murder, incest and cannibalism happen routinely in the animal kingdom and the animals are not being immoral because of such behaviours. A zebra has no more right to life than a lion has to eat it. But human beings are unlike animals. Our moral experience tells us that human life is sacred for what it is, and that is why we are right to react with horror at the violent gang rape and murder of Nirbhaya. Atheist philosopher Michael Ruse writes,

> The man who says that it is morally acceptable to rape little children is just
> as mistaken as the man who says, 2+2=5.[5]

But what about the first premise? If there is no God, then there will be no objective moral truths. Human beings, in the absence of God, arrived on the scene as random by-products of Darwinian evolution.[6] As Ruse admittedly points out,

> [H]umans are typical products of evolution. Of course, we are unique. But,
> then, so is *Drosophila melanogaster* (a species of fruit-fly).[7]

If there is no God, then we are the accidental by-products of nature. The universe is here for no purpose and has no value and no meaning for its existence – and so are we. As the atheist biologist Richard Dawkins admits,

[T]here is at bottom no design, no purpose, no evil, no good, nothing but pointless indifference...We are machines for propagating DNA...It is every living object's sole reason for being.[8]

Thus a world without God will lead to a world without ultimate meaning, value and purpose. And in a world without meaning, value and purpose, morality cannot be affirmed objectively. If I decide to rob your car and feel that I am right in doing so, then who are you to judge me wrong? You can take me to court or take revenge on me. But if I can get away with it (and even if I didn't), then I have not wronged anybody. You may *feel* that I have wronged you, but I don't. Well, maybe the whole world might feel that I have wronged you. So does the majority win? Not at all if it's still just their *feelings*. As the atheist philosopher Paul Kurtz says assuming atheism,

The moral principles that govern our behavior are rooted in habit and custom, feeling and fashion.[9]

But such a view of morality is contrary to our moral experience. Consider the following three statements:

1.　I *feel* that child abuse is wrong.

2.　I *think* that child abuse is wrong.

3.　Child abuse *is* wrong.

When we encounter cases of abhorrent and horrendous crimes committed by one human being against another, we don't want to say that we feel or think that they are wrong. Our hearts cry out saying that they *are* wrong – objectively wrong. Consider, for example, that there has occurred a catastrophic event on earth leaving behind only an adult man and a three year old young child. The man, out of frustration, begins to torture the child by all means possible. He feels and thinks that he is not doing anything morally wrong. The child has no cognitive capacity to judge the action but is only convulsing in pain. Nobody else is there on earth to feel or think that the child abuser is wrong. Will his actions, therefore, lose its moral wrongness? Since only his feelings prevail, will his actions be justified? I don't think so. Regardless of what he feels or thinks, his actions are wrong. This goes to show that moral wrongness and rightness cannot be based on feelings or intellect. There needs to be an external standard for evaluating moral actions. That external standard is provided by God's own perfect nature. God, as the greatest conceivable being, is a morally perfect being. He is by nature loving, kind, generous and self-giving. Any human action that conforms to God's essential nature would be morally right and any human action that deviates from God's essential nature would be morally wrong. The existence of objective moral truths is, therefore, evidence that there is a morally perfect God whose own perfect nature is the objective standard for morality. And more than that, the intrinsic value and dignity we see in every human being can only be explained by inferring a God who created man that way. The more serious we take human evils as moral abominations, and the more serious we value human life, the more serious the evidence becomes for the existence of God.

The second premise of the argument is nearly uncontroversial: we can all agree that morality is not merely a social construct, but something real and objective. Even deniers of objective moral truths, when asked penetrating questions, like "So do you say that torturing innocent children for fun is morally permissible if nobody is there to condemn it?," will admit that objective moral truths do exist in our world. We want to raise our voices and cry out against child trafficking, injustice, rape and murder. But such a reaction would be appropriate only if morality is objective and real. Even many leading atheists of today concede that moral truths are objective. J.L. Mackie, one of the leading atheists who challenged God's existence based on the evils in the world, says this:

> [W]e might well argue...that objective intrinsically prescriptive features, supervening upon natural ones, constitute so odd a cluster of qualities and relations that they are most unlikely to have arisen in the ordinary course of events, without an all-powerful god to create them.[10]

Now let's look at a couple of common objections to the first premise of the argument. First, it might be said that objective moral truths, if they cannot be based on feelings or intellect, can be grounded in pain. Certainly, the pain experienced by the sufferer is real and therefore causing unnecessary pain is morally wrong. But the problem with this reasoning is that animals routinely cause unnecessary pain to each other and their actions are not morally wrong. William Lane Craig says,

> When a great white shark forcibly copulates with a female, it forcibly copulates with her but it doesn't *rape* her--for none of these actions is forbidden or obligatory. There is no moral dimension to these actions.[11]

Since, if there is no God, human beings are merely evolved primates, how did human actions acquire moral significance which is lacking in their primitive cousins? And if pain is the indicator for moral rightness and moral wrongness, then what about slaying a man while he is asleep or euthanizing him to death without any pain? Will that remove its moral wrongness? I don't think so.

Second, it may be argued that anything that promotes human health and well-being can be said to be morally good and anything that destroys human health and well-being can be said to be morally wrong. But this criterion would only lead us to speciesism – that is, the unjust favouring of the human species over against the non-human species. Speciesism is the assumption that being human is a good enough reason for human species to have greater moral rights than non-human species. It is exactly analogous to racism, sexism and other forms of discrimination that we find in our own species and is, therefore, arbitrary. Why favour whites over blacks, males over females or humans over mosquitoes? If destroying the health of a man is morally wrong, then so should the destruction of the health of mosquitoes.

In our biological world, assuming that there is no God, there aren't any morally relevant differences between humans and non-humans. Creating such a difference and imputing moral significance only to human health and well-being is a purely subjective and an arbitrary construct. In the end, every attempt to try to affirm objective moral truths without reference to God fails. If God does not exist, then moral truths cannot be affirmed objectively. But our moral experience tells us that moral truths do exist objectively. It, therefore, follows that God exists.[12]

Endnotes

[1] Her real name was Mary Anne Evans. Geroge Eliot is a pseudo-name under which her books were published.

[2] Friedrich Nietzsche, *Twilight of the Idols and the Anti-Christ* (Penguin Books, NY, 1968), p 69.

[3] *Ibid.*, p 55.

[4] Mark D. Linville, "The Moral Argument" in *The Blackwell Companion to Natural Theology* by William Lane Craig (Editor) and J.P. Moreland (Editor) (Blackwell Publishing Ltd., UK, 2009), pp. 431-432.

[5] Michael Ruse, *Darwinism Defended* (London: Addison-Wesley, 1982), p. 275.

[6] I am emphasizing the word 'Darwinian' because a non-Darwinian theory of evolution is compatible with the existence of God. Theistic evolutionists believe that God was actively involved in the evolutionary process of human beings from lower animals. Hence evolution itself is not incompatible with God's existence. It is *Darwinian* evolution (natural selection acting on random mutations) that is incompatible with God's existence. In what follows, therefore, I will use the word evolution to mean Darwinian evolution.

[7] Michael Ruse, "Evolutionary Theory and Christian Ethics: Are They in Harmony" (Chapter 10) in *The Darwinian Paradigm: Essays on its history, philosophy, and religious implications* (London: Routledge, 1989), p 252.

[8] Richard Dawkins, *River out of Eden: a Darwinian View of Life* (New York: Basic Books, 1996), p. 133 and Richard Dawkins, "The Ultraviolet Garden," Lecture 4 of 7 Royal Institution Christmas Lectures (1992), http://physicshead. blogspot.com/2007/01/richard-dawkins-lecture-4-ultraviolet.html. Last accessed on 03/10/2015.

[9] Paul Kurtz, *Forbidden Fruit: The Ethics of Secularism* (Buffalo, N.Y.: Prometheus Books, 1988) p. 73.

[10] J.L. Mackie, *The Miracle of Theism* (Oxford University Press, NY, 1982), p 115.

[11] William Lane Craig in his debate with Sam Harris on the topic, "Is the Foundation of Morality Natural or Supernatural?" held at the University Of Notre Dame, Notre Dame, Indiana, United States – April 2011. For a transcript, see http:// www.reasonablefaith.org/is-the-foundation-of-morality-natural-or-supernatural-the-craig-harris. Last accessed on 04/10/2015.

[12] What makes this argument even more powerful is that it excludes demi-gods of polytheistic religions that are believed to possess less than perfect moral natures. The argument also excludes impersonal gods of polytheistic religions. This is particularly relevant in a country like India where many believe in a so-called

'Higher Power' that lacks the essential characteristics of personhood such as self-consciousness, thinking and acting. They believe God is some sort of a vague 'Energy' that cannot be defined. But objective moral truths cannot be affirmed by reference to these gods. This is because for God to be the source of moral values, he has to be morally perfect. And for God to create persons like you and me, he too has to be personal.

II

An Analysis of Religious Responses to the Problem of Evil

5
Buddhism:
Escaping the Problem

The Buddha is often compared to a physician. It is believed that he first diagnoses the problem, finds out its cause, sees the cure and then prescribes the needed therapy to end the problem. This quadrupled analysis is known as the Four Noble Truths of Buddhism. In its most simple form, it is as follows:

1. There is suffering.

2. There is a cause for suffering.

3. There is a cure for suffering.

4. There is a path to end suffering.

The first truth is pretty straightforward: like it or not, life will present you with suffering. The Buddha says,

> What is the noble truth of suffering? Birth is suffering, old age is suffering, death is suffering, grief, lamentation, pain, despair, and distress are suffering; not getting what one wants, that is suffering. In brief, the five aggregates of attachment are suffering.[1]

The second truth finds three root causes of all suffering: self-centered desire (or craving), ignorance (or delusion) and hatred (or aversion). These three intertwining causes of suffering are the three 'poisons' (or 'fires') that make us suffer. The first poison – craving – is of three types: craving for the pleasures of the five human senses, craving for existing in the world and craving for not existing in the world. They cause one to become attached to world. The Buddha says,

What is the noble truth of the origin of suffering? That craving which leads to rebirth, accompanied by pleasure and lust, finding delight in this or that, namely, craving for sensual pleasure, craving for becoming, and craving for non-becoming.[2]

Such forms of craving occur primarily because of another poison – ignorance. Ignorance of what? Ignorance of the three marks of existence: suffering, impermanence and non-self. According to Buddhism, these are the three facts of the world. Although many people live their lives pretending to deny that there are actually terrible forms of suffering in our world, the bottom line is that life is marked by suffering. Life is also marked by impermanence (or change). Nothing in the world is permanent. Everything changes. 'Change' is the only thing that will not change. Today I might be in good health. But tomorrow that might change. And if my health doesn't change tomorrow, it will definitely change some other day. People suffer because they are not willing to accept this fact in their practical lives. The third mark of existence is non-self. You and I, according to Buddhism, have no permanent self or soul within us. We are simply a matter of impermanent impersonal psychophysical aggregates heaped up together to form what we are. Ignorance of this fact leads to suffering.

Finally, ignorance and craving together lead to the third poison – hatred (or aversion). Fueled by self-centered desire and ignorance, we develop hatred towards others which cause them to suffer when we act upon our hatred. In sum, suffering, both for us and for others, is caused by the three poisons of selfish desire, ignorance and hatred.

So what now? Is there a hope to end suffering? According to the Buddha, yes there is. If the causes of suffering are the three poisons, then the solution to end suffering is to remove the three poisons from our lives. Rather than seeking to please our own selves, we should strive to centre our lives on helping others. That will decrease selfish desire and reduce suffering for us. We also ought to educate ourselves of the facts about the world that this world is not permanent and filled with suffering and that there is no real 'you' or 'me' that exists. Coming to terms with these truths will reduce the sufferings of us and others. Lastly, in order to control our hatred, we ought to practice meditation that will help focus our minds in the right direction and which will, in turn, reduce suffering for others. So how does one go about doing all this? The fourth Noble Truth provides the answer:

> What is the noble truth of the path going to the cessation of suffering? It is this Noble Eightfold Path, namely: right view, right intention, right speech, right action, right livelihood, right effort, right mindfulness, right concentration.[3]

Also called the 'Middle Way,'[4] this Noble Eightfold path to end suffering is grouped into three major categories: wisdom, ethics and meditation.

The Four Noble Truths

1. Life is suffering.

2. The causes of suffering are desire, ignorance and hatred.

3. The way out of suffering is to extinguish the fires of desire, ignorance and hatred.

4. The path to end suffering is the Noble Eightfold Path.

The Noble Eightfold Path

Wisdom

1. Right View – understanding the Four Noble Truths, Karma and reincarnation.

2. Right Intension – Resolving to live out a life consistent with the right view.

Ethics

3. Right Speech – Speaking the Truth and avoiding lies.

4. Right Action – Avoiding actions that hurt other living beings and other unethical conducts.

5. Right Livelihood – Making one's living in such a way that is moral and avoids hurting other living beings.

Meditations

6. Right Effort – Attempting to live a noble life centered on Buddhist doctrines.

7. Right mindfulness – Being alert and conscious of our every effort and thought and action.

8. Right concentration – Focusing the mind on one of the other meditation object to achieve states of calmness and peacefulness.

The one who sincerely journeys on the Middle-Way Path will eventually achieve a state called *Nirvana*. The word means to blow out or extinguish. When the fires of desire, ignorance and hatred are extinguished, there obtains a calm and peaceful state of mind that is unaffected by the perils and dangers of the world. But we would still be living on earth. Such a state is called *nirvana with the remainder* of life[5]. In this state, though we continue to exist in the world, we will not be bothered by the pain and pleasure that this ever-changing world offers us.

> [Nirvana] literally means "cooled" and is analogous to a fire that's no longer burning. Thus, when there is cessation, your mind no longer burns in response to the arising of pleasant and unpleasant in your life; it isn't reactive or controlled by what you like or dislike.[6]

After this state of blissful blindness to the pain and pleasure of life in this world, and upon the death of the individual, the person is said to achieve *nirvana without the remainder* of life. He is freed from the cycle of karma and rebirth and enters into a state of blissfulness that is characterised as neither existence nor non-existence. No words in our vocabulary can indicate what happens to the person who enters nirvana without the reminder[7]. Hence the question of what becomes of the person who has attained the second state of nirvana falls under the category of the 'Noble Silence'[8]. But what happens to the person who doesn't attain nirvana? He is swept into the cycle of rebirth fueled by his own actions (karma). The goal of life, according to Buddhism, is to escape from being born into the world as undesirable creatures – including human beings – and go somewhere else, away from the pain and misery that this world brings us. There are a total of six realms where you could be reborn. They are, from the highest to the lowest,[9]

1. Realm of gods[10]

2. Realm of humans

3. Realm of Titans

4. Realm of ghosts

5. Realm of animals

6. Realm of hell

The aim in life is to go beyond the realm of the gods and away from being reborn. Good karmic deeds help you attain a better life in your next birth and bad karmic deeds send you off to the lower end of the spectrum. So if I am in a miserable situation today, that is probably because of my bad karmic deeds in my past life. I say 'probably' because the doctrine of karma doesn't say that *all* our fortunes and misfortunes are the result of our actions. Many things that happen in life – good or bad – may simply be accidents. And also the karmic fruits of our actions are amendable to change. If, for example, being born in a low socioeconomic status is a karmic curse wrought upon me, then I could come out of the curse and live a better life if I am persistent and hardworking.

Buddhism, therefore, is obsessed with the fact that life is studded with sufferings and that the only way out of it is to attain nirvana through proper wisdom, ethics and meditation. My response to Buddhism shall be focused on three of its aspects:

1. The nature of nirvana

2. The cause and the cure

3. Karma and rebirth

First is the nature of nirvana. When a person attains nirvana with the remainder of life, he is said to be freed from the fires of self-desire, hatred and delusion. This, it is believed, would lead to freedom from all forms of mental pain. The enlightened person would still experience painful feelings. But since he is not attached to the notion of the self as in thinking, "It is *I* who is in pain," he is free from "mental pain."[11] But can he really be free from all mental pain? Buddhist sources narrate that even the Buddha, after attaining nirvana with the remainder of life, was "unhappy/discontent/fed up/uncomfortable/dissatisfied" when he was unable to reunite two parties of monks in Kosambi.[12] If mental pain can affect even the Buddha after his enlightenment, pity on us! We cannot avoid the problem of pain by trying to detach our thoughts from our painful experiences.

What about nirvana without the remainder of life? It is said to be a condition that is unthinkable and indescribable[13], and yet we have it thought through and described:

> That sphere *(ayatana)* exists, monks, where there is no earth, no water, no heat and no wind, where the sphere of infinite space does not exist, nor that of infinite consciousness, nor that of neither-perception-nor-non-perception; there is neither this world nor the other world, neither moon nor sun; there, I say, there is no coming and going, no duration (of life, to be followed by) death and rebirth; it is not stationed, it is without occurrence (s), and has no object. This, indeed, is the end of suffering.[14]

Ultimate nirvana is a state where "there is absolutely no 'becoming', and experiences have 'become cool'."[15]

> [T]he early sources describe nirvana [without the remainder] in predominantly negative terms such as 'the absence of desire', 'the extinction of thirst', 'blowing out', and 'cessation'. A smaller number of positive epithets are also found including 'the auspicious', 'the good', 'purity', 'peace', 'truth', and 'the further shore'. Certain passages seem to suggest that nirvana is a transcendent reality which is 'unborn, unoriginated, uncreated and unformed' *(Udāna* 80), but it is difficult to know what interpretation to place upon such formulations. In the last analysis the nature of final nirvana remains an enigma other than to those who experience it. What we *can* be sure of, however, is that it means the end of suffering and rebirth.[16]

Contemplating on all these 'descriptions' of nirvana without the remainder of life, all one gets to know is that it is the ultimate cessation of suffering with the turning off of all our experiences. This leads us to ask, "Should I aspire to attain this nirvana?" If there is no longer going to be 'me' as an individual and if 'I' am no longer going to experience anything good or bad, but simply going to exist as some non-personal indescribable *something*, then certainly I wouldn't be happy about reaching such a state. Yes, my sufferings would cease. But so would I, along with all the joys and goodness of this life. Besides, I have no clue as to what to expect of that state, because I am left only with descriptions of what *not* to expect: no earth, no water, no heat and no wind, no space, no consciousness, no perception, no time, no object, no emotions, no feelings, no speech, no thought and no suffering. Other than the absence of suffering, ultimate nirvana doesn't look so bright to me.

Secondly, let us analyse the Buddhist doctrines of the cause and the cure. We shall discuss it under two headings:

1. Practical problems

2. Philosophical problems

As to the practical problems, the Second Noble Truth claimed that suffering arises because of self-centered desire, hatred and delusion. Hence the Fourth Noble Truth showed the path of self-sacrifice, benevolence and understanding that can be traversed in order to end suffering. Accordingly, Buddhist scholar Peter Harvey writes,

> It is seen as in the nature of things [in Buddhism] that behaving ethically reduces suffering and increases happiness, for oneself and those one interacts with.[17]

But is it really the case that good behaviour reduces suffering. I think quite the contrary is true. The world is filled with cases where good people are bullied by the bad ones. Those who live honest lives are the ones who suffer because of those who exploit them. Those who extend their love towards the undeserving are the ones who suffer because of it. I can tell you that because of the life experience of my mother. Recently she happened to spot a lady lying on the floor in the busy sidewalk of a street. Being a doctor, she noticed a thyroid swelling in the lady's neck and this added more sympathy towards her. When she called her and learnt that she was without a house, a job or family, my mother bought her new sets of clothes and welcomed her into our own home, only to be disappointed at the fact that the lady had become a thief in our own home. My mother can narrate numerous personal incidences like this where helping others only leads to *more* suffering for us.

Right speech, right action and right livelihood (Noble Path 3, 4 and 5) are pathways that lead *towards* suffering for many people, and not away from it. As a Christian, I take Jesus Christ as the exemplar of what I am saying. He spoke what is good, practiced what is right and lived a righteous life. And they killed him for that. Yet the peace that he offers to those who suffer is a peace that nobody else can offer (John 14:27).

What about Noble Paths 1 and 2? Buddhism claims that having the right view and the right thought about the world and ourselves will reduce suffering for us. In other words, believing that this world is marked with suffering and is impermanent, and that we are simply an aggregate of five impermanent stuffs will reduce our sufferings. Who are we as individuals? We are simply five component parts assembled together with no intentionality.

While seeking enlightenment, the Buddha analyzed himself in search of an intrinsic, permanent self (atman). He found only an ever-changing configuration of component parts, or skandhas. The five skandhas are form, feelings, conceptions, dispositions, and consciousness. Form refers to the physical properties of an individual. In this context, feelings include the raw sensory perceptions of external things, while conceptions are the mental images drawn from the sensory data. Dispositions are the likes and dislikes formed in relation to conceptions and encompass the emotions. Consciousness means the mental workings commonly referred to as conscious thought.[18]

Each one of us is made up of:

1. Form

2. Feeling

3. Conception

4. Disposition

5. Consciousness

But we now know that 2-5 are not individual "parts" that make up a whole. Rather they are *functions* of the brain, which is also a form. So in the end we are just large and complex animated chunks of matter. Does that sound encouraging or depressing? Perhaps encouraging to some and depressing to others – and that's the point. Coming to realise the Buddhist doctrinal truths of suffering, impermanence and non-self, as well as karma and rebirth will not *always* guarantee less mental suffering for *everyone*. Some people may find that their mental stress is reduced if they believe that nothing is permanent and that the self doesn't exist while others might find those same doctrines causing uneasiness and mental discomfort. It is not going to work the same way for everyone.

Piecing back the Eightfold Path to nirvana, let us delve into some philosophical problems with it. First, the Eightfold Path (which includes ethics) is given as a *recommendation*, and not obligatory. Here, says the Buddha, is the Path you can take *if* you want to end suffering. But there is nothing mandatory about it. When a doctor diagnoses that his patient is sick because of a particular disease, he can only recommend the treatment. There is nothing that mandates the patient to be treated. Likewise if a person refuses to follow the ethical component of the Eightfold Path, and decides to hurt other human beings, he cannot be said to have done something morally wrong because he did not violate any objectively binding ethical standard. Of course, he causes suffering for others and perhaps he himself might suffer because of it. But that doesn't make his actions morally wrong. If there is no transcendent moral law and a divine Lawgiver, then what makes it *wrong* to cause pain? As I have argued in the previous chapters, ethics loses its objective meaning in the absence of God.

Second, morality is recommended, not because it is good in itself, but because some other benefit can be obtained, namely nirvana. This is a deficient view of ethics. As philosopher Bruce Reichenbach notes the same point in another context,

> Why ought I to do such and such? Because it will bring me certain desirable things or have advantageous consequences for me…What is commended

is no longer morality itself or the virtues themselves but the advantage one can get from them.[19]

Third, in making human beings a random composition of five aggregates, there is no way Buddhism can confer human rights and dignity to people. Damien Keown, professor of Buddhist ethics, writes,

> On the whole, however, traditional sources have little to say about the kinds of questions which are now regarded as human rights issues...In many religions human dignity is said to derive from the fact that human beings are created in the image of God. Buddhism, of course, makes no such claim. This makes it difficult to see what the source of human dignity might be.[20]

Indeed it is difficult to find a source for intrinsic human value and dignity. Buddhism, like atheism, faces the problem of affirming the intrinsic worth of being human.

We now come to our analysis of karma and rebirth. It faces a practical problem and a philosophical problem. On the practical side, it is said that one important reason for moral motivation to do good deeds is that they guarantee a higher rebirth and thus takes us a step closer to attaining ultimate nirvana. By contrast, bad deeds make us less fortunate human beings in our next birth or worse, they make us animals. But if I am not going to carry forward my memories into the next birth, then what sort of motivation will I have for behaving ethically? And what will demotivate me from behaving unethically? Suppose I continue to become richer by unfair means and I find happiness in that. I then learn that dealing unfairly would cause me suffering in this life, rebirth into undesirable circumstances in the next life and the loss of ultimate nirvana. But I have my excuses for each of them: I am rich and happy now in this life, I don't care if I am born as a tadpole or a poor man in my next life as I won't be knowing that it is because of my bad karma, and I don't want to attain the glooming nirvana after death because I find it equivalent to annihilation. Now there is nothing left to hinder me from acting immorally, not even a bad rebirth. With no conscious continuity between my various lives, past, present and future, I begin every life afresh as if that was the only life I ever lived.[21] Who cares what becomes of "me" in my next birth? Is it even appropriate to talk about "me" in my next life if there is no self-conscious identification of my previous life?

The philosophical problem with karma and rebirth pertains to its origin. Are my past lives finite or infinite? If finite, who was I in the beginning? How was I created? What did I do that initiated this process of karma and rebirth? Was there even an "I" to begin with? If my past lives are infinite, then how did I arrive at my present birth? Did I pass through an infinite number of lives with no starting point to reach this one? How is it logically possible to get to the present if there is no starting point in the past? In the end, the doctrine of karma and rebirth leaves us with more questions than answers.

Although Buddhism portrays a very realistic portrait of suffering and analysed the problem fairly well, the solution it offers as the Noble Eightfold Path is redundant.

Endnotes

[1] John J. Holder (Editor and Translator), *Early Buddhist Discourses* (Hackett Publishing Company, Indianapolis, IN, 2006), p 51.

[2] *Ibid.*, p 52.

[3] *Ibid.*, p 56.

[4] Because this path is a balance between the two extremes of total involvement with the world and total asceticism, both of which lead to suffering.

[5] Rupert Gethin, *The Foundations of Buddhism* (Oxford University Press, NY, 1998), p 76.

[6] Phillip Moffitt, *Dancing With Life: Buddhist Insights for Finding Meaning and Joy in the Face of Suffering* (Rodale Inc., NY, 2012), p 159. First published in hardcover by Rodale Inc. in 2008.

[7] Walpola Rahula, *What the Buddha Taught* (Grove Press, NY, 1974), p 41. The first edition was published in 1959.

[8] Victoria Kennick Urubshurow, *Introducing World Religions*, E-book (Journal of Buddhist Ethics Online Books, PA, 2009), p 337.

[9] Damien Keown, *Buddhism: A Very Short Introduction*, second edition (Oxford: Oxford University Press, 2013), p 35-7. First edition was published as an Oxford University paperback in 1996.

[10] There are a total of 31 levels. Levels 6-31 are the realm of the gods.

[11] *Steven Collins, Nirvana and Other Buddhist Felicities* (Cambridge Studies in Religious Traditions) (Cambridge: Cambridge University Press, NY, 1998), p 156.

[12] *Ibid.* Collins therefore says, "So even enlightened Buddhas can sometimes find things irksome, uncomfortable."

[13] *Ibid.*, p 163.

[14] *Ibid.*, p 165.

[15] Peter Harvey, *The Selfless Mind: Personality, Consciousness and Nirvana in Early Buddhism* (London: RoutledgeCurzon, 2004), p 181. First published in 1995 by Curzon Press.

[16] Damien Keown, *Buddhism: A Very Short Introduction*, second edition (Oxford: Oxford University Press, 2013), p 58. Square brackets mine. Emphasis original.

[17] Peter Harvey, *An Introduction to Buddhism: Teachings, History and Practices*, second edition (Cambridge University Press, NY, 2013), p 264. Brackets mine.

[18] Helen J. Baroni, *The Illustrated Encyclopedia of Zen Buddhism* (Rosen Publishing Group, Inc., NY, 2002), p 93-94. Brackets original.

[19] Bruce R. Reichenbach, *Evil and a Good God*, fourth printing (Fordham University Press, NY, 2001), p 78-79. First published in 1982 by Fordham University Press.

[20] Damien Keown, *Buddhism: A Very Short Introduction* (Oxford: Oxford University Press, 2013), p 120. First edition was published as an Oxford University paperback in 1996.

[21] Of course, there are reports of people who have claimed to "remember" their past lives. And the Buddha too is reported to remember his past lives. But such reports, even if true, are very rare. The majority of practicing Buddhists do not remember anything of their previous lives.

6
Hinduism:
Ignoring the Problem

In the place where I live, Hinduism is everywhere. You can find local shrines in almost every street you enter in. Most temples have brightly coloured alternating strips of red and white painted on their outer walls. There are numerous festivals that are celebrated each year that bring together families and friends and send out helping hands and healing hearts. It is indeed refreshing to be a part of the culture. Hinduism is seen more as a way of life than a religion. In fact, the word 'Hinduism' was coined only in the eighteenth century by British writers.[1] Even the word 'Hindu' was designated by Greek travelers to the Indus Valley who called the people *'indoi'* in the Greek language.[2] Nevertheless the beliefs and practices of Hindus today have textual sources, most notably the Vedas, the Upanishads and the Bhagavad Gita. It is into these ancient texts we shall delve into now.

The four Vedas are the oldest extant texts of India and they contain praise and ritualistic formulas directed towards the gods of nature. In the Indian tradition, they belong to the category of *śruti,* which is "something heard," presumably from the divine realm. They are contrasted with the category of *smṛti,* which is "something learnt" and is believed to have been written down without any divine intervention.[3] Of interest to us right now are the themes of theology and eschatology as found in the Vedas. What exactly are the Vedic gods? They are simply personifications of the natural phenomenon of the world. The evidence that nature was personified and turned into gods is from the description of the gods in

terms of the physical elements they represent. For example, the Vedic
sun god Surya is described as follows:

> The turbid darkness fled...up rose the bright beam of celestial Morning.
> Surya ascended to the wide expanses, beholding deeds of men both good
> and evil.

Rig Veda 4.1.17[4]

Likewise the god Agni, a personification of fire, is always connected to
the burning property of fire:

> Rise up, O Agni, spread thee out before us: burn down our foes, thou who
> hast sharpened arrows. Him, blazing Agni! who hath worked us mischief,
> consume thou utterly like dried-up stubble.

Rig Veda 4.4.4

However, in later Hindu literature such as the epics, what were initially
personifications of nature became independent gods that are totally
disconnected from their original referent. Thus concerning the god Agni,
the scholar Arthur Berriedale Keith writes,

> [T]he gods have long ceased to be nearly as closely connected with their
> natural bases as in the Rigveda, and Agni can figure as the main personage
> in tales which never had any relation to the fire as an element.[5]

Thus the beginning of the Vedic religion is marked by natural phenomena
acquiring personalities and being given hands to bless and to curse and a
mind to feel, think and act. The scholar A.A. Macdonell writes,

> Everything that impressed the soul with awe or was regarded as capable
> of exercising a good or evil influence on man, might in the Vedic age still
> become a direct object not only of adoration but of prayer. Heaven, earth,
> mountains, rivers, plants might be supplicated as divine powers; the horse,
> the cow, the bird of omen, and other animals might be invoked; even
> objects fashioned by the hand of man, weapons, the war-car, the drum,
> the plough, as well as ritual implements, such as the pressing-stones and
> the sacrificial post, might be adored.[6]

Such is the pantheistic understanding of the polytheistic gods in the
Vedas. However, within the polytheism of the Vedas, there is a primitive
attempt to unify the gods into one ultimate reality:

They call him Indra, Mitra, Varuna, Agni, and he is heavenly nobly–winged Garutman. To what is One, sages give many a title they call it Agni, Yama, Matarisvan.

Rig Veda 1.164.46

What exactly is this oneness is open to speculation and indeed, later Hindu texts provide their own concepts of the oneness of God based on the Vedas. For example, the Upanishads offer a monistic oneness whereas the Bhagavad Gita offers both a panentheistic oneness and a monotheistic oneness. Before we get into the Upanishads and the Bhagavad Gita, we have to look into the concept of the eschatological afterlife in the Vedas.

According to the Vedas, depending on one's moral behavior and the way one performs ritual sacrifices in their present lives, people go to heaven, hell or anywhere in between the two. Heaven is conceived as a mirror image of earth with all imperfections removed.

[The Vedic heaven is] a realm of 'inextinguishable light', joy, freedom and fulfilled desires, flowing with cosmic waters, where the deceased are 'fed and satisfied', and cared for by the Lord of the Dead, Yama...[It] is 'adorned by days, waters and nights', suggesting that it follows earthly cycles, and is an idealized mirror-image of earth, with horses and pastures, grass and trees (X.14.1–9, 10.56).[7]

Conversely, hell is a place of gloom and doom, a land of no return.

[Hell is] 'a deep place'...a 'monstrous abyass'...This abyss is said to be located 'below the three earths' (X.152.4), the same location as Naraka, the hellish realm, in the Epics and Puranas. There are also prayers against 'falling into the pit', for protection from 'the devouring wolf', and for the flames of Agni (god of fire, light and the sun) to annihilate evil-doers by burning them 'to nothingness' (II.29.6; X.87.14)....[M]oral transgressors proceed to hellish realms called Parava'tas (XII.5.64). They encounter danger from lightning, from Yama's dogs...and from descending into darkness and to 'the house infernal' from which there is no return. There one encounters 'a fiend with snapping jaws', 'wild-haired women,' 'dismal howlers', 'Decay', witches, 'evil ghosts' (VIII.1.3; 1.9–19; 2.10-24), and various other terrors (cf. VIII.1.12). The immoral are also described as sitting in a river flowing with blood, eating hair (V.19.3; VIII.4.9).[8]

After their death, "the deceased might also travel to the sky, the earth, the ocean, the sun, the dawn, 'the flowing streams of light,' plants, mountains, 'the whole moving universe,' 'distances beyond the beyond,' the past and the future (X.58)."

This picture of the Vedic afterlife is complicated by the fact that sometimes heaven and hell are not eternal abodes but are rather temporary places where one goes, enjoys or suffers rewards or punishments, and then is reborn again somewhere in the universe – and the cycle repeats itself infinitely.[9]

None of the Hindus I know, even devout ones, perform the prescribed Vedic sacrifices. And yet, according to the Yajur Veda[10], there awaits severe punishment in the afterlife for those who fail to perform the correct prescribed ritual sacrifices. And even when the correct procedures are followed and one behaves ethically well, there is no guarantee that heaven will be one's eternal reward. Since one had done only a finite amount of good deeds on earth, one's reward in heaven will also be finite. He will be hurled back into the world of suffering and start from scratch once again. Such a view of the afterlife is depressing and that is indeed why later literature such as the Upanishads and the Bhagavad Gita emerged to solve the problem of eternity.

The Upanishads and the Gita offer ways to transcend the three domains of heaven, earth and hell and find permanence in a Supreme entity. In the Upanishads, this Supreme entity is the *Brahman* – the single unchanging and permanent ground substance of all reality. All the diversities we see around us, including plants, trees, rocks, rivers, birds, animals and human beings, are because of *Maya* – illusion. As long as we live in this illusory world, we suffer. Therefore, the ultimate goal in life is to seek *Moksha* – liberation, and be united with the singular Brahman.[11] This view of the afterlife is called *Advaita Vedanta* – non-dualism, and is the widely discussed Hindu view of life after death in the Western world. According to Vedanta Hinduism, this Brahman is identical to the *Atman* – the soul within each of us. By realising that we are one with the Brahman, we shall escape this world of suffering and illusion and merge with the Brahman. The Upanishads proposes *knowledge* as the key to liberation. Those who have the knowledge that the individual soul and the Supreme Soul are one and the same will attain union with the Brahman. This knowledge is even greater than virtue which only leads to rebirth again in this world. Performing proper sacrifices and behaving ethically took you to the highest of heavens in the Vedas. In the Upanishads, however, they only expel you back to earth after a temporary enjoyment in heaven (Mundaka Upanishad 1.2.10). Only the man who is focused on Brahman can transcend heaven and earth altogether and escape this world of suffering. The metaphor used is that of a bow and arrow and a target. The bow is the word 'OM', the arrow is your soul (atman) and the target is Brahman. Using the bow and focusing on the target, one must shoot himself into the Brahman and be lodged in it forever (Mundaka Upanishad 2.2.4). Interestingly, such an endeavour is a retreat to the primitive state of existence. In the beginning, all that existed was the undifferentiated singular Brahman/Atman shaped like a man (Brihadaranyaka Upanishad 1.4.1). This thought to itself,

> 'Let me become many. Let me propagate myself.' It emitted heat. The heat thought to itself: 'Let me become many. Let me propagate myself.' It emitted water. Whenever it is hot, therefore, a man surely perspires; and thus it is from heat that water is produced. The water thought to itself: 'Let me become many. Let me propagate myself.' It emitted food. Whenever it rains, therefore, food becomes abundant; and thus it is from water that foodstuffs are produced...Then that same deity thought to itself: 'Come now, why don't I establish the distinctions of name and appearance by entering these three deities here with this living self *(atman)*, and make each of them threefold.' So, that deity established the distinctions of name and appearance by entering these three deities here with this living self *(atman)*, and made each of them threefold.[12]

There is yet another creation story in the Upanishads in which the Brahman/Atman, finding no pleasure in being alone, split his body into two, thereby creating a woman and repeatedly copulated with her until all living things from human beings to ants were born (Brihadaranyaka Upanishad 1.4.3-4). Regardless of how the world was created, Brahman is described as the cause of this world of suffering.

We now have to ask the question of what exactly this Brahman is. According to the Upanishads, Brahman is perception and bliss

(Brihadaranyaka Upanishad 3.9.28), truth, knowledge and bliss (Taittiriya Upanishad 2.1.1), one without a second (Chandogya Upanishad 6.2.1-2), ungraspable, undecaying and unattached (Brihadaranyaka Upanishad 3.9.26, 4.2.4, 4.5.15), unborn and eternal, primeval and everlasting (Katha Upanishad 2.18), all-pervading, bodiless and stable (Katha Upanishad 2.22), what cannot be seen and without sight or hearing (Mundaka Upanishad 1.1.6), the breath, speech and mind of individuals (Mundaka Upanishad 2.2.2), that which knows and observes all (Mundaka Upanishad 2.2.7), stainless and partless, consisting of brilliant lights (Mundaka Upanishad 2.2.9). From these descriptions of the Brahman, some say that the Brahman is a personal being, some say it is an impersonal entity and still some say that the Brahman is beyond the two categories of reason. Whatever be this Brahman, we have to ask ourselves whether it is desirable for us to be merged with it. If this Hindu doctrine is true, then upon my death, my unique identity as an individual, with my self-consciousness and personality, will disappear like a river merging with the ocean (Mundaka Upanishad 3.2.8-9). There will no longer be 'me' as an individual. I love chocolates. But I don't want to become a chocolate and lose my identity, do I?[13] The way of escape which the Upanishads offer is far from desirable. I would rather preserve my identity in a world of suffering than lose it in a world without suffering.

What, now, about the activity of Brahman? Existing as an undifferentiated reality, why did it wish to disperse itself as this illusory world? And why does the Brahman/Atman now want to revert back to its primitive state of undifferentiated singleness? The second creation story seems to indicate that it was for the need to have a companion and seek pleasure that the singular Brahman created this diversity of the world around us. The Brahman, therefore, is the creator of illusion and the cause of suffering. Ironically, the same Brahman is also the rescuer of its own self as it tries to become single again.

Finally, if everything is Brahman, then what about the polytheistic gods of the Vedas? They too are Brahman and are no different from human beings in their ontological status. Because the only way to liberation is through the knowledge of the Singularity which is Brahman, those who worship the gods are breaching the doctrine of monistic singularity by considering the gods as separate from themselves. Hence, according to the Upanishads, people who worship the Hindu gods are deluded and become devouring food for the gods.

> 'Sacrifice to this god. Sacrifice to that god'—people do say these things, but in reality each of these gods is his own creation, for he himself is all these gods...If a man knows 'I am *brahman*' in this way, he becomes this whole world. Not even the gods are able to prevent it, for he becomes their very self *(atman)*. So when a man venerates another deity, thinking, 'He is one, and I am another,' he does not understand. As livestock is for men, so is he for the gods. As having a lot of livestock is useful to a man, so each man proves useful to the gods. The loss of even a single head of livestock is painful; how much more if many are lost. The gods, therefore, are not pleased at the prospect of men coming to understand this.[14]

This passage of the Upanishads voices against worshipping gods and sacrificing to them and a lot of Hindus will find it difficult to accept this Upanishadic teaching. What is also voiced against by the Upanishads is the all-embracing slogan that all religions are the same, that they are all different paths to the same destiny. The Upanishads holds that only *its* views of the Ultimate Reality and the afterlife are true, which therefore implicitly falsifies other religious views of God and the afterlife. All religions are not the same, at least according to the Upanishads.

Dissatisfied with both the Vedas and the Upanishads, the Bhagavad Gita emerged as fresh literature that integrated the teachings of both the Vedas and the Upanishads into its own new doctrinal teaching. The Gita's ultimate teaching is what the Upanishads had previously condemned: worship and devotion to God. Ultimate Reality is no longer Brahman, but is Lord Krishna, whose womb is now Brahman. According to the Gita, there are many ways that lead to the cessation of suffering, and often they are confusing and contradictory. However, for convenience sake, I have outlined the Gita's pathways to liberation from suffering in an understandable manner in the following image.[15]

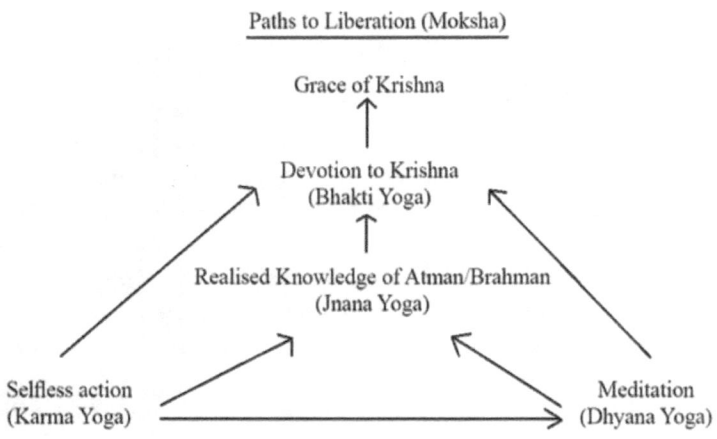

Paths to Liberation (Moksha)

Grace of Krishna

Devotion to Krishna
(Bhakti Yoga)

Realised Knowledge of Atman/Brahman
(Jnana Yoga)

Selfless action   Meditation
(Karma Yoga)   (Dhyana Yoga)

The central theme of the Gita is to obtain liberation from the cycle of
rebirth that causes suffering. The Gita works on the assumption that
there is a central core in all living beings called the Atman, which is one's
true self – immaterial and immortal (Gita 2:18, 30). The Pandava warrior
Arjuna has come to meet his own family members in the battlefield to
receive back the rightful share of the kingdom. His charioteer is none
other than Lord Krishna. Hesitant to fight his own family members, Arjuna
puts down his bow and arrows and questions Krishna of the rightfulness
of his actions. The entire Bhagavad Gita is Krishna's attempt to make
Arjuna take back his weapons and fight his own blood relations. And
the very first reason that Krishna gives in order to fight in the battlefield
is the immortality of the soul. The man who kills someone never really
kills the true self of that person because the true self, the Atman, cannot
be killed (Gita 2:19). The next response which Krishna gives is that any
action done without selfish motivation is morally right as long as dharma
is preserved. Dharma means both personal duty and virtuous conduct.
Concerning personal duty, however, several forms of personal dharma
can be in conflict with each other, which is clearly the case with Arjuna:
should he fulfil his varna-dharma (social duty) by fighting to establish
righteousness in the land or should he fulfil his kula-dharma (duty towards
family) and jati-dharma (duty towards caste) by *not* engaging in battle?

Arjuna belongs to the social class of the Kshatriyas whose duty is to fight to preserve the integrity of the land and the people against evildoers (Gita 2:31). However, aligning himself to his varna-dharma would be a breach of his other two dharmas: he is going to cause the destruction of his own family and caste and would therefore be a destroyer of his kula-dharma and jati-dharma (Gita 1:40, 43). Krishna's response to the dilemma is straightforward: *varna-dharma takes priority*. The entire human race is divided into four varnas (social classes): Brahmins who exemplify wisdom, Kshatriyas who exemplify bravery, Vaishyas who exemplify work and Shudras who exemplify service (Gita 18:40-44). Any one of these varnas is going to be dominant in each human being which is in turn determined by his or her previous karma. Like atoms that come together and make up the physical stuffs that exist in our universe, so the varnas (contained in the Gunas), determined by previous karma, come together during the rebirth of a person and make up his spiritual DNA. Hence a person is duty-bound to carry out his inbuild varna-dharma, which therefore takes predominance over other forms of dharma. Hence Krishna urges Arjuna to fight this battle.

Is this to say that other forms of dharma are irrelevant? The Gita tackles this question by offering the way of karma-(buddhi)-yoga – desireless action (Gita 2:47-53, 71, 3:1-26). By performing an action in a spiritually detached manner, with no selfish motivation and no desire for the outcome of that action, the action becomes ethically right. Arjuna is not fighting this battle to gain superiority or to loot the property of his relations. His fighting is going to be driven by no selfish motivation and will be in line with his varna-dharma. Hence, even if he kills all his family members, it will be as if he did not kill anybody (Gita 18:17). And he will not accumulate any sin upon himself. In fact, to the contrary, performing such a desireless action will take him up the ladder of attaining Moksha. Hence Arjuna is both duty-bound to fight (because of his varna-dharma) and by fighting without selfish motivation (karma-yoga), he will gain liberation from rebirth in this world.

But karma-yoga as a way of liberation from the cycle of rebirth is often times difficult to perfect. Hence Krishna offers another way to

Moksha: dhyana-yoga, that of meditation. Karma-yoga required that you go out there in the streets and perform desireless actions. But dhyana-yoga can be done right where you are. It requires withdrawing one's senses from worldly ambitions, the same goal which karma-yoga directed, and then directing one's focus into one's inner self, the Atman. The method of meditational yoga is given in Gita 6:10-18, which requires one to stay in a secluded place, remain alone, abandon all dreams and aspirations, prepare a seat for himself in a clean place, sit there, hold his body, head and neck in a straight line and without moving, concentrate on the point of his and fix his mind on the Atman, his inner self. When one engages in this form of dhyana-yoga, he becomes unaffected by the fluctuating tides of joy and pain and attains inner peace in this life and Moksha in the afterlife. However, this way of meditation is also difficult to perfect because the mind is unsteady and bringing the mind to control is like trying to control the wind (Gita 6:34). Hence the third way to Moksha is suggested: the way of realised knowledge (jnana-yoga) of the Atman's identity with Brahman (Gita 4:33-42, 5:16, 19, 21). This is similar to the Upanishadic doctrine of the oneness of the Atman with Brahman. The Gita, however, takes this doctrine further and includes Krishna himself within the oneness such that, now, the Atman, Brahman and Krishna are one and the same (Gita 6:27, 29, 30, 31, 10:12, 10:20, 13:2, 15:8-10). By acquiring this knowledge, one is liberated from the cycle of rebirth.

The fourth and the best way to Moksha is by means of devotion to Krishna – bhakti yoga (Gita 12:2). By worshipping Krishna by singing songs and bowing down to him (Gita 9:14), offering sacrifices and concentrating on him (Gita 9:22), by loving him (Gita 10:10) and by constantly talking about him and enlightening one another about him (Gita 10:9), one attains Moksha. And those who follow the path(s) of Moksha are ultimately delivered by the divine grace of Krishna (Gita 10:11, 12:7, 18:56, 66).

The four paths of Moksha outlined above are complicated by the fact that they are not mutually exclusive and they significantly overlap each other. Karma-yoga, involving action combined with the mental renunciation of all personal desires, overlaps dhyana-yoga, involving the shutting down of all senses to the external world and looking within ourselves to find the Atman/Brahman (Gita 6:1-9). And both karma-yoga and dhyana-yoga lead up to jnana-yoga (Gita 4:33-34, 38-39). Jnana-yoga in turn leads up to bhakti-yoga (Gita 9:15) and bhakti-yoga leads to jnana-yoga (Giita 18:55). In fact, even karma-yoga and dhyana-yoga lead straight up to bhakti-yoga (Gita 4:23, 9:27, 12:6-7, 18:46). And bhakti-yoga is the best of all yogas (Gita 12:2). Absolute devotion to Krishna is the deepest mystery and the ultimate teaching of the Bhagavad-Gita (Gita 18:64-65). The Gita even urges all dharma to be abandoned in favour of total devotion to Krishna (18:66). And the Gita promises Moksha to all those who teach this mystery to others (Gita 18:67-68).

Hence, according to the Gita, there are two ultimate paths to Moksha: devotion to Krishna and knowledge of Brahman (Gita 12:1-5), the former being superior to the latter. But these two paths themselves overlap each other because the one to whom we are devoted to is in fact our very self, the Atman, which is Brahman! The Gita thus offers an ill-fitting integrated path to liberation from suffering rebirth in this world. The book ends with Arjuna being convinced of his duty to fight his own family. And as the Mahabharata continues (the Gita is a part of the epic, Mahabharata), the bloodbath begins and by the end of the battle, Arjuna's side emerges victorious, all thanks to Krishna.

We shall now analyse the Bhagavad-Gita and I propose to offer seven responses to the Gita as a whole:

1. Critique of karma-yoga

   • Loss of objective morality

   • Liberation as motivation

2. The nature of morality

3. Contradictions in the Gita

4. Philosophical problems with God

5. The narrow way of salvation

6. The problem with dharma

7. The problem of determinism

My first issue is with that of karma-yoga. According to the Gita, actions that have no motive of pleasure or self-gain, and done merely as a dharmic duty is morally right and leads to liberation. Let's suppose now that my social class is Shudra: serving others is written into my DNA. I am a medical doctor by profession and I have three patients who are critically ill and who are in need of immediate organ transplantations. And so, without any kind of selfish motivation of personal gain, I decide to freely do the procedure for my patients...at the cost of a healthy adult. Not worried about the outcome of my actions, I anaesthetise the healthy adult without consent, remove his kidneys and liver and give life to three people at the expense of one. According to the Gita, since I have acted in accordance with my dharma and have abandoned all mental attachments to my actions and its consequences, I haven't really killed the healthy adult and I did not commit any crime. No sin has accumulated over me and I have climbed up the ladder of liberation from rebirth. Morality, therefore, becomes subjective to my mental condition and personal dharma. And by this way, a lot of obviously immoral actions can be justified by the doctrine of karma-yoga.

Karma-yoga also insists that we be devoid of all selfish motivations in order to obtain liberation from rebirth. But the endeavour to attain liberation is itself a selfish action and it is driven by selfish motivation, offering incentive at the end. Thus the underlying motive for following the path of desireless action is desire for liberation and is therefore self-refuting.

The second issue with the Bhagavad-Gita concerns its take on morality. As I have already explained, the Gita offers a subjective view of morality because it places the moral rightness and wrongness of an action, not on the nature of the action itself, but on the motive behind the action. If the motive behind an evil act is pure and free from egotism, unattached to the outcome of the action and in line with varna-dharma, then the evil act becomes good and would have to be encouraged. Devastating wars, extreme human experiments, severe forms of social Darwinism and so on can be justified based on the morality purported by the Gita.

The third problem with the Gita is that of contradictions. At the same stroke where it says that knowledge is superior to meditation (Gita 12:8-9), the Gita also says that meditation is superior to knowledge (Gita 12:12). Likewise meditation is superior to desireless action in Gita 12:9, 11, and the order is reversed in Gita 12:12. Earlier we had seen that desireless action, meditation and realised knowledge all lead to liberation, but all these three paths lead to bondage because they are of the nature of *sattva* (Gita 17:11, 17, 20, 18:9, 23, 18:20, 33).[16]

The fourth problem with the Gita is philosophical. Is Krishna a personal deity or an impersonal force? The answer tips in favour of the former: Krishna is a personal deity who loves his devotees (Gita 12:14, 16, 17, 19, 20). But he also devours everyone because he is death itself (Gita 10:34). The entire universe emanates from him (Gita 10:8) and he is the very substance of the universe (Gita 9:16-19, 10:20-42). Krishna brings the universe into existence and destroys it again, and the cycle repeats itself ad infinitum (Gita 9:7-8). But why is Krishna doing it again and again? What is the purpose behind the repeated never-ending cycle of creation and destruction? Is he doing it out of his own free will or is it simply mechanical? And if the universe has been created and destroyed an infinite number of times in the past, how did we arrive at this present situation? As I had already mentioned, the problem with an infinite past is that one can never get to the present because there would have been no starting point in the past from whence we journey on into the present. Moreover, if everything emanates from Krishna, then all evils are also borne of Krishna. Since Krishna is the Atman within all beings (Gita 10:20), the implication is that all human atrocities are committed by Krishna himself. Natural disasters are also the manifestations of the divine. This also raises the question of why Krishna has to incarnate time and time again into this world in order to preserve dharma (Gita 4:7) because, in a sense, it would mean that Krishna would be incarnating within himself to save himself from himself!

When Arjuna requested Krishna to show his eternal, unchanging and divine form (Gita 11:4), Krishna grants his request. And what does Arjuna see? He sees a terrifying God with many faces on all sides (Gita 11:11), many mouths, eyes (Gita 11:10) (the sun and moon are his eyes as well – Gita 11:19), many arms, many bellies (Gita 11:16), many teeth, many thighs and many feet (Gita 11:23). The celestial bodies are his ornaments (Gita 11:11). The entire world and all the gods are there within his body (Gita 11:13, 15). The great Brahman of the Upanishads is now the womb which Krishna impregnates to give birth to all the living in this material universe (Gita 14:3). There is no limit to this universal form of Krishna (Gita 11:16). This is the thing that created the entire universe and fills it with energy and also devours everything (Gita 11:30) and brings about complete destruction (Gita 11:32). This is not a graceful picture of God we would like to see. This form is fearsome, destructive and terrifying and Arjuna is in terror and confusion (Gita 11:23-25). Those who are worthy of Moksha will attain *this* state of existence with Krishna (Gita 8:5, 14:19), situated in Brahman (Gita 5:19). What is interesting to note is that this unchanging and eternal form of Krishna is simply a majestic anthropomorphic projection of God. The criticism of the ancient Greek philosopher, Xenophanes, might apply here, who argued that if cows and horses could paint, they would paint their gods in their own image, making the shapes and the bodies of their gods in a similar form that they themselves are.[17]

The fifth point to raise is about the exclusiveness of the way of Moksha. According to the Gita, those who worship gods other than Krishna go to the celestial world where the gods reside and enjoy their rewards temporarily, following which they have to return back to earth in their next birth (Gita 7:23, 9:20-21, 24-25). But if Krishna is the source of all that exists (Gita 10:8), then aren't the gods also extensions of Krishna, just like you and me are? So worshipping other gods would indirectly mean worshipping Krishna. This is a point agreed by the Gita in 9:23. Nevertheless, according to Krishna, worship and sacrifice directed to other gods are wrong and done without understanding (Gita 9:23). Their reward is going to be temporary and limited. As with the Upanishads, this means that not all religions lead to God. Even within the Hindu religion, exclusive Krishna-worshippers alone will attain eternal salvation. The popular Indian slogans, "All religions are same" and "All religions lead to God" will thus have to be abandoned in light of the textual evidence from the Bhagavad Gita.

The sixth objection concerning the Gita is the problem with dharma, or righteous duty. There is a great deal of emphasis on preserving dharma in the Gita by acting in a morally good manner. But what is this nature of goodness? Is an action morally good because God commands it, or does God commend an action because it is morally good? This is the famous Euthyphro's dilemma discussed in the literature today and I think it would apply to the Gita as well. Krishna insists that Arjuna has a moral obligation to slay the evil doers and establish righteousness in the kingdom. But is this morally right duty right because Krishna commands it, or does Krishna command it because it is morally right? The former would make moral rightness and wrongness arbitrary. Krishna could command Arjuna to commit the worst of all crimes and the crime would become morally right because Krishna had commanded it. The latter would make Krishna subject to a moral code superior to him and by which he himself has to abide. The classical response to this dilemma is to root moral rightness and wrongness in God's own loving and perfect nature, which requires the existence of an all-loving God who is the locus of moral values. God's own loving nature provides the objective standard for moral rightness and wrongness. But the panentheistic doctrine of God in the Gita cannot accommodate the concept of God being omnibenevolent. Although Krishna is said to love his devotees (Gita 12:14, 16, 17, 19, 20), he is also said to be the great Time (or destiny) which devours everything (Gita 11:32). He is the cause of this illusory world (Gita 7:14) and devours it from all sides by sending out his powerful scorching rays, licking them up with his blazing mouths (Gita 11:30). Such a conception of God is inconsistent with the concept of an all-loving God and hence Krishna cannot be the proper foundation of dharma.

The last objection to the Gita is the problem of determinism. In the closing lines of the Bhagavad Gita, Krishna instructs Arjuna that being a Kshatriya is not a matter of birth into a royal family, but his intrinsic nature (Gita 18:59) and all his actions, whether he likes it or not, will be dictated by his inner nature as a Kshatriya (Gita 18:60). Even virtuous and non-virtuous qualities of a person are determined by the gunas (likened to atoms) that make up a human being and one is born with these qualities rather than cultivate them in life (Gita 16:3-5). This raises the question of whether a wicked person can aspire to reform himself because his actions will be determined by the material makeup of his body, thereby putting a considerable limitation to the free will of individuals, making us mere automata.

In conclusion, we note that the three great Hindu Scriptures – the Vedas, the Upanishads and the Bhagavad Gita – began with a very mundane reflection of nature, attributing divine characteristics to the world they saw around them, and then evolved to posit a higher principle behind the physical world that would explain the complex human experiences on earth, but belittles the experiences by attributing it to maya, illusion, and offers a way out of this world that is exclusive and the final abode, a mystery.[18]

Endnotes

[1] John Stratton Hawley (editor), Vasudha Narayanan (editor) The Life of Hinduism (University of California Press, California, 2006), p 10.

[2] *Ibid.*

[3] Blackwell Companion to Hinduism, p 68.

[4] Translation by Ralph Thomas Hotchkin Griffith, a scholar of Indology. Further citations of the Rig Veda will be the translations of the same scholar.

[5] Arthur Berriedale Keith, *The Religion and Philosophy of the Veda and Upanishads*, 2 vols, Volume one (Harvard University Press, Cambridge, 1925), p 59.

[6] Arthur Anthony Macdonell, *Vedic Mythology* (Motilal Banarsidass Publishers Pvt. Ltd., Delhi, reprint 2002), p 2.

[7] Gregory Shushan, "Afterlife Conceptions in the Vedas" published in *Religion Compass*, Volume 5, Issue 6, June 2011, p 203.

[8] *Ibid.*, p 204-205.

[9] *Ibid.*, p 203.

[10] *Ibid.*, p 205.

[11] The Upanishads also contain several other views of the afterlife as shown by Gregory Shushan in "Afterlife Conceptions in the Vedas" published in *Religion*

Compass, Volume 5, Issue 6, pages 202–213, June 2011. In fact, the Upanishads is not a single philosophical system, but is rather a collection of several philosophical doctrines, some of which are logical contradictions. See Structural Depths of Indian Thought, State University of New York Press for more on this. However, Advaita Vedanta is the most popular eschatological view in the Upanishads and hence further discussion will be on this theme. For an explanation of what Advaita Vedanta is, see below.

[12] Patrick Olivelle (translator and editor), *The Early Upaniṣads: Annotated Text and Translation* (Oxford University Press, NY, 1998), p 247. The quotation is from Chandogya Upanishad 6.2.1-3, 6.3.2-4.

[13] I also love my brother. But I don't want to become my brother and lose my own identity, do I? Ultimately, we all prefer duality to singularity, don't we?

[14] Patrick Olivelle (translator and editor), *The Early Upaniṣads: Annotated Text and Translation* (Oxford University Press, NY, 1998), p 47, 49. The quotation is from Brihadaranyaka Upanishad 1.4.6, 10.

[15] In what follows, I will be relying on the translation and commentary by Nicholas Sutton in his *Bhagavad-Gita* published by the Oxford Centre for Hindu Studies in the year, 2014.

[16] See chapter 14 of the Bhagavad Gita for the description of sattva-guna causing bondage.

[17] See Robert M. Grant's *Gods and the One God* (The Westminster Press, Philadelphia, 1986), p 76-77.

[18] The ultimate abode for those who traverse the path of liberation is left vague in the Gita. It is described as the non-manifest and non-decaying, the place where Krishna himself lives (Gita 8:21). But then Krishna himself is the supreme abode (Gita 10:12). We only have a description of what not to expect: the abode is unlit by the sun or moon (Gita 15:6). The only good thing about this abode is that once attained, they are free from rebirth in this world.

7
Islam:
Controlling the Problem

The hardest definitions are the simplest ones. I remember in one of my Forensic Medicine classes, we were asked the definition of death. After a minute or two of silence from our class, the professor went on to say that there is no universally accepted layman's definition of death. In simple terms, death is simply the end of life.

Likewise, the terms 'good' and 'evil', 'right' and 'wrong' have similar problems of defining. We say that torture, child trafficking and the like are evil. But what is evil? How do we define it? Believers in God will have an easy answer: evil is a departure from God's commands. In the Bible, the word 'sin' is defined as 'missing the mark,' like an arrow that falls on the ground instead of hitting the bulls-eye of the target. In other words, there is a standard of moral goodness (the mark or the target) and evil is a departure from that. But such a definition is a religious one that will not be accepted by the atheist. So can the atheist come up with a better definition of evil? Many define evil as any bad state of affairs. But this is simply to replace the word 'evil' with 'bad.' For we can now ask what a bad state of affair is. The common answer would be any action that causes harm unnecessarily. But we can now ask, "Why is causing harm unnecessarily a bad state of affairs? What do you mean by 'bad'?" Doctors advice their patients to stop smoking because it is bad. But bad for what? Bad for their health. So there is, at the centre, human well being and flourishing and any action that departs from that central mark is considered bad. So evil is any activity that is not promoting human well being and flourishing. Some might want to add a couple of qualifying words, "unnecessary" and "for others": evil is any *unnecessary* activity that is not promoting human well being and flourishing *for others*. We say 'unnecessary' because punishing a criminal for a crime is not evil and we say 'for others' because eating rotten tomatoes is not evil. It's only when we do so *unnecessarily to others* that it becomes evil. So this seems to be a fairly good definition of evil. But notice how this definition hinges upon an unjustifiable assumption that human well being and flourishing are the objective standards against which every action is to be judged as good and evil, right and wrong: a departure from human well being and flourishing is evil/wrong and a conformity to human well being and flourishing is good/right. The atheist, here, is making the same assumption that the theist makes in saying that God's commands are the objective standards against which every actions are to be judged. Just as the atheist is justified in asking for reasons why there is a God and that he has decreed moral commands to follow, so also the theist is justified in asking for reasons why human well being and flourishing are the objective standards for moral judgement. As the Canadian John G. Stackhouse points out,

> Human beings are perfectly free to wish for more food rather than less, for more security against wild animals rather than less, and for more peace with their neighbors rather than less—but these are simply self-centered desires. They have nothing to do with the way things *ought* to be, because it is meaningless [on atheism] to say things ought to be anything other than what they are.[1]

They have nothing to do with the way things ought to be. Rightly said. On atheism, there is no objective universal law, like the law of gravity, which says that human well being and flourishing are the ways in which human activity should be oriented towards. They are simply a matter of subjective, though universal, human preference. Hence, without reference to God, actions such as rape and child abuse can never be deemed 'evil' or 'wrong' in an objective sense. These actions are simply equivalent to hitting a mosquito or disliking tea. They would have no moral significance whatsoever. This is, of course, the first premise of the moral argument for God's existence which we had explored.

Whether an atheist or theist, we can thus define evil as a departure from the way things ought to be.[2] Whenever we call an action 'evil,' we imply that it shouldn't have happened that way. We could all agree on that. The reason why I am bringing up this definition of evil under Islam is because generally in Islam, evil is not a departure from the way things ought to be. It is precisely the way God *wants* it to be.

The overarching Islamic theodicy of evil is the belief that life on earth is a test. The evils we encounter in our daily lives and in the lives of others are God-ordained with the intention of testing his people. This is a theme consistently stated in the Quran:

> Do the people think that they will be left to say, "We believe" and they will not be tried? But We have certainly tried those before them, and Allah will surely make evident those who are truthful, and He will surely make evident the liars.

> Sura 29:2-3[3]

> And We will surely test you with something of fear and hunger and a loss of wealth and lives and fruits, but give good tidings to the patient.

> Sura 2:155

> [He] who created death and life to test you [as to] which of you is best in deed - and He is the Exalted in Might, the Forgiving.

> Sura 67:2

> And We will surely test you until We make evident those who strive among you [for the cause of Allah] and the patient, and We will test your affairs.

> Sura 47:31

> You will surely be tested in your possessions and in yourselves. And you will surely hear from those who were given the Scripture before you and from those who associate others with Allah much abuse. But if you are patient and fear Allah - indeed, that is of the matters [worthy] of determination.

> Sura 3:186

> And know that your properties and your children are but a trial and that Allah has with Him a great reward.

> Sura 8:28

And do not extend your eyes toward that by which We have given enjoyment to [some] categories of them, [its being but] the splendor of worldly life by which We test them. And the provision of your Lord is better and more enduring.

Sura 20:131

Or do you think that you will enter Paradise while such [trial] has not yet come to you as came to those who passed on before you? They were touched by poverty and hardship and were shaken until [even their] messenger and those who believed with him said,"When is the help of Allah ?" Unquestionably, the help of Allah is near.

Sura 2:214

And it is He who has made you successors upon the earth and has raised some of you above others in degrees [of rank] that He may try you through what He has given you. Indeed, your Lord is swift in penalty; but indeed, He is Forgiving and Merciful.

Sura 6:165

And you did not kill them, but it was Allah who killed them. And you threw not, [O Muhammad], when you threw, but it was Allah who threw that He might test the believers with a good test. Indeed, Allah is Hearing and Knowing.

Sura 8:17

So they said, "Upon Allah do we rely. Our Lord, make us not [objects of] trial for the wrongdoing people.

Sura 10:85

Indeed, We have made that which is on the earth adornment for it that We may test them [as to] which of them is best in deed.

Sura 18:7

Every soul will taste death. And We test you with evil and with good as trial; and to Us you will be returned.

Sura 21:35

And We did not send before you, [O Muhammad], any of the messengers except that they ate food and walked in the markets. And We have made

some of you [people] as trial for others - will you have patience? And ever
is your Lord, Seeing.

Sura 25:20

Your wealth and your children are but a trial, and Allah has with Him a
great reward.

Sura 64:15

From cancers and tsunamis to crimes, God uses evil to test his people
to see if his people are worthy of going to heaven. And it is not just
the bad things in life which God uses to test people. Even good things
in life such as health, wealth, fame, family and friends are used by God
to test his people (Sura 21:35). God can even use you, by letting you
suffer, in order to test your loved ones and see if they sustain belief in
him (Sura 10:85, 25:20).

I offer five responses to the Islamic theodicy of life as a test.[4] First,
can we ever call anything 'evil' or 'bad'? Recall that whenever we call an
action 'evil,' we imply that it shouldn't have happened that way. Murder
shouldn't happen. Rape shouldn't happen. Child trafficking shouldn't
happen. They are all a deviation from the way things ought to be. But
in Islam, evils such as these are precisely the trials that God uses to test
his people. They are not deviations from the way things ought to be.
If God were to remove the evils in the world, he would essentially be
defeating the very purpose of creating humans on earth. In such a view
of the world, therefore, evil is not an aberration. It is not an anomaly
that we should hope to get rid of. Evil is that which God uses to test
his people. But such a view of evil is contrary to our daily experience in
which we abhor evil. Evil is not the way things ought to be. If we are to
define evil as a departure from the way things ought to be, we have to
reject the idea that the chief purpose on earth is to be tested by God.[5]

Second, the magnitude and perfusion of evil makes the test-theodicy
implausible. Consider the genocides that have happened throughout world
history. Who were being tested there? When an entire nation or an ethnic
race is destroyed, who are the kith and kin being tested? There are no

family members, relatives or friends to be tested for their faith because they would all have been wiped out in the ethnic cleansing.

Third, why is someone else being tortured by God to test me? Does God give an anencephalic child to test the parents? What wrong did the child commit to deserve this suffering? Would I injure my younger child to test my elder one? This would make God unjust.

Fourth, what is the point of testing someone if I already know the results? A trial or a test implies that you don't know the result. But if God, being omniscient, already knows who would pass his test and who wouldn't, then why doesn't God send us to heaven or hell directly, based on his foreknowledge, without allowing us to go through this period of testing on earth?

Fifth, the test-theodicy reduces ethics to a reward-seeking behaviour. Since life is a temporary testing field with the ultimate goal of going to heaven, ethics loses its essence. The crippled man I meet in the street, the orphans I visit after my day's work and the beggar coming up to my front door asking for alms are all challenges for me to help me go to heaven. Good works, in such a context, is not the result of an outpouring of our love *for others*, but rather it is result of our love *for ourselves*, enabling us to pass the test of life and thereby enjoy a blissful paradise in the future. Thus it reduces ethics to mere advantage.

One last consideration about the Islamic view of life in this world needs to be highlighted before we move forward. In Islam, life in this planet, apart from being a test ground, is a delusion of play and amusement:

> And the worldly life is not but amusement and diversion; but the home of the Hereafter is best for those who fear Allah, so will you not reason?

> Sura 6:32

> Every soul will taste death, and you will only be given your [full] compensation on the Day of Resurrection. So he who is drawn away from the Fire and admitted to Paradise has attained [his desire]. And what is the life of this world except the enjoyment of delusion.

> Sura 3:185

O my people, this worldly life is only [temporary] enjoyment, and indeed, the Hereafter - that is the home of [permanent] settlement.

Sura 40:39

Such a view of life on this planet removes the seriousness of the evils we encounter in this world. It comes almost close to the Hindu doctrine of Maya – the grand illusion of life in this world. Experience tells us that life is more than that. For these reasons, I believe that Islam's analysis of evil and suffering is less preferable to be endorsed.

Endnotes

[1] *John* Gordon *Stackhouse*, Jr, *Can God be Trusted? Faith and the Challenge of Evil* (Oxford University Press, NY, 1998), p 25. Emphasis original, brackets mine.

[2] The 'ought to be' for the theist would be in conformity to God's moral commands and for the atheist would be in conformity to human well being and flourishing.

[3] Translations are from the Sahih International version of the Quran.

[4] To be sure, Islam offers other theodicies as well such as the punishment theodicy (Sura 42:30, 40) and the character building theodicy (Sura 6:42). We have, however, explored and responded to the overarching theodicy of Islam, consistently stated throughout its pages as the reason why there is suffering in our world. Other theodicies fit into the larger one: in a world where God uses suffering to test his people (the overarching test-theodicy), he sometimes punishes people for their sins (the punishment theodicy) and builds up their character through the sufferings (the character building theodicy).

[5] I am cautious to use the words 'chief purpose' because the notion that God *sometimes* tests his people with evil is not incompatible with the definition of evil we had seen.

III

The Christian Response
to the Problem of Evil

8
The Theodicies of the Bible

In his book, *God's Problem: How the Bible Fails to Answer Our Most Important Question – Why We Suffer,* the agnostic New Testament scholar, Bart Ehrman, lays out the biblical answers for why God allows suffering and concludes that none of them are satisfactory. Ehrman himself started his career as a scholar, pastor and a devout Christian. His ambition was to become a full time minister for God. But sadly, Ehrman began to question his Christian faith because of the problem of suffering. He writes,

> The problem of suffering became for me the problem of faith. After many years of grappling with the problem, trying to explain it, thinking through the explanations that others have offered— some of them pat answers charming for their simplicity, others highly sophisticated and nuanced reflections of serious philosophers and theologians—after thinking about the alleged answers and continuing to wrestle with the problem, about nine or ten years ago I finally admitted defeat, came to realize that I could no longer believe in [God][1]

So Ehrman has written the book in order to

> examine the biblical responses to suffering, to see what they are, to assess how they might be useful for thinking people trying to get a handle on the reality of suffering either in their own lives or in the lives of others, and to evaluate their adequacy in light of the realities of our world.[2]

Unfortunately, however, I find his examination incomplete, his assessment inept and his evaluation inadequate. Nevertheless, since Ehrman is a popular writer whose writings can relate to many of us today, I will use his book as the ground base for critique and development and offer a novel view of the biblical answer to suffering from Christian thinkers who have themselves wrestled with this problem, as Ehrman had, but did not come to the same conclusions that he did. Ehrman explores six biblical reasons for why God allows suffering:

1. Suffering comes as punishment for sin

2. Suffering comes because of the abuse of human free will.

3. Suffering comes with redemptive purpose

   - Good comes out of suffering

   - Suffering has positive benefits: it brings God glory, it serves to extend God's purposes and it builds character.

   - Salvation depends on suffering

4. Suffering comes to test our faith

5. Suffering comes as a mystery

6. Suffering comes because of Satan

The fundamental problem in Ehrman's evaluation of these six responses to the problem of suffering is his implicit expectation of wanting to see *one* response addressing *all* the sufferings in the world. Take the first biblical response: suffering comes as punishment for sin. According to the Old Testament of the Bible, God punishes his people, Israel, for their sins by letting them suffer from military conquest. But is this a view of suffering endorsed in *all* instances of evil? Ehrman himself answers negatively:

> I should stress that the prophets themselves never state this as a universal principle, as a way of explaining *every* instance of suffering. The prophets, that is, were speaking *only* to their contemporaries about their specific sufferings.[3]

As Ehrman agrees, the punishment theodicy that permeates the Old Testament addressed the sufferings of ancient Israel alone. But Ehrman asks,

> Even if we limit ourselves to *ancient* Israel, do we really want to say that innocent people starved to death (starvation does not hit just the guilty, after all) as a divine punishment for the sins of the nation?[4]

In response, I would say that God was not punishing the innocents in ancient Israel. He was punishing the guilty. But since the agents that God used to punish his people – famine, drought, army, disease – do not discriminate between the good and the bad, innocent people are inevitably entangled into the punishing fury of God's wrath. But why does God use such imperfect agents to bring judgment upon people? Doesn't it bring so much collateral damage? Wouldn't it make God unjust right at the moment of executing his justice? I will address this problem in its due time. But for now, we should understand that God sometimes does use imperfect agents within his world to punish the wicked people, as a result of which the innocents suffer as well. The punishment theodicy doesn't have to work as a clean rule (you alone sin, you alone get punished) in order to be acceptable. Granted the interconnectedness of man and the world, we should expect several loose ends in the punishment theodicy, for which God is not to blame.

The second biblical theodicy is the free will response – the one that we have already encountered as a *defence* in the logical version of the problem of evil. Humans suffer because of harm caused by other humans. Ehrman notes two problems with this view. First, he argues that God's foreknowledge and human freedom are incompatible.

> God is typically portrayed as the all-powerful Sovereign of this world who foreknows all things, yet human beings are portrayed as responsible for their actions.[5]

If God knew that Adam and Eve would eat the forbidden fruit, if he knew that Judas would betray Jesus and Pilate would crucify him, then evidently Adam, Eve, Judas and Pilate would have no other option other than to carry out what God already foreknows, thus removing their free will to do otherwise. Thus the affirmation of human freedom and divine foreknowledge is, for Ehrman, a "paradox."

But do we really have a paradox in this situation? Does divine foreknowledge cancel out human freedom? Suppose there is an infallible weather forecasting machine that is able to predict the climate accurately. Will such a forecast remove nature's freedom to be itself? To rephrase the question, will the weather forecasting machine determine tomorrow's weather or will tomorrow's weather determine today's forecast? Obviously, it will be tomorrow's weather that will determine today's forecast. Likewise, it is human free action that will determine God's prior knowledge of that action.[6]

Ehrman's second problem with the free will theodicy is that it only accounts for evils caused by humans.[7] So what? The free will theodicy may have a small explanatory scope in accounting only for human evils. Nevertheless, it has good explanatory *power* in explaining a great deal of human injustice.

The third biblical theodicy is that suffering comes with redemptive purpose in three ways. First, something good can come out of suffering. That Joseph, as a young boy, suffered under the hands of his own brothers is redeemed to become the right-hand man of the Egyptian King is evidence that God can bring something good out of a bad situation (Genesis 37-50). Second, suffering can by accompanied by positive benefits such as by bringing God glory (the story of Moses parting the Red Sea), by enabling God's purposes to be carried forward (as with the spread of Christianity in the midst of persecution) and the building up of character in a person (Romans 5:3-5). Third, suffering becomes necessary for salvation (as with Jesus whose suffering and death becomes necessary to secure the salvation of sinners). So what is Ehrman's problem with redemptive suffering? He writes,

> Sometimes something good can come out of suffering...[But] I am absolutely opposed to the idea that we can universalize this observation by saying that something good *always* comes out of suffering.[8]

Who is he opposing? Certainly the Bible doesn't universalize the theodicy of redemptive suffering. Maybe he is opposing Christians who do universalize redemptive suffering. But why does he attack *their* views when his self-proposed task was to "examine the biblical responses to suffering?" Ehrman thinks that unless the Bible provides "the one answer" to the problem of evil that will address *all* the sufferings in the world, the Bible would have failed to answer our most important question--why we suffer. But that doesn't have to be true. The Bible could very well offer multiple reasons for why God allows a variety of sufferings which, when taken together, can address most (all?) evils in the world.

The fourth biblical theodicy of suffering is that God allows suffering in our lives in order to test our faith. The book of Job is a telling example of God testing Job by letting him suffer.[9]

The author of 1 Peter, likewise, urges Christians to hold on to their faith while being tested in their sufferings (1 Pet. 4:12–13, 19). However, Ehrman rightly discerns here as well that "suffering *sometimes* comes as a test of faith"[10]) but then goes on to say that "it is hard to believe that God inflicts people with cancer, flu, or AIDS in order to make sure they praise him to the end."[11] Since God *sometimes* uses suffering test our faith, we shouldn't be quick to suggest that God inflicts people with cancer, flu or AIDS to test his people.

The fifth biblical theodicy of suffering is found in the book of Ecclesiastes, according to which, pain as well as pleasure is fleeting and suffering, as we know it, is just the way the world is, with no explanation. While Ehrman sympathises with this view of suffering, he ignores what else the book of Ecclesiastes has to say. Although it seems as if the author offers no hope beyond death – a living dog is better than a dead lion (Ecclesiastes 9:4) – there is the seed of what, in the New Testament, is known as the just judgment of God wherein, at the final resurrection of the dead, God will "render to each one according to his works" (Romans 2:6) (ESV).

> God will bring every deed into judgment, including every hidden thing, whether it is good or evil.
>
> Ecclesiastes 12:14 (NIV)

Indeed, according to the book of Ecclesiastes , this is the reason to trust and obey God in the midst of life's miseries (chapter 12). God is able to provide the adequate compensation for the sufferings in this life.

The sixth and final biblical theodicy of suffering which Ehrman outlines, and the one which is dominant in the New Testament, is that people suffer because of demonic forces let loose in the world. A boy with epileptic seizures was brought to Jesus. Jesus rebukes the demon that caused his seizures and the boy is healed when the demon leaves him (Matthew 17:14-20). This is the apocalyptic theodicy of suffering, according to which God has allowed cosmic evil forces to pervade the earth and one day he will destroy these demonic forces in a moment of apocalypse, thereby setting up paradise on earth. Surprisingly, Ehrman finds this view of suffering "powerful and attractive"[12] but thinks that such a view will lead to social apathy. However, as I will explain later on in this chapter, the apocalyptic view of suffering, when fully understood, will lead to anything but social apathy. His other reason for rejecting this view is that people have always made wrong predictions about the time when God will make his apocalyptic entry into the world to sort all things out. But that doesn't make the biblical view of suffering wrong. It only makes people wrong! A third reason for rejecting the apocalyptic theodicy of suffering is that he believes that it is based on ancient and outdated cosmology of heaven up above and the earth down below. Well, maybe heaven is not "up there." But that doesn't mean heaven is not there at all! In the end, I find Ehrman's critiques superficial and lacking intellectual vigour in dealing with the biblical material on the problem of suffering.

We have explored Bart Ehrman's analysis of six answers which the Bible gives to the question of suffering and evil in our world. But is his list of biblical theodicies complete? In his book, *Defending God: biblical Responses to the Problem of Evil,* Old Testament scholar James Crenshaw lists even more biblical responses to the question of why we suffer.[13]

Our purpose, however, is not to explore *all* the biblical theodicies peppered throughout the Bible but instead to explore, as we did with Islam, the overarching grand theodicy of the Bible within which every other theodicy can and should be contained. But for that, we have some preliminaries to be sorted out first. We need to rethink God, the world and ourselves in light of the true narrative storyline of the Bible and it is this task we shall take up in the next chapter.

Endnotes

[1] Bart Ehrman, *God's Problem: How the Bible Fails to Answer Our Most Important Question – Why We Suffer* (HarperCollins, NY, 2008) p 3-4.

[2] *Ibid.*, p 16.

[3] *Ibid.*, p 53.

[4] *Ibid.*, p 54.

[5] *Ibid.*, p 120.

[6] For a detailed analysis, see William Lane Craig's *The Only Wise God: The Compatibility of Divine Foreknowledge & Human Freedom* (OR: Wipf and Stock, 1999), Reprint edition. Previously published by Baker Book House, 1987.

[7] Although Ehrman doesn't mention it in the book, he did mention it in his public debates.

[8] *God's Problem*, p 155. Emphasis original.

[9] Ehrman suggests two theodicies in the book of Job. The first is the test-theodicy and the second is the mystery-theodicy. But I will explain later why such an analysis is wrong.

[10] *God's Problem*, p 171. Emphasis mine.

[11] *Ibid.*

[12] *Ibid.*, p 258.

[13] James L. Crenshaw, *Defending God: Biblical Responses to the Problem of Evil* (Oxford University Press, NY, 2005). For example, he examines Exodus 34:6-7 and other passages to argue that God "is described as conflicted precisely because of an inner desire to retain a balance between strict justice and gracious mercy." p 19.

9
The Narrative Storyline of the Bible

The Bible contains many stories, by which I mean dynamic narratives that move from one scene to another without remaining static in a single situation. It begins with God creating the world and Adam and Eve eating from the forbidden tree. Things get so bad as sin and violence increase on earth that God decides to flood the earth, sparing Noah and his family. They populate the earth again but sin and violence take a downward spiral from there. God calls Abraham, enters into a contract with him to make him the father of many nations. To Abraham is born Isaac and to Isaac is born Jacob. Jacob has twelve sons who eventually become the twelve tribes of the nation of Israel. The nation is enslaved in Egypt and Moses is called to lead them out of slavery into a land flowing with milk and honey. Moses gives them the Torah – God's holy commandments – for the people to follow. Moses then dies and Joshua takes over the leadership and leads the people into the promised land. After Joshua, God raises up Judges – temporary military leaders – who protect and fight for God's people. The people protest for a King and God gives them King Saul, King David and King Solomon. The people continue to rebel against God and one another, thereby leading to their exile from the promised land. Prophets like Elijah, Isaiah, Jeremiah and Micah emerge to warn Israel of the dangers of rebellion and urge them to turn back to God with the promise that God would once again bless them and return them back to the land flowing with milk and honey. There ends the Old Testament of the Bible. Then suddenly, out of the blue comes Jesus, apparently breaking the smooth narrative of the Old Testament and offering, instead, the Kingdom of

Heaven for those who repent from their sins and turn to God. There are no land promises reiterated. Instead, Jesus prepares a place for us in Heaven. He takes the penalty of our sins and thereby opens up the doorway to Heaven. He was raised from the dead and went to Heaven. He will one day come again, after a series of cataclysmic events, to judge the world, destroy it, send bad people to hell and call his chosen people to Heaven. At least, this is what most Christians believe about Jesus and this is what I once believed about Jesus too. Such an understanding of the New Testament, however, makes the Old Testament look odd and irrelevant: leaders, Kings, prophets, land, exile, exodus – what were they all about if the goal was to leave the earth and go to Heaven? And so we have a sharp discontinuity between the two Testaments, with the Old Testament engaging on a horizontal plane and the New Testament on a vertical plane. The way many Christians come to terms with such a disjunction between the Testaments is to arrange them, not one next to the other as a continuous sequence, but one behind the other with the Old Testament serving simply as the background to the New Testament. With such an understanding of the Bible, which is dominant in so much of Western theology and has found its way into the East as well, the Old Testament is seen and read in a couple of ways. First, it is read simply as a set of prophesies about the coming of Jesus and his mission which would unfold in the New Testament. And second, it is seen as a reminder to the people back then that there are all basically sinners who cannot pull themselves up by their moral bootstraps and so are in need of a perfect Savior.

Apart from being unbiblical – a contention which I will substantiate soon - the belief in heaven as the final destiny of humans complicates the problem of suffering in a significant way by making earthly progress irrelevant. In fact, it questions the very reason why God created the earth in the first place. God could have very well created Adam and Eve in Heaven, planted a spiritual tree and prohibited them from eating from it. Once they disobeyed and ate from the tree, God could have provided the required sacrifice immediately by dying on a spiritual cross and secured their salvation instantly. Had he wanted more people, he could have created as many of us as he had wanted with the snap of his fingers (metaphorically) and allowed us to share in his Heavenly Kingdom as well. And for the disobedient ones, he could have directly sent them to hell without going through hell on earth.

The irrelevancy of world history comes to a telling focus by the relatively recent attempts to make 'the end of the world' come soon. In 2011, when I was pursuing my M.B.B.S. course in a medical college, one of the top news was the prediction of the end of the world on May 21 by a Christian evangelist by the name Harold Camping. Dailymail titles the news, "Will Saturday be the end of the world? Evangelists party like there's no tomorrow."[1]

The belief was that prior to the destruction of the world, God's chosen people would suddenly disappear from the earth and be teleported to Heaven - an event called the Rapture of the Church – following which the earth would undergo a serious of natural disasters until it is finally smashed to smithereens. The news gained international coverage and many Christians left their jobs, family and friends to travel worldwide to announce the 'awesome news.' One of the pictures posted was of a man speaking out loud through a microphone and behind him, a vehicle with a poster depicting the world being burnt up by fire with a text that read, "The Bible Guarantees it." May 21, 2011 had come and gone but the end had not come. Nevertheless, the belief in the Rapture of Christians and the destruction of the world remain the dominant views today, generating popular novels, films and preachings in the pulpits. The consequence of having such a view, as already stated, is the diminution of world progress: from the Stone Age, the Bronze Age, the Iron Age all the way to the present age of science and technology, all are utterly irrelevant with regard to God's own purposes for us and the world, which is simply to reap souls fit for Heaven.

So what is the true biblical story and how does it relate to the problem of suffering? To begin, I propose that we consider ourselves as myopic and thereby in need of the right spectacles through which can see the problem more clearly and so come up with a satisfying theodicy. To get the appropriate spectacles, we need the appropriate frame and the appropriate lens that can fit into the frame. It is our task, now, to create the appropriate frame by sketching, with broad brushstrokes, the true, single and coherent narrative storyline of the Bible, stretching seamlessly from the Old to the New Testament.

We begin by looking at the beginning and the end of the biblical narrative. In the beginning God creates the heavens and the earth (Genesis 1:1). In the end he will create the *new* heavens and the *new* earth (Revelation 21:1). The phrase 'heaven and earth,' in both these texts, means the material Universe.[2] So we have, as the two bookends of the narrative, creation in Genesis and new creation in Revelation. But how do we move from creation to new creation? Is God going to destroy the present creation and start a new creation from scratch or is God going to transform the present creation into the new creation? We will now look at a third text to answer our question: Romans 8:21.

Romans 8 is a densely packed chapter written by the apostle Paul. In context (8:18-30), Paul talks about the triad of creation, humans and the Spirit of God like three concentric circles, one inside the other. The outer circle is creation, inside which are humans and inside whom is the Spirit. The three, says Paul, are crying. God's creation is crying because it is subject to decay (8:22), God's children are crying because of the sufferings they go through (8:23) and, astonishingly, God's own Spirit comes into our lives and cries with us (8:26). And then the whole scene is transformed from the inside out: God's Spirit will eventually bring about the resurrection of God's children (8:11) who will, in turn, bring about the restoration of creation (8:21).

> The creation itself will be liberated from its bondage to decay and brought into the freedom and glory of the children of God.

> Romans 8:21 (NIV)

The creation will be freed from all that corrupts and destroys it. This includes freedom for the plants and animals, rocks and sand as well. Death, which is written in every atom in the universe, will be abolished once and for all and new creation will emerge. We have here, as clearly stated as possible, not the destruction of the world, as popular Christianity has it, but its transformation. Indeed, when we go back to Revelation 21, we read, not that man will go up to live with God in Heaven, but that God will come down to live with man on earth (21:3) so that the earth is turned into paradise, with no more death or mourning or crying or pain (21:4). This is the grand narrative of the Bible and unless we get this picture right, every other step we take to address the problem of suffering will certainly mislead us. It is our task, therefore, to ward off common misconceptions about the renewal of the earth in the next chapter.

Endnotes

1 http://www.dailymail.co.uk/news/article-1388972/Judgment-Day-Rapture-Parties-planned-evangelist-Harold-Camping-predicts-huge-earthquake.html, by David Gardner for MailOnline. Updated: 18:12 GMT, 20 May 2011 (Last accessed on June 14, 2015).

2 In Genesis 2:1, the text reads, "Thus the heavens and the earth were finished, and all the host of them," thereby implying that what was created in Genesis 1 (that is, the material Universe) is being described as the heavens and the earth in 2:1 and 1:1. As to Revelation 21:1, since it is describing the old heavens as passing away, it could not be talking about the heavenly realm where God is believed to dwell because God's dwelling is believed to be perfect and eternal, without any need for change or destruction. It is a reference to the material Universe. Moreover, the new heavens and the new earth is phrase derived from Isaiah 65:17 which goes on to talk about the restoration of earthly life and no reference to the heavenly realm.

10
Heaven Vacated and the Earth Restored

There is a familiar old Christian hymn that goes like this:[1]

> I'm but a stranger here,
> Heaven is my home;
> Earth is a desert drear,
> Heaven is my home;
> Danger and sorrow stand
> Round me on every hand;
> Heaven is my fatherland,
> Heaven is my home.

The idea that this human body is a temporary dwelling place on earth and that our ultimate abode is somewhere away from this earth is well established, as we had seen, in Hindu and Muslim Scriptures. But contrary to popular opinion, the Bible stands unique in its eschatological promise. According to the Bible, God honours the human body and desires to restore it to its perfect glory along with the restoration of this world. The ultimate destiny for humans is not heaven, but *this earth*. This may come as a surprise to many Christians today because this was simply not taught in our Sunday schools or preached in the pulpit.

We shall now look at ten common biblical passages that are often misread as offering an other-worldly hope in the afterlife, noting how we bring so many presuppositions into these texts that are simply not warranted.

1. Our citizenship is in Heaven (Philippians 3:20-21)

But our citizenship is in heaven. And we eagerly await a Savior from there, the Lord Jesus Christ, who, by the power that enables him to bring everything under his control, will transform our lowly bodies so that they will be like his glorious body.

Philippians 3:20-21 (NIV)

If I travel to a different country, meet a person there and tell him, "Hi, I'm Dr. Jerriton and I'm a citizen of India," will he respond by asking, "So that means you're going back to India, right?" I think not. Just because my citizenship is in India, that doesn't have to mean that I will be going back there. And yet so many of us, when reading this passage about our citizenship being in Heaven, have come to the conclusion that Heaven is our home and the earth is simply a temporary place of visitation. New Testament scholar N.T. Wright explains,

"'We are citizens of heaven,' Paul declares in verse 20. At once many modern Christians misunderstand what he means. We naturally suppose he means 'and so we're waiting until we can go and live in heaven where we belong'. But that's not what he says, and it's certainly not what he means. If someone in Philippi said, 'We are citizens of Rome,' they certainly wouldn't mean 'so we're looking forward to going to live there'. Being a colony works the other way round. The last thing the emperors wanted was a whole lot of colonists coming back to Rome. The capital was already overcrowded and underemployed. No: the task of the Roman citizen in a place like Philippi was to bring Roman culture and rule to northern Greece, to expand Roman influence there."[2]

Being a citizen of Heaven does not mean we go back to Heaven as the place of our eternal abode. It means that we bring the civilisation of heaven to the earth we live in. We are citizens of heaven colonising the earth.

2. Meeting Jesus in the air (1 Thessalonians 4:16-17)

For the Lord himself will come down from heaven, with a loud command, with the voice of the archangel and with the trumpet call of God, and the dead in Christ will rise first. After that, we who are still alive and are left will be caught up together with them in the clouds to meet the Lord in the air. And so we will be with the Lord forever.

1 Thessalonians 4:16-17 (NIV)

A famous passage that is often used to support the so-called Rapture of the Church – of Christians being 'caught up' or stolen from the earth to go to Heaven – this passage says nothing of that sort. Paul says that we will be caught up in the clouds and meet Jesus in the air. Apparently, we won't be suspended in the air forever. So the statement 'and so we will be with the Lord forever' is assumed to be saying that we will go with Jesus *from* the air *to* Heaven and so we will live with him in Heaven forever. The problem is that the text doesn't tell us where we will be going once we meet Jesus in the air. There is, however, a strong contextual reason for thinking that we will return back to earth once we meet Jesus in the air since Paul, being a Roman citizen, might be having in mind the analogy of the Roman Emperor returning back to his city after going out to battle his enemies and the people going out of the city to meet and welcome him back into the city. Regardless of that, the only point we need to note is that there is no heavenly hope mentioned in 1 Thessalonians 4:16-17.

3. The unseen and the eternal (2 Corinthians 4:17-18)

For our light and momentary troubles are achieving for us an eternal glory that far outweighs them all. So we fix our eyes not on what is seen, but on what is unseen, since what is seen is temporary, but what is unseen is eternal.

2 Corinthians 4:17-18 (NIV)

What I see is this earth. What I can't see is Heaven. So this earth is temporary but heaven is eternal. I have to fix my eyes on going to Heaven. It may be so natural for many of us to read the passage this way. The reason why such a reading remains natural to us is because we have already sold ourselves to a vertical eschatology. But what does the text really mean? The same author who wrote this passage also wrote another passage we had already explored: Romans 8:21. In that passage, we noted that Paul talks about the pain of the world eventually giving way to the renewal of creation. And in Romans 8:18, he writes,

> For I consider that the sufferings of this present time are not worth comparing with the glory that is to be revealed to us.

Romans 8:18 (ESV)

When we compare our present sufferings to the future glory that will be ours at the renewal of creation, all our sufferings will appear infinitesimally small as if they are a tiny dot in the vast ocean. That is essentially what Paul says. He makes a similar statement before talking about the state of the seen and the unseen:

> For our light and momentary troubles are achieving for us an eternal glory that far outweighs them all.

2 Corinthians 4:17 (NIV)

What Paul has in mind in 2 Corinthians 4:18 is not a vertical eschatology of heaven and earth, but a horizontal eschatology of creation and new creation: that which is seen is this present condition of earth, full of corruption and decay and that which is unseen is the future condition of earth in its pristine perfection, free from corruption and decay and which will be eternal. Fix your eyes, says Paul, on *that*!

4. Heavens burnt up and the earth destroyed

> But the day of the Lord will come like a thief, and then the heavens will pass away with a roar, and the heavenly bodies will be burned up and dissolved, and the earth and the works that are done on it will be exposed. Since all these things are thus to be dissolved, what sort of people ought you to be in lives of holiness and godliness, waiting for and hastening the coming of the day of God, because of which the heavens will be set on fire and dissolved, and the heavenly bodies will melt as they burn!

2 Peter 3:10-12 (ESV)

Perhaps this is the most famous passage for the belief in the end of the world. There are three entities that are described as being involved in this passage: the heavens, the heavenly bodies and the earth. The heavens will be set on fire, dissolve and will pass away, the heavenly bodies will be burnt up and melt away, and the earth, interestingly, will be "exposed." Old translations, such as the KJV, say that the earth will also be "burnt up." But present manuscript evidence has led modern translations, such as the NIV and the ESV, to say that the earth will be 'exposed' or 'laid bare.' The earth and its works will be exposed or found out. And what will happen after such a cataclysmic event takes place? There will appear, to the surprise (and perhaps dismay) of many, *the new heavens and the new earth* (2 Peter 3:13). The key to understanding this passage as a whole is, as always, the context. Earlier in the same chapter, Peter had talked about how the earth was "destroyed" by the flood during the days of Noah (2 Peter 3:5-6). How was the earth destroyed during the flood of Noah? Did God shatter the whole earth into pieces and create a whole new earth once again or did God just clean the surface of the earth with the flood? Obviously, it is the latter that God did. The purpose of the flood was not to destroy the earth but the ungodly people. So too, says Peter, the earth will once again be "destroyed" (that is, there will be a surface cleansing), not by water, but by fire, with the aim of destroying the ungodly (2 Peter 3:7). A coherent picture now begins to emerge. The graphic description of the heavens disappearing, the heavenly bodies melting away and the earth exposing the ungodly people by their destruction are all a cleansing process that will eventually give way to the new heavens and the new earth. Far from being the end of space and time, this passage is about the ultimate purification of heaven and earth from all that corrupts it.

5. This world is passing away (1 John 2:15-17)

> Do not love the world or anything in the world. If anyone loves the world, love for the Father is not in them. For everything in the world--the lust of the flesh, the lust of the eyes, and the pride of life--comes not from the Father but from the world. The world and its desires pass away, but whoever does the will of God lives forever.

1 John 2:15-17 (NIV)

The popular understanding of this passage is that the world will disappear and those who do the will of God will live forever in Heaven. The passage, however, doesn't tell us *where* we will live forever. Heaven is assumed to be the place where we will live forever. Likewise, the passing away of earth doesn't necessarily have to be by means of destruction. If we are to understand this passage in light of other passages like Revelation 21:1,

Romans 8:21 and 2 Peter 3:10, we would be led to conclude that John, like the rest, is talking about the end of wickedness on the earth and the new life in God's new world where "nothing impure will ever enter it, nor will anyone who does what is shameful or deceitful, but only those whose names are written in the Lamb's book of life" (Revelation 21:27). John, in 1 John 2:15-17, is talking about the moral cleansing that will take place on earth, in line with what Peter says in 2 Peter 3:10-12.

6. The heavenly country and city (Hebrews 11:14-16)

For people who speak thus make it clear that they are seeking a homeland. If they had been thinking of that land from which they had gone out, they would have had opportunity to return. But as it is, they desire a better country, that is, a heavenly one. Therefore God is not ashamed to be called their God, for he has prepared for them a city.

Hebrews 11:14-16 (ESV)

The author of Hebrews seems to say that the Israelites who were exiled out of Israel, their homeland, did not want to go back to the same land on earth. Instead, they desired another homeland, a heavenly country, a city whose builder is God. Hence it is understood by many modern readers to be talking about Heaven as our homeland. The problem, however, is that those who died are still waiting to receive the promise of their heavenly homeland (Hebrews 11:39). The Homeland, Country or City is not something to which we will go, but which, according to Revelation 21:1-4, will one day come down to receive us on earth. Those who have died are still waiting to receive *that* promise at their resurrection (Hebrews 11:19, 35).

7. Going to my Father's House (John 14:2-4)

In my Father's house are many rooms. If it were not so, would I have told you that I go to prepare a place for you? And if I go and prepare a place for you, I will come again and will take you to myself, that where I am you may be also. And you know the way to where I am going.

John 14:2-4 (ESV)

One of the (apparently) clearest passages for Heaven-goers, John 14:2-4 immediately comes to our minds when thinking about our eternal destiny. Jesus, in the clearest fashion, seems to be talking about leaving his disciples behind and going to Heaven. He encourages his disciples not to lose heart because he is going to come once again to receive his people to himself in Heaven. A careful analysis of the context and a word study of the *Father's House* will clear away such a misconception. First let us look at the context. Where is Jesus going? Is he going to the Father or the Father's House? Jesus begins to talk about his departure from John 13:33 (ESV),

> Little children, yet a little while I am with you. You will seek me, and just as I said to the Jews, so now I also say to you, 'Where I am going you cannot come.'

Simon Peter asks him, "Lord, where are you going?" (John 13:36) (ESV). But Jesus doesn't give a direct reply to his question but instead says, "Where I am going you cannot follow me now, but you will follow afterward" (John 13:36). But later on, Jesus tells them where he is going: he is going to the Father (John 14:6, 28, 16:10, 28, 20:17). But isn't the Father in his 'House,' which is Heaven? John uses the same phrase, "Father's House" in John 2:16 to refer to the physical Temple in Jerusalem. This means that the "Father's House" in John 14:2-4 must somehow relate to the Jewish Temple in Jerusalem. A careful study of the ancient Jewish Temple shows that it had three divisions:

1. The Holy of holies

2. The Holy place

3. The outer courtyard

The Holy of holies was hidden from view by a curtain and it lodged the Ark of the Covenant which is described as God's footstool (1 Chronicles 28:2). It represented the invisible heavenly realm. The Holy place had the curtain which was blue, purple and scarlet in colour with designs of winged creatures representing the visible sky and the birds of the air. The Holy place also had ten lamp stands with each lamp stand containing seven burning candles. Against the dark background of the hall, they would have appeared as 70 lights that represented the stars, planets, sun and moon. The outer courtyard had a large washbasin called the 'sea' with designs of fruits etched on the basin. The whole basin stood on 12 oxen (2 Chronicles 4:2-4).The sea, the fruits and the animals of the basin represented the whole earth. From these observations, the Bible scholar G.K. Beale concludes that the Jewish Temple that was in Jerusalem during Jesus' day stood as a miniature model of the entire creation.[3] This means that the Father's House into which Jesus will welcome us when he will "come again" in the future is the renewed creation. If we were to add brackets into the text of John 14:2-4 to bring out the intended meaning of the text, it would be like this:

> In my Father's house (that is, the new creation) are many rooms (places of residence). If it were not so, would I have told you that I go to (my Father in Heaven to) prepare a place for you (in my Father's House, the new creation)? And if I go (to Heaven) and prepare a place for you (in the new creation), I will come again (from Heaven) and will take you to myself, that where I am (that is, the new creation) you may be also. And you know the way to where I am going.

Such a reading of this passage also does justice to the overall theme of John's Gospel. John begins his Gospel by invoking creation imagery found in the creation account of Genesis: God creates the world 'in the beginning' and creates 'light' which shines in the darkness (Genesis 1:1-2, John 1:1, 5). John then has Jesus standing on trial before Pontius Pilate on the sixth day with Pilate exclaiming, "Behold the Man!" (John 19:5). This echoes the creation narrative where God made man on the sixth day (Genesis 1:26). The way John has structured the crucifixion of Jesus is also fascinating. According to John's Gospel, Jesus is crucified in between two gardens: the garden of Gethsemane and the garden tomb. He is hung on a tree at the centre of the two gardens and Mary and the male disciple are standing in front of the wooden cross (John 19:26), like Adam and Eve standing before the Tree of the knowledge of good and evil. At his resurrection, Jesus is deliberately mistaken for a gardener since Adam was a gardener in Eden. Adam is the man of creation. Jesus is the man of new creation. Thus for John, new creation is at the heart of his theology.

8. Earthly tent and heavenly building (2 Corinthians 5:1)

For we know that if the earthly tent we live in is destroyed, we have a building from God, an eternal house in heaven, not built by human hands.

2 Corinthians 5:1 (NIV)

Many consider the human body as nothing but a closed prison for the soul, and the earth a larger prison for body. The idea that the real thing in you is the soul or spirit and this human body is simply a temporary habitation for you dates back all the way to the pagan Greek philosopher Plato, who lived in the late fifth and early fourth century B.C. and is also the main theology of the Upanishads and the Bhagavad Gita.[4] According to Plato, the true self in you, which is the soul or spirit, when released from the prison house of the body, will travel to a place of blissful immortality. The human body is simply a bad covering that needs to be shed off. Since many of us today unknowingly live with such a platonic worldview, it is easy for us to read 2 Corinthians 5:1 to mean exactly that: our present bodies are tents that contain our souls and one day the tent will be destroyed and we will go to our eternal house, which is heaven. But neither this passage nor its context says even remotely that. The building or the house that Paul talks about in this verse is not Heaven. It is the imperishable resurrected body imagined like clothing reserved in heaven for us. The aim is not to come out of the tent of our present bodies and inhabit Heaven. The aim is to put on the immortal resurrected body *on top of* the present earthly body.

For while we are in this tent, we groan and are burdened, because we do not wish to be unclothed but to be clothed instead with our heavenly dwelling, so that what is mortal may be swallowed up by life.

2 Corinthians 5:4 (NIV)

Just as the human body without the skin is incomplete, so too our present bodies are incomplete without immortality. It needs an additional layer to be added on so that the whole body would be transformed altogether. That additional layer, which Paul says is the house or building, is at present reserved for us in heaven. The day will come when God will clothe us with the resurrected body so that these present dying bodies of ours would be swallowed up by immortal life. When that happens, we will be *more physical* than we are today. It should be noted, however, that it is not the human body that goes up to Heaven to receive its resurrected body. It is the exact opposite of that: the resurrected body will be given to us from Heaven to transform our lives on earth.

So what is the role of heaven in biblical thought? We already noted that Heaven is the place where our future bodies are stored for us, ready to be given to us at the moment of new creation. But what happens to the soul in between death and resurrection? Many of us confuse life after death with resurrection. I recently heard a wonderful Easter sermon being preached in a hospital chapel. The preacher eloquently spoke about the Christian hope of the resurrection with words like, 'Jesus conquered death,' 'Jesus is alive' and 'Jesus offers eternal life.' But sadly he went on to speak of Jesus' resurrection as securing a believer's life in heaven. For many people today, that's what resurrection means: life beyond death in heaven. But is that what resurrection is all about? Consider Jesus in his resurrected state: He had flesh and bones (Luke 24:39), was mistaken for a gardener (John 20:15) and a traveller (Luke 24:13-35) and ate broiled fish (Luke 24:41-43) in front of his disciples! It seems as if his body is more suited to live on earth than in heaven – and indeed it is! If heaven is the destiny, then it makes no sense for resurrected individuals to be physical, as Jesus clearly was. Indeed, there would have been no need of a resurrection had the purpose been to go to heaven. Resurrection is not the disposal of the human body, but rather its glorious affirmation. It is not life after death, but rather it is, in the words of N.T. Wright, life *after* life after death.[5] The book of Isaiah gives a graphic description of what the resurrection is:

> Your dead shall live; their bodies shall rise. You who dwell in the dust, awake and sing for joy! For your dew is a dew of light, and the earth will give birth to the dead.
>
> Isaiah 26:19 (ESV)

Resurrection is the belief that ultimately the dead will be revived in their bodies and live again on earth. When a person dies, his soul or spirit departs from his body and goes to be with God in Heaven (2 Corinthians

5:8, Philippians 1:23). But such a state is only temporary. For at the resurrection, the soul or spirit that had departed from the body will be reunited with the body and the dead body would come back to life, never to die again. *That* is resurrection. It is what Paul says is the rescue of our *bodies* (Romans 8:23). And it will take place when God rescues his creation from decay (Romans 8:21). Resurrection, therefore, is the *renewal* of the human body in the context of the renewal of creation. As the theologian Jürgen Moltmann rightly says,

> Resurrection is not a consoling opium, soothing us with the promise of a better world in the hereafter. It is the energy for a rebirth of this life. The hope doesn't point to another world. It is focused on the redemption of this one.[6]

9. Our inheritance is in heaven (1 Peter 1:3b-5)

> In his great mercy he has given us new birth into a living hope through the resurrection of Jesus Christ from the dead, and into an inheritance that can never perish, spoil or fade. This inheritance is kept in heaven for you, who through faith are shielded by God's power until the coming of the salvation that is ready to be revealed in the last time.

1 Peter 1:3b-5 (NIV)

The word 'inheritance' and its cognates occur many times in the Old Testament and is regularly used to denote the physical land on earth.[7] The same meaning is retained in the New Testament Gospels as well.[8] However, when it comes to the New Testament epistles, people read the same word and assume that it is talking about Heaven.[9]

If we are to be consistent in our interpretation of the Bible, then we have to say, unless there is evidence to the contrary, that the word 'inheritance,' even in the epistles, must have a correlation to the physical land on earth. With such a hermeneutical approach, when we read 1 Peter 1:4, the imperishable inheritance that is, at present, hidden in heaven and which will one day be revealed to us on earth, could only be talking about the heavenly City, Country or Land[10] which is now in Heaven and which will one day descend to merge with the earth (Revelation 21:1-3), thereby creating a renewed world. And since we are citizens of that renewed world, we are, at present, temporary dwellers on the earth in its present condition (1 Peter 2:11, Hebrews 11:13) who long for the new world to come. A similar motif that we have already seen is the resurrection bodies of God's people kept in Heaven for the present time and which will one day descend to be clothed on to us living on the earth (2 Corinthians 5:1-5). Everything that is needed to repair this broken earth – from resurrection bodies to heavenly cities – is ready and kept in Heaven like new machine parts fashioned and kept in a machine shop. At the right moment, the new creational parts will be sent to earth to fix it so that instead of the thornbush will grow the juniper, and instead of briers the myrtle will grow (Isaiah 55:13).

> The wolf shall dwell with the lamb,
> and the leopard shall lie down with the young goat,
> and the calf and the lion and the fattened calf together;
> and a little child shall lead them.
>
> The cow and the bear shall graze;
> their young shall lie down together;
> and the lion shall eat straw like the ox.
>
> The nursing child shall play over the hole of the cobra,
> and the weaned child shall put his hand on the adder's den.
>
> They shall not hurt or destroy
> in all my holy mountain;
> for the earth shall be full of the knowledge of the LORD
> as the waters cover the sea.

Isaiah 11:6-9 (ESV)

The rising of the dead in their new bodies, the whole creation being liberated from decay, the dawn of global peace even in the animal kingdom and, ultimately, God himself coming to live with us on earth are powerful themes that have to be reclaimed to replace the pagan idea of drifting in heaven for eternity.

10. Kingdom of heaven, eternal life, and Kingdom inside

> And he said: "Truly I tell you, unless you change and become like little children, you will never enter the kingdom of heaven."

Matthew 18:3 (NIV)

In the New Testament Gospels, Jesus is portrayed, page after page, as preaching about the Kingdom of Heaven (or God). Matthew's Gospel uses the phrase, 'Kingdom of Heaven' whereas the other three Gospels replace the phrase with the 'Kingdom of God.' For example, consider the parallel between Matthew and Luke.

> Blessed are the poor in spirit, for theirs is the kingdom of heaven. (Matthew 5:3) (NIV)

> Blessed are you who are poor, for yours is the kingdom of God. (Luke 6:20) (NIV)

So what is the Kingdom of God/Heaven? A plain reading of the phrase suggests that it is a Kingdom belonging to God which is in Heaven. And so many readers come to the conclusion that Jesus was preaching about how to enter into Heaven where God is King. But was that the message that Jesus preached?

In Daniel 7, which is one of the books of the Old Testament, the author describes as seeing a terrific vision of four powerful monsters coming up from the sea and devouring everything in their way. But then God, the Judge of all the earth, takes his seat in the divine Law court and the beasts are judged. The power of the three beasts is taken away and the fourth beast is killed and burnt with fire. Then, a human figure is brought inside the divine council and he is given all the power that the beasts possessed. The vision is interpreted by an angelic figure who tells Daniel that the beasts are the pagan empires that have fought and prevailed over God's people until God came and pronounced judgment in favour of God's people "and the time came when they possessed the kingdom" (Daniel 7:22) (NIV). Jesus picks up from where Daniel left and he announces his Gospel message saying that "The time has come... The kingdom of God has come near. Repent and believe the good news!" (Mark 1:15) (NIV).

For Jesus, the Kingdom of God means the overthrow of pagan powers and the establishment of God's own power exercised through God's people. That is why he tells his followers to pray for the Kingdom of God to come *on earth*.

Thy kingdom come. Thy will be done, as in heaven, so on earth.

Matthew 6:10 (ERV)

The prayer is about God's Kingdom coming down to man and not about man going up to God's Kingdom. What will happen when God's Kingdom – His administration – fully and gloriously comes to earth? There will be a *renewal* of personal, societal and environmental life. And so Jesus talks about the renewal of all things at the end of the age:

> Truly I tell you, at the renewal of all things, when the Son of Man sits on his glorious throne, you who have followed me will also sit on twelve thrones, judging the twelve tribes of Israel.

Matthew 19:28 (NIV)

The Greek word for 'renewal' comes from two roots namely *pálin*, "again" and *genesis*, "beginning." A similar word is found in Titus 3:5 which talks about the washing (that is, the moral cleansing) that leads to a "new beginning" and renewal of our lives by the Holy Spirit. A washing away of all that opposes God will take place leading up to the regeneration and renewal of the world. That is when the Kingdom of God would be fully inaugurated on earth.

But what about the passage where Jesus says that the Kingdom of God is "within you" (Luke 17:21)? Many people look at this verse and think that the Kingdom of God is purely spiritual and refers to the rule of God in our hearts. But the problem is that, in context, Jesus is talking to the disbelieving Pharisees who have rejected him and his message. It seems strange to think that Jesus would have meant that God was ruling in *their* hearts. Another way of translating the words *entos hymon*, which many modern translations use, is to say that the Kingdom of God is "in the midst of you."[11] A third and better way of translating the phrase is to say that God's Kingdom is "within your grasp."[12] The intended meaning is that God's rule is happening here in the midst of us, being exercised through Jesus as he heals the sick, raises the dead, cleanses the lepers, discharges debtors, delivers the captives, defends the feeble and serves the unfortunate. But God's rule is not simply there to sit and watch. Jesus calls people to join him in bringing the rule of God on earth; hence

God's Kingdom is both in the midst of us and within our grasp. The rule of God has *already* burst forth into the world in Jesus but it is *not yet* complete. At the end, there will be a completion of God's Kingdom – his rule – which would result in the renewal of all things and is equivalent to the new creation mentioned elsewhere in the New Testament.

But what sort of creatures will inherit this new creation? Paul declares,

> Flesh and blood cannot inherit the Kingdom of God, nor does the perishable inherit the imperishable.

> 1 Corinthians 15:50 (NIV)

Does this mean that those who are anatomically made up of flesh and blood cannot inherit God's Kingdom? I don't think so. Paul has categorised "flesh and blood" as that which is "perishable" and the "Kingdom of God" as that which is "imperishable." The perishable flesh and blood cannot inherit the imperishable Kingdom of God. The emphasis, as the context will make clear, is not on the flesh and blood which, readers think, will have to be thrown away to enter the Kingdom of God. The emphasis is on the *perishability* of the flesh and blood. Since flesh and blood are perishable, they cannot inherit the imperishable Kingdom of God. What should happen is that the perishable flesh and blood must be converted to the imperishable flesh and blood.

> For the perishable must clothe itself with the imperishable, and the mortal with immortality.

> 1 Corinthians 15:53 (NIV)

New Testament scholar Michael Licona comments,

> One can almost see Paul grabbing his arm as he emphasizes that it is *this* body that will put on immortality as one puts on a coat. A transformation of the corpse will occur, and it will be clothed with immortality and imperishability.[13]

This is the reason why, after his resurrection, Jesus himself had flesh and bones that could walk through closed doors and disappear at will. Something has happened to his body which is still in every way human but has been converted into something imperishable. A similar conversion of the human body will one day happen to us (Philippians 3:21).

We now look at the context of 1 Corinthians 15:50. Using the metaphor of a sown seed, Paul says that the body that goes to the grave as the perishable is the same body that will be raised to life as the imperishable (1 Corinthians 15:42). It goes to the grave in dishonour and comes out in glory (15:43a). It goes in weakness and comes out in power (15:43b). It goes as a body that contains the soul and comes out as a body that contains the spirit (15:44). At this point, several translations mislead the readers by saying that the body will be raised as a "spiritual body."

> It is sown a natural body, it is raised a spiritual body.

1 Corinthians 15:44 (NIV)

The word 'natural,' in the Greek, means 'soul.' Paul says that this present body of ours is a 'soul-body.' That doesn't mean we are made up of souls with no physical stuff. Likewise when he says that the resurrection body is a 'spirit-body,' he does not mean that it will be made up of spirit alone. He means that it will be a physical body that will be controlled by the spirit. Throughout the chapter, 'bodies' are very important for Paul. He talks about heavenly bodies (sun, moon and starts) and earthly bodies (man, animals, birds and fish) and says that they are all different from one another but share the same property of being physical (1 Corinthians 15:39-41). And it will make no sense for him to suddenly shift the emphasis from physical bodies to immaterial spirits in verse 44.

Another common misunderstanding that has crept into many devotional books and sermons is the words 'eternal life' that is used regularly in the New Testament. A famous passage is from John 3:16:

> For God so loved the world that he gave his one and only Son, that whoever believes in him shall not perish but have eternal life.

The word eternal life means unending life which, many people assume, is in Heaven. But 'eternal life' refers only to the *quality* of life and not its location. It could be in heaven, earth or anywhere in between the two. For Jesus (and for Paul), world history is divided into two eras or ages: the present evil age and the future new age. A clear distinction is evident in Luke 20:34-35,

Jesus replied, "The people of this age marry and are given in marriage. But those who are considered worthy of taking part in the age to come and in the resurrection from the dead will neither marry nor be given in marriage...

And according to Paul,

[Jesus] gave himself for our sins to rescue us from the present evil age... [so that] what counts is the new creation.

Galatians 1:4, 6:15 (NIV)

Eternal life belongs to the age that is to come on earth, which is one of the many ways of talking about the new creation. The words 'New Jerusalem,' 'heavenly City,' heavenly Country, 'new creation,' 'Father's house,' 'eternal life,' 'Kingdom of God,' 'Kingdom of Heaven,' 'inheritance' and 'age to come' are used by different authors of the New Testament to mean the same future hope for the world – which is all about the renewal of God's creation - and we have to learn to resonate along with the biblical evidence.

It should have become evident by now, after dealing with potential passages that might be misread as endorsing an other-worldly hope in Heaven, that the Bible tells the sweeping story of God's creation which will be transformed into a new creation. Plants, trees, animals, birds, rocks and dust will all be a part of the new creation that God will make. Using the equation $H = ep$ (Heaven equals earth perfected), the theologian Randal Rauser makes the telling point that "the very best that we enjoy of earth are glimpses of what will be transformed into heavenly glory."[14] Rauser also comments,

We have been looking for heaven over the distant horizon when all the while the place he is preparing is right before our eyes. The world around us is being prepared for the ultimate transformation into our eternal home.[15]

With this understanding in mind, we can state that everything reported in the Bible between Genesis 1-2 (creation) and Revelation 21-22 (new creation) has relevance to the former and moves in the direction of the latter. From God flooding the world and starting afresh, his calling of Abraham to be a blessing to all nations, the promise of a land flowing with milk and honey, the multiple battles fought to extend the land of milk and honey to cover all the earth, the exiles that atoned for human wickedness and all the way through to Jesus announcing the Kingdom and dying to inaugurate it and the Church taking up the Kingdom-shaped cross and implementing it in the world, all fit into the larger meta-narrative of creation and new creation like a hand in a glove. This is the dynamic story of the Bible which needs to be reclaimed and which will enable us to see the problem of suffering more clearly and respond appropriately.

But how does the death of Jesus on the cross relate to the theme of creation and new creation? We shall pick up this question in the next chapter.

Endnotes

[1] Thomas R. Taylor, *I'm but a Stranger Here*. For the full lyrics, see http://www. lutheran-hymnal.com/lyrics/tlh660.htm (Last accessed on 20-12-15).

[2] N.T. Wright, *Paul for Everyone: The Prison Letters* (Copublished in 2004 by the Society for Promoting Christian Knowledge, London, and Westminster John Knox Press, Louisville, Kentucky), p 126. First published in Great Britain in 2002 by the Society for Promoting Christian Knowledge, London.

[3] Gregory K. Beale, *A New Testament Biblical Theology: The Unfolding of the Old Testament in the New* (Grand Rapids: Baker Academic, 2011).

[4] "The soul is imprisoned like the oyster in its shell." Plato, Phaedrus 250C.

[5] N.T. Wright, *The Resurrection of the Son of God* in "Christian Origins and the Question of God", Vol. 3 (Minneapolis: Fortress Press, 2003), p 31.

[6] Jürgen Moltmann, Jesus Christ for Today's World (First Fortress Press edition, Fortress Press, 19940, p 81.

[7] Hebrew: נַחֲלָה‎ – nachalah. Meaning: possession, property, inheritance. See, for example, Deuteronomy 4:21, Judges 20:6, , Joshua 17:4,14; Joshua 19:49, Numbers 26:53, Ezekiel 45:1, Psalm 2:8 and Isaiah 58:14.

[8] Greek: κληρονομία - kléronomia. Meaning: heritage, possession. See Matthew 21:38, Mark 12:7, Luke 12:13 and Luke 20:14.

[9] See Acts 20:32, Galatians 3:18, Colossians 3:24, Hebrews 9:5, Ephesians 1:14, Ephesians 5:5 and 1 Peter 1:4. Nowhere in these passages is there any implicit or explicit mention of heaven as the inheritance.

[10] The synonymous usage of the Land, City and Country is in Hebrews 11:14-16. As to the Land, the Old Testament promise to Abraham that he would inherit the land from the Mediterranean to the Euphrates, as in Genesis 13:14- 15; Genesis 15:18 and so on, is expanded so that the whole earth becomes the 'land' which Abraham and his family (that is, the Church) would inherit (Romans 4:13). Notice,

again, that the 'inheritance' is not Heaven. And from Romans 4:13, there is a direct connection to the restoration of creation in Romans 8:21: God's people will inherit the whole land of the earth in the renewal of creation.

[11] For example, NIV and ESV.

[12] N. T. Wright, *Kingdom New Testament* (HarperCollins, NY, 2012) p 151.

[13] Michael R. Licona, The Resurrection of Jesus: A New Historiographical Approach (Downers Grove, IL: *InterVarsity Press*, 2010) p 406.

[14] Randal Rauser, *What on Earth Do We Know about Heaven?* (Baker Books, Grand Rapids, Michigan, 2013), p 13.

[15] *Ibid.*, p 32.

The Cross and the Resurrection in the Biblical Narrative

When somebody asks us, "Why did Jesus die?" we have a stock response: he died for our sins. When we are asked to unpack what we mean by that, we would say that humans are basically sinners who have broken God's commandments are unable to please God with their good works. And God, being just, cannot forgive their sins without letting out his punishing anger on sinners. So he sends Jesus, heaps the sins of all people on him, and punishes him to let us go free. I may have oversimplified the message but this is the essence of the popular version of the Christian 'Gospel.' The problem is not with the response but with the unpacking of it. Notice the context in which the cross is interpreted: humans are sinners and God is just. The cross thus becomes the violent act of God executing his justice on the sinless Jesus in the place of sinful humans.

Such a view of the cross has opened the door to much criticism: what sort of a father would punish his own son for the crimes committed by another? Isn't this a form of child abuse? Why doesn't God simply forgive us without a blood sacrifice? These sorts of criticisms have come up because we have skewed the background of the cross. Imagine a bloodstained scalpel blade lying on the floor in a scene of crime. What thought comes to your mind? Murder, vengeance and hatred. Now imagine the same scalpel in a kidney dish inside an operation theatre of a hospital. What thought comes to mind? Love, healing and hope. The way you imagine the context will affect the way you view an object. And because we have tended to see the cross of Christ in the context of a vengeful God up there and pitiful humans down here, we have lost the essence of the cross altogether. The cross should be placed right where it belongs: in between creation and new creation. The cross is the place where all the sorrow and suffering, violence and corruption of the present creation came rushing together in order to be dealt with by the powerful love of God. It is not God up there and Jesus down here. It is God, in the face of Jesus, allowing himself to be entangled by the wires of sin and evil in order to unwind the wires from his wounded creation. The cross is the advance death certificate for the decaying state of the present creation written in blood and sealed in a tomb. This cosmic scope of the cross finds its place in many biblical passages:

> May I never boast except in the cross of our Lord Jesus Christ, through which the world has been crucified to me, and I to the world. Neither circumcision nor uncircumcision means anything; what counts is the new creation.

> Galatians 6:14-15 (NIV)

> [Jesus] gave himself for our sins to rescue us from the present evil age, according to the will of our God and Father...

> Galatians 1:4 (NIV)

> For he has rescued us from the dominion of darkness and brought us into the kingdom of the Son he loves...

> Colossians 1:13 (NIV)

> through him to reconcile to himself all things, whether things on earth or things in heaven, by making peace through his blood, shed on the cross.

> Colossians 1:20 (NIV)

> as a plan for the fullness of time, to unite all things in him, things in heaven and things on earth.

> Ephesians 1:10 (ESV)

The world has now become the Kingdom of our Lord and of his Christ, and he will reign forever and ever.... It is time to destroy all who have caused destruction on the earth.

Revelation 11:15, 18 (NLT)

Heaven, earth and time – these are all affected and transformed by the death of Jesus on the cross. Through the cross, the present world (we included), in its state of decay and corruption, has been impaled to death so that what matters now is new creation. Through the cross, God has rescued us from the present evil age where darkness rules and brought us to a whole new world where the Kingdom of God advances. It is God's plan and purpose to reconcile and bring back to a state of harmony, through the blood of Jesus, everything in the entire universe and to destroy everything that is bent on destroying God's earth. The death of Jesus, although violent and bloody in itself, takes on a whole new perspective when seen in the context of creation and new creation. It is the outpouring of the Creator's love for his creation. It is God coming into the messy world in order to transform it from the inside out. It is, therefore, a symbol of love, healing and hope.[1]

If the death of Jesus is the advance death certificate of the present creation, then the resurrection of Jesus is the advance birth certificate of new creation. We have already noted that the resurrected body of Jesus was fully human, made up of bones, flesh and blood, but was nevertheless able to walk through closed doors and disappear from sight. Paul in Ephesians 1:10 says that God's plan is to unite – to bring together – heaven and earth in Jesus. And in the resurrection of Jesus, that 'bringing-together' project has already begun. The resurrected body of Jesus was made up of substances from both heaven and earth. His muscles, bones, flesh and blood, that all come from earth, were merged with heavenly properties of incorruptibility and teleportation. The resurrected Jesus is, therefore, the beginning of God's new creation. The God who began the bringing-together project in Jesus will not rest until he brings together the rest of his creation. Heaven and earth are not meant to be pulled apart and held separate. They are made for one another. A question that might linger in the minds of readers at this point is the question of God's power: if

God is all powerful, why doesn't he complete the new creation this very second? Why has he taken it up as a long term project and allowed so much suffering along the way? To answer this question, we move to the next step of designing our spectacles and that is to create the appropriate lenses that will fit into the frame which we have been building so far.

Endnotes

[1] I do affirm the doctrine of the penal substitutionary atonement of Jesus which states that Jesus died in our place for our sins. One of the ways of making sense of the apparently unjust doctrine of the innocent dying in the place of the guilty is to consider the legal doctrine of vicarious liability which states that, under certain conditions, one person will be held responsible for another person's actions. For example, an employer will be held responsible for the mistake done by his employee, under certain conditions, because the employee would be working as a representative of the employer. The New Testament calls Jesus the Christ — the King who represents his people. He is, therefore, able to stand in our place and receive our penalty.

12

Rethinking God, the World and Humankind

Rethinking the world

The beginning three chapters of the Bible (Genesis 1-3) has God making the world in six days, creating man on the sixth day, forbidding him from eating from the tree of the knowledge of good and evil and cursing him with death for breaking the commandment. Readers of these chapters have often assumed that God had initially made the world in a perfect and flawless state until Adam and Eve sinned and therefore opened the door to death and decay, both for themselves and for the rest of creation. But what does the biblical evidence tell us? Old Testament scholar Terence Fretheim notes several subtleties in the creation narrative of Genesis that points to a world where pain and death were in-built into its very structure.[1]

1. God made the world 'good,' not 'perfect.'

2. God evaluates certain things as 'not good' within the 'very good' world that he had made.

3. The creating Spirit of God moves across the waters in a random and imprecise way.

4. God bestows creative powers to imperfect entities.

5. God takes 144 hours to create the world.

6. Adam's side, not just his rib, was removed to make a woman, necessitating bloodshed.

7. The Tree of Life in the Garden implies that eternal life was not yet given to Adam and Eve.

8. Pain of childbearing is 'increased,' not 'introduced.'

9. God's command to 'subdue' the earth implies that the earth was not yet subdued.

10. God rests from all activities and allows the world to be what it was made to be.

First, the word "good," says Fretheim, does not mean "static or perfect,"[2] requiring no further development. In context, it is an evaluative word and it means "as God intended it to be." The same word, in an evaluative context, is used in Genesis 49:15 where Jacob talks about how his son, Issachar, will evaluate a resting place as "good." But one might ask whether God would intend death for his creation. Does God intend the death of his creation? Not at all. What God intends for his creation is *progress*. Having created a world where death is inbuilt,[3] God doesn't want the world to remain that way forever. As we shall be exploring later on, God creates a beautiful small garden called "paradise," places man in it, provides the Tree of eternal life for him to become immortal at the appropriate time and commissions him to extend the boundaries of paradise to cover the whole earth so that God himself could come and live and vitalize the entire creation.[4] Fretheim writes,

> Genesis does not present the creation as a finished product, wrapped up with a big red bow and handed over to creatures to keep it exactly as originally created. It is not a onetime production. Indeed, for the creation to stay just as God originally created it would constitute a failure of the divine design. From God's perspective, the world needs work; development and change are what God intends for it, and God enlists human beings (and other creatures) to that end.[5]

Second, God evaluates Adam's loneliness as "not good" (2:18), even within the "very good" (1:31) creation that he had made, thus further supporting the point that God had not created a "perfect" world where nothing extra needed to be added. Adam's wife, Eve, is created because God evaluates Adam's celibacy as "not good." He needs a partner to complete and compliment him. Perhaps there were many other things that were "not good" in God's creation which God did not address but which were all part of the "very good" creation of God.[6]

Third, the second verse of Genesis one has the Spirit of God moving over the surface of the waters, ready to burst forth with creative activity. A couple of points should be noted. The word 'Spirit' used in this verse is not the comforting Holy Spirit of the New Testament. The word *ruach* means "wind, breath, blast, anger or energy." It carries the imagery of a violent and untamed breath that comes from forceful expiration. The other point to note is the activity of the Spirit: it *moves* over the surface of the waters. *Moved*, in Hebrew, means to flutter or shake. This word is used twice in the Old Testament in Deuteronomy 32:11 and Jeremiah 23:9. In Deuteronomy 32:11, the verse is used to describe the eagle stirring up the nest with its fluttering wings in order to make its young ones attempt to fly. In Jeremiah 23:9, it is used to describe the shaking of the bones of a drunkard man in a random fashion. In both these contexts, randomness and disorder are implied. The violent and untamed energising breath of God is vibrating violently, randomly and disorderly in an ugly, formless and waste land (see Genesis 1:2a) to create the world. Thus, Genesis 1:2 suggests that creation, in spite of the beauty, is also going to be messy. Fretheim writes,

> The spirit works in the disorder of things to bring about new life and new order, an order that is not precise or tightly woven, despite initial appearances.[7]

Fourth, in the creative activity of Genesis 1, God bestows creative power to imperfect entities such as the land and sea.

> Then God said, "Let the land produce vegetation... Let the water teem with living creatures...Let the land produce living creatures..."

Genesis 1:11, 20, 24 (NIV)

Notice that, in the creation of vegetation, sea creatures and land creatures, God speaks to the land and the waters. God doesn't say, "Let there be vegetation and living creatures." God, instead, gives the creative power to the land and the sea so that *they* become the creators of life on earth.

If I am a well trained surgeon running a hospital, then all the surgeries I do will be perfect and successful. But if I hand over the surgeries to a less competent surgeon, then the outcome of surgeries will not always be perfect and successful. Likewise, the outcome of vegetation, sea and land creatures are inevitably going to depend on the condition of the land and sea. Since the land and the sea are not perfect, as God is, then their creations are also not going to be perfect either. There will be defects and flaws in the plant and animal world because their creators, namely the land and sea, are imperfect (Genesis 1:2a). Fretheim writes,

> Earth and waters are not machines that work in precise and predictable and orderly ways.[8]

Fifth, God, who could have created the world in a fraction of a second, took 144 hours – six days! – to create the world. Regardless of how people interpret the 'days' of Genesis creation, the point is that God takes time to make the world. In other words, God wants *progress* in creation. He wants the world to take time in its development. He wants a genuine move from A to B over time in his creation, even though he is able to bring about the B without starting from A.[9]

Sixth, Genesis 2:22 says that God made Eve from the *tsela* of Adam.

> Then the LORD God made a woman from the rib he had taken out of the man, and he brought her to the man.
>
> Genesis 2:22 (NIV)

Most translations translate *tsela* as Adam's rib. But the word actually means 'side' or 'chamber.'

> God is imagined as a surgeon; God puts Adam to sleep, removes a part of his body (probably his side, not just a rib), and creates a woman (Gen. 2:22-23). A bloody process indeed![10]

Seventh, the presence of the Tree of Life in the Garden (Genesis 2:9) and God's concern that Adam, in his post-sin state, might eat from it and live forever (Genesis 3:22) is evidence that Adam was not created with *inherent* eternal life. Left to time and without eating from the tree, Adam and Eve would have eventually died even if they hadn't committed any sin. Death was a possibility even in the good world that God had created.[11]

Eighth, when Adam and Eve sinned against God, a curse fell on each of them. Adam was cursed to work hard, by the sweat of his brow, to eat his food and survive on earth. Eve was cursed with the pain of childbearing.

> I'll greatly increase the pain of your labor during childbirth. It will be painful for you to bear children...

> Genesis 3:16 (ISV)

Notice that God doesn't *introduce* the pain of childbirth. The pain of childbirth is already in-built in Eve's body even before she had sinned. God merely *increases* her pain as a curse after she had sinned.

Ninth, when God made Adam and Eve, he blessed them with five elements, summarised in Genesis 1:28:

1. Be fruitful

2. Multiply

3. Fill the earth

4. Subdue the earth

5. Rule over...all the earth

Each of the five elements implies their negation: by the time the blessing was given, Adam and Eve were not fruitful (for they hadn't yet started any activity), did not multiply (for they hadn't yet had children), did not fill, subdue and rule over the earth. The word 'subdue' means to bring into control that which is wild and uncontrolled. God made the world raw and untamed. Tsunamis, glaciers, earthquakes, forest fires, wild beasts, viruses and mutations might all have been part of the creation which God wanted humans to 'subdue' and 'rule over.'

Lastly, after God creates the world in six days, we read that God rested on the seventh day. He ends his activity and gives space for creation to be itself. Fretheim comments,

> "[God resting on the seventh day] is testimony to God's suspension of creative activity, which allows the creatures, each in their own way, to be what they were created to be...With regard to human beings, God leaves

room for genuine decisions as they exercise their God-given power...With regard to nonhuman creatures, God releases them from "tight divine control" and permits them to be themselves...[which would include natural calamities] from the movement of tectonic plates to volcanic activity, to the spread of viruses, to the procreation of animals."[12]

Thus we have, embedded in the creation narrative of Genesis, hints and pointers to a world somewhere between total chaos and perfect order. Death and decay were part of the creation of God, although they were not intended to be in God's creation forever. What God wanted was progress from death and decay to life and incorruptibility, being accomplished through his image-bearing human beings.

Before we proceed further, one potential obstacle to such a reading of Genesis 1 needs to be addressed. In Romans 5:12-21, Paul apparently talks about the entry of sin and death after Adam had sinned:

> Therefore, just as sin entered the world through one man, and death through sin, and in this way death came to all people, because all sinned...

> Romans 5:12 (NIV)

How do we understand this passage? There is innocence at first and the man is alive. God gives a commandment to Adam. But he sins by breaking the commandment and death enters the world and spreads like wildfire. Paul has a similar line of thought in Romans 7:9,

> Once I was alive apart from the law; but when the commandment came, sin sprang to life and I died.

The same sequence is noted: life, then commandment, then sin and then death. The death that Paul is talking about in Romans 7:9 is used in a spiritual sense because Paul was obviously alive while writing this letter. This is further reinforced by God's warning to Adam and Eve in Genesis about eating from the forbidden Tree:

> [O]f the tree of the knowledge of good and evil you shall not eat, for in the day that you eat of it you shall surely die.

> Genesis 2:17 (ESV)

But did Adam and Eve physically die on the day they ate from the Tree of the Knowledge of good and evil? Of course not. God's warning carries the sense that the eternal life that God wanted Adam and Eve to catch hold of (by eating from the Tree of Life) would be withheld from them and they will eventually die (physically) and rot like the rest of creation if they were to disobey God. It is likely that Paul thinks in this way too. The entry and the spread of 'death' by one human's trespass is about the withdrawal of the solution to the problem of physical death in God's creation brought about by the sin of Adam. It's like a man carrying a cure to a terrible disease that has infected everyone in his village, including him, but slips and falls to the ground and thereby spills the cure on the ground and ruining it. Death, now having taken a whole new meaning as the *withdrawal of life,* has entered the village through one man and death spread to all people in the village.[13]

To restate the point I'm trying to make, it is relatively more plausible, given the evidences we have seen so far, that God had created a beautiful world where suffering and progress were integral to the unfolding of creation. God wanted genuine progress from creation to new creation, rather than create the new creation in the beginning.

Rethinking God

A fresh understanding of God emerges out of our rethought world. Old Testament scholar John Walton notes that Genesis 1 is about the inauguration of the universe as a Cosmic Temple. Recall that we had already established that the physical Temple that stood in Jerusalem was a small replica of the entire creation. The whole creation is a Cosmic Temple for God to live in. God creates the world in six days and then rests on the seventh day. People have often asked why God rested on the seventh day. But few people have asked the question of *where* God rested. We assume that after creating the Universe, God rested on his throne in Heaven. But the language of God's 'resting place' is used elsewhere in the Bible to speak of God's *enthronement on earth* (Psalm 132:7-8, 13-14). After creating the world in six days, God himself comes down to take up residence on earth. After Adam and Eve had sinned, God still would live with sinners in the pillar of cloud by day and the ball of fire by night (Exodus 13:21). He would continue to live with them in the Jewish Temple (2 Chronicles 5:14, 7:2, 1 Kings 8:11, Isaiah 6:1-4). His ultimate desire is to flood the whole earth with his glorious presence (Numbers 14:21, Habakkuk 2:14, Isaiah 11:9) because, after all, God had created the Universe as a Cosmic Temple for the very purpose of living in it and fructifying it with life and beauty. Walton writes,

> The most central truth to the creation account is that this world is a place for God's presence.[15]

It is, therefore, no surprise that we see God's visitations on earth in the form of clouds, fire, smoke, thunder and ultimately in the form of a crucified Jesus. Hence the first point about God: he is not an ultra-transcendent deity who refuses to stain himself from the mess of his creation. The second point about a rethought God flows from the first. Although God's ultimate intention is to come down to his world and transform it, he will do so *from within the world*. A good example is God's concern for the suffering Israelites in Egypt seen in the dialogue between God and Moses in the story of the burning bush.

> The LORD said, "I have indeed seen the misery of my people in Egypt. I have heard them crying out because of their slave drivers, and I am concerned about their suffering. So I have come down to rescue them from the hand of the Egyptians and to bring them up out of that land into a good and spacious land, a land flowing with milk and honey... So now, go. I am sending you to Pharaoh to bring my people the Israelites out of Egypt.
>
> Exodus 3:7-8, 10 (ESV)

God himself has personally come down from Heaven to rescue his people from slavery. At this point, we would expect God to appear directly in a vision to Pharaoh and convey his message and miraculously rescue the people. But, instead, God sends Moses as his representative:

> Then the LORD said to Moses, "See, I have made you like God to Pharaoh, and your brother Aaron will be your prophet.
>
> Exodus 7:1 (NIV)

And perhaps the exemplifying event demonstrating this attitude of God is seen in the life and death of Jesus Christ. In Isaiah 52, there is the wonderful and vivid description of God, in all his glory and splendour, returning *physically* to his people after centuries of being absent from them.

> The voice of your watchmen—they lift up their voice; together they sing for joy; for eye to eye they see the return of the LORD to Zion... The LORD has bared his holy arm before the eyes of all the nations, and all the ends of the earth shall see the salvation of our God.
>
> Isaiah 52:8, 10 (ESV)

The chapter immediately goes on to talk about a servant who shocks the entire world, including kings, by his wounded appearance – wounded beyond human resemblance (Isaiah 52:14). He is the bared holy arm of God extending into the world (Isaiah 53:1) but lacking the majesty and glory that characterizes God (Isaiah 52:2). He is rejected by men – a man of sorrows and well familiar with grief (Isaiah 53:3). This one bears our sins and suffers pain for us (Isaiah 53:4). We are healed by his wounds (Isaiah 53:5). When the magnificent God enters space and time to intervene in the world, he will empty himself and work from within the world, through agents, to bring about healing and hope.[16]

The third point about God comes out of the second. If God's desire is to come and inhabit the world in order to take control and rule over it, and if such an act would involve his self-emptying and the use of agents to accomplish his task, then God is inevitably going to take time to do what he wants to do in and for the world. He will not do his work by the snap of his fingers. Rather, as we had seen in the creation narrative, God will take time and leave room for progress in the world. We believe in a God who believes in progress. Blood and history matter to God. Many Christians believe that God had waited for 2000 years, from Adam to Jesus, only to bring out the point that humans are basically sinners who needed a Saviour. But that is not the God we encounter in the Bible. God is deeply involved in the unfolding of world events and relies on human beings to carry out his task. Such a commitment to his creation will consume centuries of time with lots of frustrations and failures.

When Adam sinned and refused to carry forward God's purposes for the world, God takes the Adamic blessing to multiply, fill, subdue and rule the earth (Genesis 1:28) and gives it to Noah and his family (Genesis 9:1). When they mess up, he calls Abraham and 'blesses' him with the same task (Genesis 12:2, 17:2, 6, 8, 16, 22:8). The 'blessing' is then transferred to Isaac (Genesis 26:3-4, 24), Jacob (Genesis 28:3-4, 14, 35:11-12, 48:3, 15-16) and Israel (Genesis 47:27, Deuteronomy 7:13, Exodus 1:7, Psalm 107:38, Isaiah 51:2) until, finally, the 'blessing' falls upon Jesus, the last Adam (1 Corinthians 15:45), who becomes fruitful in his task, whose family is multiplied worldwide as Christians fill the earth, who subdues creation (Matthew 8:27, 29) and rules over it (1 Corinthians 15:25). The failures and frustrations in between Adam and Jesus were necessary in the unfolding of the great narrative of human history, not to mention the environmental and cosmological history. As God's purposes for humans and the world passed on from one person to another on one side, on the other side, cultures developed, technologies increased, knowledge and wisdom grew, climates changed, volcanoes erupted, glaciers melted, viruses replicated, stars fell and planets revolved. These are not irrelevant things that happened (and are happening) on earth. These are all important and necessary events in the progress of God's creation to the new creation of Revelation 21-22.

Lastly, if all this is said about God – that is, if God will come down, empty himself, use agents and consume time to work in the world, then God is best imagined as a Cosmic Artist with the brush of creativity and messiness in his hands. Many people imagine God as a Cosmic Engineer who is expected to make this universe neat and perfect. Because of such a conception of God, any defect or flaw encountered in creation is seen as carelessness or lethargy on God's part. But as we have seen in our exploration of the creation narrative in Genesis, God paints on the cosmic canvas with the brush of his turbulent breath (Genesis 1:2). Below is a world famous painting by Jasper Johns created in 1959 and sold for $17 million in 1988.[18]

The painting is described thus:

> False Start does not seem to use color; it is about color...The stenciled
> labels for colors draw attention, since these are often "wrong" - the word
> GRAY is painted in red letters on a patch of yellow, and so on. Much
> critical commentary has been devoted to the contradictions inherent in this
> mislabeling. The commentary itself is paradoxical; nearly everyone begins
> by saying the device is uninteresting, and then discusses it at length.[19]

No form, wrong labels and erratic borders, all of which hint towards carelessness, lethargy, imprecision, inefficiency and immaturity. And yet the artist has taken intentionality, maturity and creativity to bring about this painting, which is why it has been sold for millions of dollars. God is like that. When God paints creation into existence, there will be unnecessary brush strokes and splattered paint in the wrong place. But that neither means that God is inefficient nor does that mean that God is careless. For God is like an Artist and not like an Engineer. The only way God differs from artists is in the compensation that God can provide for all the loss suffered by the creatures in his creation. He is able to give back life in its fullest and most colourful form to creatures that find themselves in areas of splattered paint where there is suffering and death.

Rethinking humankind

When God made humans, he created them in divine image (Genesis 1:27). In the hospital that I once worked at, there is a huge idol of the Hindu deity Ganesha at the main entrance. To the people who worship in front of it, the idol mediates the presence and blessings of the deity and the place where they stand becomes sacred ground. God made a similar idol in Genesis. But this idol was not immobile. It could walk. It was not mute. It could talk. It was not deaf. It could hear. It was not blind. It could see. The idol was named 'mankind.' The idol was made to represent God on earth and to extend God's presence and rule in the world. After analysing the Egyptian and Mesopotamian context of the role of images/idols in ancient culture, the Old Testament scholar Richard Middleton concludes that they provide the most plausible set of parallels for interpreting the 'image' in Genesis 1. He writes,

> Humanity in Genesis 1 is called to be the representative and intermediary of God's power and blessing on earth.[20]

Since humans are made in the divine image, they are called a 'Royal Priesthood' (1 Peter 2:9). To be 'royal' is to be like a king, exercising authority over creation. To be a priest is to be like a servant, mediating the blessing of God to creation. And so Adam, carrying in himself the divine image, was placed by God in the Garden of Eden to "cultivate" (Priestly role) and "guard" (Kingly role) the Garden (Genesis 2:15).

The guarding of the Garden is not separate from the priestly role of cultivating the Garden. The same word for 'guard,' used in Genesis 2:15, is also used in Numbers 3:8 as the duty of priests to guard the Temple. G.K. Beale notes,

> When these two words [serve and guard] occur together later in the OT, without exception they have this meaning and refer either to Israelites serving and guarding/obeying God's Word (about 10×) or, more often, to priests who serve God in the temple and guard the temple from unclean things entering it.[21]

Beale also notes that in Ezekiel 28:12b-15, which is a passage often misinterpreted to refer to the devil before he sinned, Adam is portrayed as being in Eden, the Garden of God, wearing precious stones as his covering, and anointed as a guardian in the Garden.

> The jewels that are said to be his "covering" in Ezek. 28:13 are uniquely listed in Exod. 28:17-21, which describes the jewels on the ephod of Israel's high priest, who is a human and not an angel.[22]

With several other evidences at hand, Beale concludes that Adam was created as a Priest in Eden, the Temple.[23]

Adam's task was to expand the boundaries of the Eden-Temple to cover the whole earth. That is the essence of the 'blessing' of Genesis 1:28 which was originally given to Adam and then transferred to several Adam-like figures until, finally, it was fulfilled by the last Adam, Jesus Christ. This fits well into the wider context of God's entire creation, heaven and earth included, being created as a Cosmic Temple. God begins his work of cleaning up this Cosmic Temple by placing his own 'image' in a small Garden on earth and then commissioning him and his descendants to make the whole earth a sacred place wherein the divine presence can come and live with humans in a loving relationship forever. What Adam failed to do is taken up by Jesus, who is the 'image' of the invisible God (Colossians 1:15), who is the Temple of God (John 2:21) and the one who will unite heaven and earth through his death and resurrection (Ephesians 1:10). The point about humans can now be made: humans were created as Royal Priests who will reflect God's activity into the world. But what sort of royalty and priesthood are we talking about? We will explore the life and teachings of Jesus to answer this question. Jesus is identified by the New Testament as King and Priest (Revelation 19:16, Hebrews 4:14). We often associate kingship with domination and priesthood with service. But listen to how Jesus uniquely blends the two in his conversation with James and John in Mark 10:35-45 (NIV):

35 Then James and John, the sons of Zebedee, came to him. "Teacher," they said, "we want you to do for us whatever we ask."

36 "What do you want me to do for you?" he asked.

37 They replied, "Let one of us sit at your right and the other at your left in your glory."

38 "You don't know what you are asking," Jesus said. "Can you drink the cup I drink or be baptized with the baptism I am baptized with?"

39 "We can," they answered.

Jesus said to them, "You will drink the cup I drink and be baptized with the baptism I am baptized with, 40 but to sit at my right or left is not for me to grant. These places belong to those for whom they have been prepared."

41 When the ten heard about this, they became indignant with James and John. 42 Jesus called them together and said, "You know that those who are regarded as rulers of the Gentiles lord it over them, and their high officials exercise authority over them. 43 Not so with you. Instead, whoever wants to become great among you must be your servant, 44 and whoever wants to be first must be slave of all. 45 For even the Son of Man did not come to be served, but to serve, and to give his life as a ransom for many."

James and John – the ones who had been following Jesus – knew who Jesus was. He was the 'Christ,' who is God's appointed Leader to usher in the Kingdom of God by defeating all oppressing forces on a political and spiritual level. That would include the overthrow of the Roman Empire, under whose government they were in, and the establishment of global peace under one God and his Christ. They knew that Jesus was going to do all this. They imagined the day when it will all happen and Jesus sitting on the royal throne where the Roman Emperor, Caesar, was seated at present. When that day comes, they wanted to sit at the right and the left of Jesus in superiority. Four chapters later, we read that Jesus was actually enthroned as 'The King of the Jews' on a wooden cross (Mark

15:26). But those who were seated to his right and his left, ironically, were not James and John but, instead, two rebels who probably had the same ambition as James and John (Mark 15:27). Jesus understood that James and John had a wrong conception of power and authority. So he calls all his disciples together, including James and John, and explains to them that true power lies, not in the ability to bully others, but in the gift of serving others – even to the point of death. It is in the *expenditure* of life, and not in the *expansion* of life, that real power is manifested. Such a person is said to be truly alive. Philosopher and theologian Arthur C. McGill, in his book, *Suffering: A Test of Theological Method*, explains thus:

> When a man lives as Jesus did, and spills out his life for others, either in one decisive moment or gradually over a whole lifetime of daily attrition and impoverishment, then he is truly alive. If he lives to expand himself rather than to expend himself, he is empty and dead.[24]

For this reason, the crucifixion and death of Jesus Christ is said to be the power and wisdom of God that shames all human power and wisdom (1 Corinthians 1:18-25). This power, in its self-consumption, *gives* life rather than take it away. It displays the wisdom by which God made the world and how he will redeem the world. Thus, to be a kingly priest is to be – as Jesus was – in the place which the world tries to avoid, namely weakness, suffering and death, and empty our lives for others. Although such a complete expenditure of life is practically impossible for most of us, we are to consider true life as being *oriented* towards that end. The more our lives are pushed in that direction of self-emptying, either by volunteering or by compulsion by natural circumstances such as disease or poverty, the more our lives will shine with the holy life and power of God and take us into the new world that God is making.

> Whoever tries to keep their life will lose it, and whoever loses their life will preserve it.

Luke 17:33 (NIV)

> Very truly I tell you, unless a kernel of wheat falls to the ground and dies, it remains only a single seed. But if it dies, it produces many seeds.

John 12:24 (NIV)

Anyone who loves their life will lose it, while anyone who hates their life in this world will keep it for eternal life.

John 12:25 (NIV)

Through suffering, our bodies continue to share in the death of Jesus so that the life of Jesus may also be seen in our bodies.

2 Corinthians 4:10 (NLT)

We have so far explored how God, as the Cosmic Artist, created the world artistically, with several fluffy borders of suffering, but intends to take his creation forward to extreme perfection through redeemed humankind by their own self-emptying for the sake of others. We are now ready to sketch the ultimate reason why God allows suffering in the next chapter.

13
The Grand Theodicy of the Bible

We have, at last, created the spectacles through which we can see and better understand the problem of evil and suffering from a Christian perspective. In our eager expectation of what lies ahead, we quickly wipe the glasses clean and wear our spectacles. What we see, to our surprise, is a garden. We see a well fenced garden with a rich green lawn, over which are evergreen shrubs and shrubbery, climbers and creepers, flower beds, plants and trees. There are fountains and ponds, paved paths, rockery and soil. I propose that we see the Christian answer to the question of suffering as garden shaped. And as such, I will call it the Garden Theodicy. We will incorporate all that we have been saying so far about God, the world and man and synthesize a rich variegated grand Theodicy (with a capital T) which will contain and be in dialogue with other theodicies of the Bible which we had already explored.

So why does God allow evil and suffering according to Christian theology? We begin by looking at the fence of the Garden. The fence is the outer wall that defines the boundaries of the Garden. The fence *encloses* the Garden. Likewise, as the outer defining border that encloses everything else is the fact that the world has been created with the freedom to be itself. The ocean will be itself, thereby opening up the possibility of people drowning. The land will be itself, thereby hurting people who fall on it. Fire will be itself, thereby burning those who touch it. Ice will be itself, thereby melting into glaciers and destroying villages when the temperature falls. The human body will be itself – a product of dust (Genesis 3:19) – and thereby be vulnerable to the forces of the external environment of nature and also the internal milieu of the body, leading to blood cancers and bone fractures. God does not, as a rule, micro-manage the world in terms of removing the destructive capacity of creation whenever it tries to hurt people. After all, it is God who made the world like this in the first place. For him to modify what he had already made – like, for example, turning fire into smoke whenever someone tries to touch it - would amount to a failure of the original divine plan. No – God made fire, water, land, ice and chromosomes - with their capacity to destroy - and judged the overall condition to be 'good.' If human beings have the free will to do what they want, then creation can be said to have 'free process' to do what *they* want, only without intentionality as humans do.[1]

Take the life of the biblical character named Job. His property is lost, his children die and he himself is stricken with a terrible disease. His wife tells him to curse God and die. When Job calls God out of his distress to answer his questions on why the innocent suffer, God comes and speaks to him through a whirlwind – a symbol of chaos and the cause of natural disaster – and invites Job to ponder upon the complexity of God's creation and find in it the divine answer to his suffering (Job 38-41). Accordingly, Fretheim writes,

> The book of Job explores various factors related to his suffering and will finally emerge with the viewpoint that his experience of suffering has to do with the nature of God's creation.[2]

Fretheim also writes,

> [O]ne clear response as to why Job is suffering is that God's created order has significant chaotic elements that carry much potential danger to human health. *And* God has chosen not to manage this world to make sure that no one gets hurt by it. God will let the creatures be what they are created to be, and in their finitude, human beings will have to struggle to work with that reality...[For Job] to understand his personal suffering, he must revise his evaluation of the nature of creation and the way in which God has chosen to work on and through it.[3]

The world is a complex piece of creation and frailty humans can often get caught up in its uproar, even without any divine intent behind it. As the biblical author of Ecclesiastes puts it,

I have observed something else under the sun. The fastest runner doesn't always win the race, and the strongest warrior doesn't always win the battle. The wise sometimes go hungry, and the skillful are not necessarily wealthy. And those who are educated don't always lead successful lives. It is all decided by chance, by being in the right place at the right time.

Ecclesiastes 9:11 (NLT)

This is because we are interconnected with each other and the rest of creation. As Fretheim writes,

> Because humans are part of this interconnected world, we may get in the way of the workings of these [non-human] creatures and be hurt by them.[4]

Take the biblical examples of God's judgments on people. For example, God sends several plagues in Egypt because of the Pharaoh's refusal to let the Israelites go free. Frogs, lice, wild animals, locusts, disease and thunderstorms are some of the plagues that he sends. But these agents do not discriminate between the good and the bad people in Egypt. The disease that affects an evildoer will be transmitted to the innocent one who goes to help him. The wild animals that kill the evildoer will also kill the innocent. This is because people live as a community and are interconnected to nature. And hence many times the innocent suffer unjustly and randomly because of the guilty.

But there isn't a total randomness in everything. There is order in the universe, which is why science has developed so much today. Light continues to travel at the same speed and gravity continues to operate at the same strength. And the man who shoots himself in the head will always die. There are some things that are predictable and some that aren't. God has made the world somewhere in the spectrum between total chaos and perfect order and continues to work towards the latter through human collaboration.

A couple of questions emerge from such an analysis of God and his dealings with the world. What about the miracles that God performed according to the Bible? Aren't they evidence that God can break the rules of the created order if he wanted to? It is true that in many times God has broken the norms of the workings of creation and intervened to rescue people in times of trouble. Consider the miracle of God parting the Red Sea for the Israelites to walk on dry land. That is indeed a great miracle. But even when God was holding back the waters from falling on the Israelites, as thousands of people crowded the pathway, it was possible for old people to have died of suffocation and little children to have been trampled by the crowd. There would have been suffering and death even in the middle of a miracle! When edible food fell from heaven for the Israelites to eat (Exodus 16:14-35), people who would have suffered from a fever or a heart disease would have continued to suffer from the same. When the sun stood still on behalf of the Israelites (Joshua 10:12-14), people would have continued to faint from heat exhaustion. When the widow's oil multiplied (2 Kings 4:2-7), she still had to live with the pain of being a widow. When Elisha's bones revived the dead (2 Kings 13:21), Elisha still remained dead! Miracles are not complete reversals of the workings of creation. Even in the midst of miracles, God's creation continues to work the way it was designed to work, with suffering and death inbuilt into it. Miracles are like little leaflets that fall on muddy ground that do not alter or remove the ground but simply cover the ground until the wind blows it away. Hence the fact that God works miracles in the world does not mean that he is playing double standards with his creation by both allowing the creation to run its natural course, thereby entailing human suffering and death, but also intervening whenever he wants to break the natural course of events in the world by performing miracles.[5] The other question is this: why did God make the world in which natural calamities, death and decay are built into its very structure? Fretheim admits,

[I]t is not entirely clear why God created this kind of world.[6]

He suggests that only a world with potential suffering and death could be productive of genuine life and create space for novelty, surprise and creative activities on the part of God and his creation. He also suggests that God is committed to the 'free process' of the non-human world in the same way he is committed to the 'free will' of human beings: both are needed for his world to take momentum and move forwards and not remain as "a drab, ever-the-same world."[7]

I have to admit that I am unsatisfied with his two suggestions. Novelty, surprise, creative activity and dynamism can be achieved even without suffering and death, as it will be in the new creation. I propose, instead, that the reason why God, who is all powerful and all loving, made this kind of world has to do with *who* he is – that is, his character. We shall look at four aspects of God's character – his attitude – to understand why God made the world like this.

First we shall discuss God's omnipotence. Yes, God is all powerful. He can do whatever he wants. But 'can' doesn't necessarily imply 'will.' Just because God *can* do whatever he wants doesn't mean he *will* do whatever he wants. Arthur McGill writes,

> God has a specific character, a special kind of powerfulness within himself. He can no more dissociate himself from that mode of power than he can dissociate himself from his own inner reality...[This] power of God reveals itself in and *as* Jesus.[8]

New Testament scholar Richard Hays agrees:

> God has chosen to save the world through the cross, through the shameful and powerless death of the crucified Messiah. If that shocking event is the revelation of the deepest truth about the character of God, then our whole way of seeing the world is turned upside down...[God] refuses to play games of power and prestige on human terms.[9]

The decisive mark of God's power, in human terms, is *weakness* and which, in divine terms, is stronger than human strength (1 Corinthians 1:25). God's power is made complete in what the world perceives as impotent and weak (2 Corinthians 12:9). God will work from the state of weakness, as with the crucifixion of Jesus, to bring about the strength the world glories in. God's creation has such marks of 'weaknesses' in it, which would include suffering and death. This is not a denial of the omnipotence of God – as some thinkers like the Jewish Rabbi Kushner have argued.[10, 11] It is only to say that God has a specific character to him that inclines him to manifest his power differently. By this proposal of mine, we can maintain that God is still "God," with omnipotence as one of his defining characteristics, but affirm a more biblical picture of

God that will (and should) displace the 'God of philosophers' that creeps up into discussions of the problem of evil.

The second character of God relevant in our discussion of the problem of evil is his omnibenevolence. If God is an all-loving God, shouldn't we expect to see his creation in pristine perfection, free from defects and suffering? In what sense can we say that God is love in the light of natural and moral evils? Herein we import our renewed understanding of God as the Cosmic Artist. Good artists do not necessarily paint their masterpieces in a precise, clean and crisp fashion. Rather, they create and work with the mess to bring about beauty and enhancement at the final outcome. Even the child born with terrible birth defects is fearfully and wonderfully made in the divine image (Psalm 139:14a). His works are 'wonderful' (Psalm 139:14b). The word 'wonderful,' interestingly, has a combination of positivity and negativity to it.[12] Hence the evils and sufferings in the world do not automatically invalidate the existence of an all-loving God. Rather, they only invalidate the way we conceive about the character of God as the abstract Engineer whom we expect to have created a flawless world running like a cosmic machine.

The third character of God is his predisposition to work from *inside* the world. God is so deeply involved with worldly affairs that he will become an inside character in the story of the world rather than stand outside and make sure all goes well. This explains much of the frustrations that he goes through from having to put up with sinful humans who always seem to mess up the narrative script for the world. For example, consider the regret of God in making man when he sees how evil people can be:

> The LORD saw how great the wickedness of the human race had become on the earth, and that every inclination of the thoughts of the human heart was only evil all the time. The LORD regretted that he had made human beings on the earth, and his heart was deeply troubled.

> Genesis 6:5-6 (NIV)

Far from lacking omniscience, this is a God who participates in the unfolding of world events and is deeply affected by them. He is not the director who stands outside the scene and watches the play. He joins in as a character of the story and thereby limits his power of involvement in the world and creates space for other characters to do their own role. But such a commitment to work from inside the world and *through* agents in his creation will entail a lot of evil and suffering because the agents are not puppets that bend to every command of his.

Lastly, it is God's character to rejoice in the progress of the world. This would include social and cultural development, technological development, the development of nature and cosmic development of planets and stars. Rather than say that progress is essential for the world not remain as 'a drab, ever-the-same world,' as Fretheim suggests, I suggest we say that progress is written into the character of God. God *wants* progress in his creation. He wants his creation to be molded into a beautiful sculpture beginning from a formless ball of clay. He wants creation to progress to the new creation over time, rather than make the new creation instantly.

These four defining characters of God – namely the cross shaped power of God, the artistic love of God, the inward working of God and the progress-seeking of God – sufficiently explain the reason why God made the world the way it is today, with suffering and death as a part and parcel of it.

We have looked at the fence of the Garden and seen elements of disorder, randomness, ambiguity and unpredictability as part of God's creation. But the fence is not made of concrete. It is made up of post and rail, in which case, not *every* instance of suffering and death can be characterized as random and purposeless. There are other reasons for why evil and suffering exist in our world, which we will explore now; but they are all contained within a world where natural and moral evils sometimes take place without any specific divine intention or purpose.

Sometimes suffering comes as God's punishment for our sins (punishment theodicy). A thief who regularly escapes from being arrested is one day suddenly caught red-handed and pays for all the crimes he had done. He then repents of his crimes and turns over a new leaf. Maybe God had actively intervened in this case to manipulate the circumstances around him to make him get caught and pay the price. But at the same time, another thief keeps stealing and is never caught in his lifetime. We shouldn't assume that God is arbitrarily choosing whom to punish and whom not to. Underneath his every active action in the world, there is a complex web of divine reasons for acting in one situation and not in another because his thoughts are nothing like ours and his ways are far beyond anything we could imagine (Isaiah 55:8). Sometimes suffering comes because human free will is taken to the extreme level and God's active intervention is absent (free will theodicy). Sometimes suffering comes with a redemptive purpose. A man indifferent to justice in the society is met with an accident, becomes quadriplegic, is converted and spends the rest of his life advocating for road safety measures and social justice (good coming out of suffering). Sometimes a man who is born without limbs finds peace and strength in God, testifies to the unfailing love of God in spite of his tragedy and thereby brings God glory and praise among people and he himself leads an undefiled and holy life before God (suffering that comes with positive benefits). Sometimes suffering comes to test our faith in God. God may allow a person to lose his most valuable job, even after he had prayed for it a million times, with the intention of testing his faithfulness to God. And sometimes suffering comes as a result of satanic activities in the world. According to the Bible, there are dark semi-divine, sub-personal forces that are active in the world. These forces are anti-creational and are bent on thwarting God's purposes from moving forward. The well known entity in this category is called the *Satan* and there are a lot of misconceptions about this character which we have to address now.

The Satan is believed to have a name, Lucifer, and a title, Morning Star, and is believed to be one of the angelic creatures created by God to serve as the Chief Musician in Heaven (Ezekiel 28:13). Although God had given him a very high status in the Heavenly council, he wanted to take the position of God himself.

> You said in your heart,
> 'I will ascend to heaven;
> above the stars of God
> I will set my throne on high;
> I will sit on the mount of assembly

in the far reaches of the north;
I will ascend above the heights of the clouds;
I will make myself like the Most High.'

Isaiah 14:13-14 (ESV)

But God knew better. He rejected Lucifer and condemned him to Hell – a place of eternal torment prepared for him. But Lucifer wouldn't go without a fight.

> Then war broke out in heaven. Michael and his angels fought against the dragon, and the dragon and his angels fought back.

Revelation 12:7 (NIV)

Lucifer had managed to convince a third of all the heavenly angels to fight for his cause. However, the victory belonged to God and Lucifer, along with the one-third of angels who sided with him, was cast down from Heaven to earth (Revelation 12:4, 9, Luke 10:18). Unfortunately, this happened to take place just before God was in the business of making human beings on the sixth day of creation. Having come to realize his defeat, and because of the thought that God was going to send him and the rest of the angels further down the earth to Hell (Jude 1:6), his anger towards God turned to humans instead, who were the crown of God's creation. So he takes the form of an innocent looking snake and convinces them to eat from the forbidden Tree (Genesis 3:1-6). When God comes to know of what had just happened, he decided not to condemn humans to Hell for their rebellion in the same way he had condemned Lucifer. Instead, God will himself come as a human, by being born as a descendant of Eve, to avenge Lucifer and send him to his rightful place of eternal punishment (Genesis 3:15). Because of this fate, Lucifer has become even more furious to torture and kill humans and prevent God from entering into the world in the flesh of Jesus Christ. That is why humans suffer: Lucifer and his angels bring suffering on us because of their nightmares with God.

This is the popular version of the Satan's story. Unfortunately, however, the story is erroneous from start to finish. The main problem with this story is that the verses taken out of the individual books of the Bible to synthesize a coherent story are ripped out of their contexts and woven into a new context which is foreign to the Bible. First, the name Lucifer itself doesn't exist in the original Hebrew Bible. We get his name from a mistranslation of Isaiah 14:12 by the KJV of the word *helel*, meaning the morning star. The translation was rendered from the Latin translation of the Bible, called the *Vulgate*. It is not a proper name, but is itself a title. Second, he wasn't a musician in Heaven because Ezekiel 28: 12-16, as I had mentioned earlier, is talking about Adam as the Great Priest and not the Satan. Adam was created with wisdom and beauty, placed in Eden – the Garden of God, adorned with precious stones as priestly clothing, given musical instruments to praise God (as priests do), anointed to guard the garden, corrupted his 'wisdom' by eating from the Tree of wisdom and was driven out of the mountain of God. Third, the Satan did not crave the position of God and, as a result, thrown down from Heaven because Isaiah 14 is talking about the King of Babylon, not the Satan. The King had oppressed Israel and taken the nation as captives of war. However, God promises to give them rest from their oppression by destroying the King who "ruled the nations in anger with unrelenting persecution" (Isaiah 14:6). The King would be brought so low that even the dead people, whose souls are in the underworld, will greet him and say, "You too have become as weak as we! You have become like us!" (Isaiah 14:10). Then the chapter goes on to describe the King's former state of sovereignty, pride and glory and contrasts it with his present situation where he has been down to the grave.

> You said in your heart, 'I will ascend to heaven; above the stars of God.
> I will set my throne on high...

Isaiah 14:13a (ESV)

The verse immediately explains what this means:

> I will sit on the mount of assembly, in the far reaches of the north.

Isaiah 14:13b (ESV)

The King wasn't thinking of literally flying up to Heaven and sit on the throne of God. Rather, he wanted to sit enthroned on a mountain and be sovereign over the entire earth, all the way to the north. By his rule, he made the world into a desert, over threw cities and did not let the prisoners go free (14:17). But he was brought down to the pit because of his arrogance and pride (14:15). He doesn't even receive a proper burial. His corpse is trampled by foot instead (14:19). And people who see the fate of this King will be shocked and say, "Is this the man who made the earth tremble…" (14:16). Yes, Isaiah 14 is talking about a *man*.

Fourth, there was no battle in Heaven between God and the Satan because Revelation 12 is talking about Israel, Jesus and the Church. Using heavy picture language, the author is describing the history of Israel, the coming of Jesus and the beginning of the Christian era. The pregnant Woman clothed with the sun, with the moon under her feet and a crown of twelve stars on her head is the nation of Israel (12:1). The Child whom she carries is, of course, Jesus – the one who "will rule all the nations with an iron sceptre" (12:5). The dragon with seven heads that comes and stands in front of the woman, waiting to kill the child the moment he was born (12:4b), is none other than the city of Rome, founded on seven hills and which was bent on destroying the Jewish state of Israel. Hearing the news that Jesus had been born, the Roman King, Herod, took extreme measures to kill the child (Matthew 2). The Woman ultimately gives birth to a male child – Jesus is born to the nation of Israel – who is taken up to Heaven to be with God (the ascension of Jesus after his resurrection as reported in Acts 1:1-11). All of these 'signs' appeared in Heaven (Revelation 12:1). Since the child is out of reach, the dragon comes to kill the Woman. But the Woman is given two wings of an eagle to fly from heaven to a desert on earth where she will be kept safe for a short period of time (Revelation 12:6, 14), which probably refers to the Jews in exile during the Roman rule. The dragon, instead of following her to the earth, goes up beyond the sky to kill Jesus who is seated at the right hand of God in Heaven. But the chief angel, Michael, meets the dragon and a bloody fight is started: "Michael and his angels fought against the dragon, and the dragon and his angels fought back" (Revelation 12:7) (NIV). But the dragon was no match for Michael, and he was hurled down to earth along with his angels – where the Woman is (Revelation 12:8-9). There is a great celebration in Heaven because of securing the victory over against the dragon (Revelation 12:10-12). The dragon then remembers that the Woman is still hiding on earth. He goes to her and opens his mouth and spews water like a river, to overtake the woman and sweep her away with the torrent (Revelation 12:15). But the earth opens up its mouth and swallows up all the water (Revelation 12:16). The dragon is enraged at this and goes, instead, for the Woman's other children – the Christians (Revelation 12:17).

The first thing to note is that this chapter uses highly coloured picture language: a Woman clothed with the sun and standing on the moon, a dragon with seven heads and ten horns, thousands of starts falling on earth and the earth still remaining in one piece, the formation of wings for the Woman clothed with the sun and the river of water flooding out from the dragon's mouth are not – and could not! – be taken literally. What is literal is the message that lies underneath such a cosmic picture language: Rome (and behind it, the Satan) flexes its muscle and has brought great oppression for Israel, Jesus and the Church, but nevertheless the final victory belongs to all those who stand firm in their faith in God, even if it means they will have to be killed as martyrs (Revelation 12:11). The other thing to note is the direct link between Michael and his angels in Heaven with God's people on earth:

> Then war broke out in heaven. Michael and his angels fought against the dragon... The great dragon was hurled down... They triumphed over him by the blood of the Lamb...
>
> Revelation 12:7, 9, 11 (NIV)

Who are "they" who triumphed over the dragon? The answer is clear: Michael and his angels (12:7). But verse 11 goes on to say that "they did not love their lives so much as to shrink from death." Who are "they" now? Answer: those followers of Jesus who are persecuted and martyred for their faith. The suffering of Jesus' followers caused by Roman persecution is projected on to the cosmic screen of Heaven as the battle between Michael and the dragon. This was taking place during the first century A.D. under the Roman rule of the Emperor Nero. But the popular reading of this passage disconnects the earthly reality of the heavenly battle and teleports the heavenly battle way back into the past where man had not yet been created. A similar misreading of the text by ripping the context is Luke 10:18 where Jesus says to his disciples, "I saw Satan fall like lightning from heaven."

In context, Jesus appoints 72 followers of his and sends then two by two to every place which he was going to visit (Luke 10:1). They are commanded to heal the sick and announce the invasion of God's Kingdom on earth (10:9). They do as they are told and report to Jesus saying, "Lord, even the demons submit to us in your name" (10:17) (NIV). This is the report to which Jesus replies, "I saw Satan fall like lightning from heaven." He then goes on to explain what that means:

> I have given you authority to trample on snakes and scorpions and to overcome all the power of the enemy; nothing will harm you.

Luke 10:19 (NIV)

Here again, the Satan's fall from heaven is linked to the miracles performed by the 72 followers of Jesus because of the authority given to them. We shouldn't disconnect the earthly reference to the Satan's fall and allow it to float into the past. Such biblical gymnastics should be avoided at all costs.

Lastly, the Satan was not present in the Garden of Eden. Although it is tempting to see the serpent in the Garden of Eden as the Satan, interacting with Eve and deceiving her into eating from the forbidden Tree (Genesis 3:1-6), the context doesn't allow us to make any such identification. The serpent is one of the wild creatures that God had created on the sixth day and saw that it was "good" (Genesis 3:1, 1:24-25). Outside Eden, the beasts were undomesticated and wild. God had created it that way. And Adam and Eve, as Royal Priests, were commissioned to safeguard the Garden from foreign intrusion by these beasts. But because the serpent didn't look so wild (it appeared subtle, prudent, crafty), Eve was tricked into believing the lie of the serpent. This explains why, in later texts, the Satan comes to be associated with the serpent: he too is a deceiver of the nations (Revelation 12:9). But there is no indication in the text of Genesis that the serpent was in fact the Satan.

Who or what, then, is the Satan? What is his role? Why did God create him? Why hasn't God destroyed him? We will attempt to provide biblical answers to these questions. The word 'Satan' literally means, 'The Accuser.' He is the one who is supposed to bring *legitimate* charges against everyone who disobeys God's commandments. Hence he is likened to someone who holds the position of the Director of Public Prosecutions.[13]

The clearest evidence of this is in the book of Job. There is a meeting held in the Heavenly lawcourt and God, the King and Judge, has called all his angels to report their duties to him. Along with the angels comes *the Accuser.* God had given him the role of a professional accuser – a spy – whose task was to travel the globe and look for people who commit sins and bring it to God's notice. The scholar James Wharton gives us an analogy from the ancient world:

> Every emperor in the ancient world required agents who moved throughout the empire looking for signs of treason or malfeasance that required the emperor's attention.[14]

In the book of Job, contrary to popular belief, the Satan is not God's enemy – the devil. He was created and appointed by God to bring legal charges against those who disobeyed God and hence was instrumental in maintaining law and order in the world. But as time goes by, and for some unknown reasons, he overplays his role as *the Accuser* by bringing *false* accusations against people. He also lures people into committing sins so that he can bring *true* accusations against them as well. That is why the Bible calls him the accuser of our brothers and sisters:

> Then I heard a loud voice in heaven say: "Now have come the salvation and the power and the kingdom of our God, and the authority of his Messiah. For the accuser of our brothers and sisters, who accuses them before our God day and night, has been hurled down..."

> Revelation 12:10 (NIV)

Day and night he accuses us before God, bringing both false as well as true charges before God. But God still holds him in position of authority because ultimately, God will use the Satan, the Accuser, to purify the world of all wickedness and then the Satan will be destroyed. In the book of Revelation, after the Satan is bound up for a thousand years – a symbolic imagery in itself, he is let loose for a short period of time during which he will gather the whole world to participate in a bloody battle against God's chosen people.

> But fire came down from heaven and devoured them. And the devil, who deceived them, was thrown into the lake of burning sulphur...

Revelation 20:9b-10a (NIV)

This dramatic event is followed by the Great Judgement of God where every single shred of wickedness is abolished (v11-v15) which then results in the new heavens and the new earth (Revelation 21-22). N. T. Wright comments,

> [T]he release of the satan, though unexpected and unwelcome to us, seems to be part of the strange divine plan to ensure that all evil, every trace, is rooted out of the world, allowing the great transformation into 'new heaven and new earth' to take place. The satan, the accuser, must do all he can, and then he too must be destroyed. It is as though, faced with a farmyard full of infected material, one were first to find the ideal broom with which to sweep the yard clean, and then were to throw the broom itself into the fire, its horrible work done.[15]

And so the point can be made that *sometimes* (many times? most times?) suffering falls on people because of the activities of the demonic, which are themselves allowed to dominate the world in accordance with the divine purposes of God for the world. Note the emphasis I make: *sometimes* suffering comes as a punishment, *sometimes* suffering comes randomly, *sometimes* it comes as the abuse of the free will, *sometimes* it comes to glorify God, *sometimes* it comes to edify the soul and build up moral character, *sometimes* it comes with a hope of some greater good, *sometimes* it comes to test our faith in God and *sometimes* it comes because of diabolical forces in the world. Just as the Garden has flowers in *some places*, trees in *some places*, footpaths in *some places*, fountains in *some places*, ponds in *some places*, sand in *some places* and grass in *some places*, so too God's reasons for allowing evil and suffering have their own places in the grand purposes of God.

But this isn't like any other garden. This Garden has, at its centre, a Tree. This Tree keeps shedding forth its leaves to all the places in the

Garden. And there is rejuvenation and healing taking place wherever the leaves of the Tree fall. Somehow the whole Garden is nourished and sustained by this Tree. As the Bible puts it,

> The leaves of the tree were for the healing of the nations.

> Revelation 22:2 (ESV)

Regardless of the reasons we suffer, which may appear either just or unjust to us, there is this Tree that keeps reminding us of hope, healing and love. Somehow the justice and injustice of our sufferings are healed by the continual withering of this Tree. In other words, the death of Jesus on the cross is the central event in history that justifies the apparently unjustifiable sufferings down through ages past, present and future. All our anger, frustration, dissatisfaction, sorrow, tears and confusion, which suffering has wrought upon us, can be taken up to this Tree to be comforted there. The cross thus becomes the centre of interpretation for the Bible as a whole. As Richard Hays comments,

> The claim that Jesus' death and resurrection is the central decisive act of God for the salvation of humankind means that the cross becomes the hermeneutical center for the canon as a whole.[16]

In Jesus, we see every aspect of human life – love, joy, peace, hate, betrayal, bereavement, abandonment, physical and mental torture, unjust suffering and death – transformed into something eternal and worthwhile. And we get to inherit *his* story. As the Bible says,

> But rejoice inasmuch as you participate in the sufferings of Christ, so that you may be overjoyed when his glory is revealed.

> 1 Peter 4:13 (NIV)

The word for 'participate' means to join oneself as an associate and become a partner with him and therefore "we share in his sufferings in order that we may also share in his glory" (Romans 8:17b) (NIV). And yet again, Paul declares,

> I want to know Christ--yes, to know the power of his resurrection and participation in his sufferings, becoming like him in his death, and so, somehow, attaining to the resurrection from the dead.

> Philippians 3:10-11 (NIV)

It is only by sharing the form and pattern of his death will we arrive at the final resurrection from the dead. And the suffering and death of Jesus on the cross show that from God's angle, this was the only way to pull creation from its present state of decay into the new creation. The philosopher Dr. Vince Vitale gives us a good analogy from his personal experience:

> Dr. Frasco – a topflight vascular surgeon – found my family in the hospital waiting room and told that he needed to operate [my dad], and that although there wasn't time to explain why due to the complexity of my dad's condition, there was a good chance he would have to amputate my dad's leg. Despite Dr. Frasco's qualifications, it was tempting in this situation to question him, to be suspicious of his prognosis and his chosen course of action. My dad looked perfectly healthy from the outside. Maybe this surgeon was taking the easy way out. Maybe he'd rather get an amputation over with now rather than have to battle operation after operation so my dad could keep his leg...But suppose Dr. Frasco had come to my family and said that during the operation, my dad was going to need a significant number of blood transfusions, and that they were having trouble finding a suitable donor. And suppose further that Dr. Frasco – out of compassion for my father and my family – offered to donate his own blood. And suppose even further that Dr. Frasco did this at the risk of his own life, perhaps because such a large quantity of blood was needed. Now, in this situation, my response to Dr. Frasco would change markedly...[I]f Dr. Frasco had offered my dad his own blood, I would have been convinced that he was for us. I would have been convinced that we could trust him, and I would have been rightly convinced of this.[17]

This is a remarkable example. If the doctor had taken the extreme measure of risking his own life for the benefit of his patient, then regardless of the clinical prognosis of the patient, we can rightly say that from the doctor's perspective, his chosen course of action was indeed the one and only one – and the right one. If the doctor would have found other ways of rescuing the patient's limb which wouldn't have involved donating several units of his blood to his patient, then isn't it reasonable to think that he would have chosen those less risky ways? The fact that he has chosen this extreme measure of sacrificing his life for his patient shows that he is deeply committed to rescuing his patient by the only way possible. Likewise, the fact that God, in Jesus, has taken the extreme measure of pouring out his own life's blood on the cross shows the necessity of such a sacrifice.

> Was it not necessary that the Christ should suffer these things and enter into his glory?

> Luke 24:26 (ESV)

Yes, the sacrifice of Jesus is both *necessary* and *inevitable* if God's creation has to be rescued from its present state of death and decay to its future state of new creation. Thus the cross of Jesus Christ, symbolised by the Tree at the centre of the Garden, provides consolation *in* all suffering, justification *for* all suffering and redemption *through* suffering. The character of God (that is, the artistic love of God, the inward working of God and the progress-seeking of God) that led him create a world where unjust suffering and death are inbuilt into the very structure of his creation (but weren't intended to remain like that forever) has led him to stand at the centre of his creation and bleed for it. The God who painted the world into existence with the warm breath of his nostrils (Genesis 1:2b) has come to paint the world into a new existence once again – this time with his blood.

This is the Garden Theodicy I propose: that we look at the reasons for suffering as a multicoloured, multitextured and multidimensional garden with the healing power of the cross located right in the middle of it. But there are three very important precautions we ought to take while handling this Garden Theodicy. *First, do not dismantle the Garden Theodicy.* For any instance of suffering, we dare not say, "Well, that's because of the abuser's free will that he suffers." This is because there could be multiple reasons for a person's suffering. A man could suffer because of a complex combination of the abuser's free will, the randomness of the created order, the growth of the person's spirituality, the testing of God and so forth. Hence we shouldn't take one bit of the Garden Theodicy and label it on the person's suffering. I suggest that for any instance of suffering or death, we apply the Garden Theodicy *as a whole* and not as individual parts. *Second, do not generalise any of the parts of the Garden Theodicy.* By claiming that *all* suffering is due to a single reason – be it randomness, free will, satanic activities, for the greater good or to test one's faith – we insult both God and the sufferer. In fact, the very search for a one-size-fits-all theodicy should be ridiculed back and avoided at all costs. Sadly, pastor theologian Timothy Keller, in criticising the common theodicies offered for why God allows suffering, creates just that generalisation in order to critique it.[18] He writes that the soul-making theodicy suffers from "glaring weaknesses"[19] because many types of sufferings kill its victims rather than make them morally and spiritually stronger and that it doesn't account for the death of animals and little children. Or again, he criticises the free will theodicy by saying that it explains "only a certain category of evil"[20] and that the theodicy assumes that God puts up with the horrendous evils of history for merely sustaining the freedom of choice among human beings.[21] Keller wants "the only or main reason"[22] why God allows evil and sees that the common theodicies on offer fail to meet his criteria. He writes,

> [E]ach theodicy provides some plausible explanations for some of the evil in the world – but they always fall short, in the end, of explaining all suffering.[23]

But Keller is clearly missing the point. He blurs the distinction between the explanatory power of a theodicy and its explanatory scope. As I have explained in chapter 3, theodicies are provided for their explanatory power (that is, *how well* they are able to explain why God allows suffering) and not for their explanatory scope (that is, *how much* of the varieties of suffering they are able to explain). Hence we shouldn't generalise any particular theodicy.

Third, do not use inappropriate parts of the Garden Theodicy. The free will theodicy should not be applied to an infant dying of pneumonia. The theodicy of testing the faith of a person should not be used in a situation where the person is killed in a car accident. Even critiques should not discredit a theodicy by trying to show that they are inappropriate in some circumstances. The Garden Theodicy should be looked as a whole and be used appropriately.

Having suggested the ways not to handle the Garden Theodicy, I will now suggest the way to handle it. As we gaze upon this Garden and enter it, our spectacles slowly begin to disintegrate. We are inside the garden but we can no longer see which part of the Garden we are standing on. Our hands are lacerated by the fence while climbing into the garden. Our feet are ulcerated by the stones we stumbled upon. Our back is bruised by the crowded trees we dashed upon. We are injured everywhere we walk. And since we no longer have our glasses, we cannot see what hit us. All we are allowed to see in the Garden is that Tree which was located at the centre of the Garden. This tree has now been stripped of all its branches. Its glory has faded away. A wounded man is hanging on it and is bleeding to death. He happens to be the gardener who had been looking after the Garden for all these years. My proposal is that since we are unable to see, among the list of reasons we have explored so far, what reasons God has in allowing a particular suffering, we shouldn't speculate the reasons why God allows suffering and evil in our lives and in the lives of others. We should not speculate where, in the Garden, we (or others) are standing. A rapist killing an innocent victim, a plane crash killing hundreds of passengers, an epidemic disease killing thousands of villagers, a dictator killing millions of civilians and all the other varieties of all evil, suffering and death should not be placed under a microscope in order to see what reasons exist behind their occurrences. Let God have his own reasons for allowing suffering from the list we had explored. What we are called to do is to look at the Tree with the man hanging on it, fall on our knees and pray for his Kingdom to come and his will to be done on earth as in Heaven, and then get up and *do* the Kingdom work, which leads us into the area of Christian ethics.

Endnotes

[1] John Polkinghorne, *Quarks, Chaos, and Christianity: Questions to Science and Religion* (New York: Crossroad, 1994), p 46-47.

[2] *Creation Untamed*, Kindle location 1115, p 66. Fretheim argues that the satanic figure who appears in the beginning of the book of Job as the cause of Job's suffering is, in fact, the symbol of the chaos of creation which the latter chapters insist is the cause of Job's suffering.

[3] *Ibid.*, Kindle location 1390 and 1349, p 86, 83. Emphasis original. Brackets mine.

[4] *Ibid.*, Kindle *location 443, p 27. Brackets mine.*

[5] For those who are interested in knowing how God is still active in the world by performing miracles, I would suggest reading the book by the New Testament scholar Craig S. Keener, titled *Miracles: The Credibility of the New Testament Accounts*, 2 vols. (Grand Rapids: Baker Academic, 2011).

[6] *Creation Untamed*, Kindle location 1393, p 86.

[7] *Ibid.*, Kindle location 1395, p 86.

[8] *Suffering*, p 79, 60. Emphasis original. Brackets mine.

[9] Richard B. Hays, *First Corinthians: Interpretation* (Louisville, KY: *John Knox* Press, 2011), p 27, 36. Brackets mine. Originally published in hardback in United States by Westminister John Knox Press in 1997. Louisville, Kentucky.

[10] *Harold Kushner, When Bad Things Happen to Good People* (New York: Schocken Books, 1981).

[11] Sadly, even Arthur McGill hints in that direction when he writes,

"[T]he God revealed in Jesus Christ is not just any God, or even a being who is endowed with all sorts of supreme attributes. This God is very peculiar, and in a fundamental way very ungodlike." –*Suffering*, p 61. I disagree with his characterisation of God and I am proposing a way to hold on to God's 'supreme attributes' of omnipotence, omnibenevolence and omniscience even in light of the 'very ungodlike' God we meet in Jesus Christ.

[12] Compare Judges 13:19 and Job 10:16.

[13] "It is clear the world *satan* is a title, an office: he is the "accuser," the director of public prosecutions." - N.T. Wright, *Evil and the Justice of God* (Downers Grove: InterVarsity Press, 2006), p 69. Emphasis original.

[14] James A. Wharton, *Job* (Louisville, KY: *John Knox* Press, 1999), p 16.

[15] N. T. Wright, *Revelation for Everyone* (Louisville, KY: *John Knox* Press, 2011), p 182-183.

[16] Richard B. Hays, *The moral vision of the New Testament: community, cross, new creation: a contemporary introduction to New Testament ethics* (N.Y.: Harper Collins, 1996), p 309.

[17] Dr. Vince Vitale (co-author), *Why Suffering? Finding Meaning and Comfort When Life Doesn't Make Sense* (Faith Words, New York, Boston, Nashville, 2014), Kindle location 1004-1014, p 84-85.

[18] In Timothy Keller's *Walking With God Through Pain and Suffering* (Hodder & Stoughton, London, 2013), Kindle Edition.

[19] *Ibid.*, Kindle location 1525.

[20] *Ibid.*, Kindle location 1548.

[21] *Ibid.*, Kindle location 1576.

[22] *Ibid.*, Kindle location 1583.

[23] *Ibid.*, Kindle location 1607.

14
The Ethics of the Kingdom of God

W
hen the concept of ethics is placed within the context of creation and new creation, a whole new dimension of human attitude and behaviour will emerge. God has crafted man in the divine image and appointed him to be his representative on earth so that he can carry out his intentions for the world through his image-bearers. Man is given the role of being a 'Royal Priest' whose task is to be the hands and feet of God in the shaping of the world. He is called to *"rule over"* God's creation (Genesis 1:28). Such a rule begins from the inside of the human heart:

> Do not offer any part of yourself to sin as an instrument of wickedness, but rather offer yourselves to God as those who have been brought from death to life; and offer every part of yourself to him as an instrument of righteousness.

Romans 6:13 (NIV)

The word 'instrument' literally means weapons of warfare. God had commissioned humans to *"rule over"* all that he had made. But, ironically, we have allowed sin to *"rule over"* us. It is time, says Paul, to use our body parts – our eyes, our mouth, our ears, our brain, our hands and our feet – as *weapons of warfare* to rule over all sinful thoughts and behaviours. Humans were also called to "subdue" – to bring to control - God's creation (Genesis 1:28), which also begins from the inside of the human heart:

> [W]e take captive every thought to make it obedient to Christ.

2 Corinthians 10:5b (NIV)

The word for 'captive' means to "subdue" (that is, to bring to control). In order for man to shape the world the way God intends, he has to begin by shaping his own heart in the right way. He needs to be in the process of overcoming sin in his life and be in a right relationship with God *so that* he can be who he was truly created to be: a Royal Priest in God's earth. Many Christians emphasise the former and ignore the latter. They believe that all that matters in life is to have a personal relationship with God and stay like that until they die so that they can go to Heaven. Thus Christianity has become a private activity as something which you do behind closed doors inside Churches and homes. It has come to have no relevance to the outside world of science, politics, technology, medicine and the environment. But the whole point of Christian spirituality – of praying on our knees, meditating on the Bible, singing praises to God and leading a holy life, which are all part of the being a (Royal) Priest – is to be energised so as to extend the royal rule of God into every nook and corner of the world. Paul declares in 2 Corinthians 5:17, "*ei tis en Christō kainē ktisis*" – if anyone in Christ, new creation![1]

One day God is going to make the whole universe a new creation. But he creates little pieces of new creation – you and me! - in advance so that they can join the larger project, which is the original Adamic project, of making the earth into paradise so that the divine presence can come and life fully and nourish every atom in the world.[2] We have to have this double vision of salvation: God saves us from our sins *so that* we can be the saving people for the world. This means that, as God's people, we are to engage in the activities that take the world forward into the new creation. Since there will be no more death or suffering, crying or pain in the new creation, we should engage in activities that alleviate pain and suffering and work towards the health of human and animal life. Since there will be no more injustice, poverty and violence in the new creation, we should be fighting against them now and work for justice, equality and peace. Since there *will be* trees, plants, mountains and rocks in the new creation, we should be engaged in the preservation of the environment in the present. Since there *will be* buildings and pavements in the new creation (Revelation 22:2), we should be working towards technological developments in the present. To take Christianity seriously means to be actively engaged in areas of science, politics, technology, medicine, sociology, ecology and so on. But they all begin with an undefiled personal relationship with Jesus Christ. What Jesus achieved on the cross and in his resurrection isn't something that will automatically bring about the renewal of creation. If it did, we should be living in a pain-free world right now! No – Jesus achieved something unique on the cross and in his resurrection which needs to be *implemented* in the world. N.T. Wright comments,

> The call of the gospel is for the church to *implement* the victory of God in the world *through suffering love*. The cross is not just an example to be followed; it is an achievement to be worked out, put into practice.[3]

Imagine an old and abandoned house where the paints in the walls and doors have faded and they are covered all over with dust and dirt. Somebody has placed a paint bucket full of colourful paint in the centre of the house. Now just because there is paint in the house doesn't mean that the house will automatically become colourful. There needs to be a paint brush and someone who will dip the brush into the bucket and paint the house efficiently. Or imagine someone creating a vaccine that can cure a deadly disease. Simply creating the vaccine in a laboratory and keeping it inside a refrigerator is not going to transform the world. It requires implementation. Likewise, in the death and resurrection of Jesus, God has achieved a unique victory over the powers of evil. But that victory needs to be implemented in real life by *us*. But why us? The answer is because right from the beginning of creation, God is committed to work *through* his image-bearers to perform his actions in the world. God has worked through Jesus and Jesus now works through his followers to propel the creation forward into its new mode of existence. Since Jesus works through imperfect people like ourselves to transform the world, creation is not going to move forward in a linear progression. There will be ups and downs in the progress of creation, as evident in the history of Christianity down through the centuries. Nevertheless God, in Jesus, will achieve his intended plan for his creation. As the familiar old hymn says,

Jesus who died shall be satisfied, and earth and Heav'n be one.[4]

Hence the point can be made: the idea of man created as a Royal Priest and standing in between creation and new creation provides the *commitment and the energy* for *both* personal holiness *and* public engagement. A further aspect of being a Royal Priest on earth needs to be mentioned. An ideal King and Priest will not cling to his life when his life is demanded from him. He will give it up, as did Jesus himself, for rescuing others. In our minds, the fullness of life consists in accumulating all wealth and health to ourselves. Hence suffering and death seem so far away and disconnected from what we imagine the fullness of life to be. But as I have already argued earlier, the fullness of life as a Royal Priest is oriented *towards* suffering and death, not away from it. This may be counter-intuitive to many of us, but the cross of Christ demands such radical revisions of our intuitions. Many times we may be squeezed at our brush-tips to spill out the paint required to fill the canvas of the earth. God can even work through tragedies in our lives to bring the transformation he intends for the world. For example, people's lives can change and an entire community can be affected by the life of someone who had been so intimate with God even in the midst of being bedridden for ten years and dying of cardiac arrest. Royal Priests can perform their God-given tasks even in their suffering and death. In fact, according to Jesus, *that* is life lived at its fullest potential (John 12:24).

In conclusion, the doctrine of humans being a Royal Priesthood is stark contrast with Buddhist and Hindu doctrines which encourages its followers to remain callous to the ever-continuing world of suffering and pain and provide the way of *escaping* this dark and gloomy world. Christianity also stands in contrast with the Islamic teaching of *accepting* this world as it is (that is, as a testing filed) where pain and suffering will always remain until God destroys this world and takes us to Heaven.

Endnotes

[1] This is the literal translation from the original Greek text of the New Testament.

[2] "God has brought this judgment into the middle of history, precisely in the covenant-fulfilling work of Jesus Christ, dealing with sin through his death, launching the new world in his resurrection, and sending his Spirit to enable human beings,

through repentance and faith, to become little walking and breathing advance parts of that eventual new creation." - N.T. Wright, *Justification: God's plan and Paul's Vision* (Downers Grove, IL: InterVarsity Press, 2009), p 251.

[3] N.T. *Wright, Evil and the Justice of God* (Downers Grove, IL: InterVarsity Press, 2006), p 98.

[4] Maltbie D. Babcock, This is My Father's World. http://cyberhymnal.org/htm/t/i/tismyfw.htm (Last accessed on 20-12-15).

15
A Call to Faith

One of the great stories I had read as part of my high school curriculum was Oscar Wilde's wonderful story of the Selfish Giant.[1] I came to realise its powerful Christian theme only in recent months. None of my teachers who taught us the story had ever mentioned the Christian theme behind it. In Wilde's story, there is this Giant who is so possessive of his garden that he wouldn't allow the children to come play in it. "He was a very selfish Giant."[2]

One day, when the spring season had come, the selfish Giant looked out at his garden and found that his garden alone was still covered with snow and frost. "I cannot understand why the spring is so late in coming,"[3] he said to himself as he was looking out at his cold white garden. But one day, to his surprise, he saw that the long awaited spring had at last come to his garden, only because the children found a way to enter into the garden without his permission. "In every tree that he could see there was a little child. And the trees were so glad to have the children back again that they had covered themselves with blossoms, and were waving their arms gently above the children's heads."[4]

But in one corner of the garden, winter still prevailed because there was a little child standing under a tree, unable to climb over its branches. The Giant's heart melted for the little child and he went and helped the child sit on one of the branches of the tree. The little child hugged and kissed him in return. And spring immediately filled the entire garden. Every day the children went up to play in the garden but the little child who made the Giant's heart melt in sympathy was no more to be found. "Years went over, and the Giant grew very old and feeble."

It was the winter season yet once again and his garden was cold white all over. "Suddenly he rubbed his eyes in wonder, and looked and looked. It certainly was a marvellous sight. In the farthest corner of the garden was a tree quite covered with lovely white blossoms. Its branches were all golden, and silver fruit hung down from them, and underneath it stood the little boy he had loved."[6] The Giant was overjoyed to see the little child who had gone missing for years. When he ran close to the child, his joy turned into sorrow mingled with anger. "For on the palms of the child's hands were the prints of two nails, and the prints of two nails were on the little feet."[7] The Giant cried out to the child saying,

> Who hath dared to wound thee? ...tell me, that I may take my big sword and slay him.
>
> 'Nay!' answered the child; 'but these are the wounds of Love.'[8]

The child happened to be a divine child. He smiled at the Giant and said, "You let me play once in your garden, to-day you shall come with me to my garden, which is Paradise."[9] The next day, as the children come to play in the garden, they found the Giant lying dead in his garden and covered all over with white blossoms.

Such a fascinating story! I offer a couple of reflections from the story. First, about the child who came. The Giant lived a very selfish life, not wanting to share any of his property with others. The three most sought after things in our world are money, sex and power, and they reflect the self-centered character of human beings that has been the cause of so much suffering. And yet the Son of God chose to come into this world to confront it with the power of *wounded love*.

"He came. He entered space and time and suffering. He came, like a lover. Love seeks above all intimacy, presence, togetherness. Not happiness. "Better unhappy with her than happy without her"—that is the word of a lover. He came. That is the salient fact, the towering truth, that alone keeps us from putting a bullet through our heads. He came... In coming into our world he came also into our suffering... Are we broken? He is broken with us...Does he descend into all our hells? Yes... he came into life and death, and he still comes. He is still here...He is gassed in the ovens of Auschwitz. He is sneered at in Soweto. He is cut limb from limb in a thousand safe and legal death camps for the unborn strewn throughout our world, where he is too tiny for us to see or care about. He is the most forgotten soul in the world. He is the one we love to hate. He practices what he preaches: he turns his other cheek to our slaps. That is what love is, what love does, and what love receives. Love is why he came. It's all love. The buzzing flies around the cross, the stroke of the Roman hammer as the nails tear into his screamingly soft flesh, the infinitely harder stroke of his own people's hammering hatred, hammering at his heart—why? For love. God is love, as the sun is fire and light, and he can no more stop loving than the sun can stop shining. Henceforth, when we feel the hammers of life beating on our heads or on our hearts, we can know—we must know—that he is here with us, taking our blows. Every tear we shed becomes his tear. He may not yet wipe them away, but he makes them his. Would we rather have our own dry eyes, or his tear-filled ones? He came. He is here. That is the salient fact. If he does not heal all our broken bones and loves and lives now, he comes into them and is broken, like bread, and we are nourished. And he shows us that we can henceforth use our very brokenness as nourishment for those we love...There is, as we saw, one good reason for not believing in God: evil. And God himself has answered this objection not in words but in deeds and in tears. Jesus is the tears of God."[10]

Jesus is love, not in theory, but in action. He is Immanuel, God with us. The problem of evil requires that we not only look at it from an intellectual perspective, as we have done in this book, but also that we look at it on an emotional level. A lot of people, when faced with real-life experiences of suffering, do not want logical answers to why we suffer, but emotional answers that can comfort them and offer them hope. But, of course, the emotional answers shouldn't offer a *false* comfort and a *false* hope to the sufferers. The emotional answers must be grounded in reality. I will address how the cross of Jesus Christ addresses the emotional problem of suffering and is also grounded in historical truth.

I had already hinted earlier that the crucifixion of Jesus Christ offers consolation *in* all suffering, justification *for* all suffering and redemption *through* suffering. First, the element of comfort. The thought that God himself – the Creator of the cosmos – has come into our suffering world in weakness, in the person of Jesus Christ, to share our suffering is a source of remarkable comfort for us.

> [He] emptied himself, by taking the form of a servant, being born in the likeness of men.
>
> Philippians 2:7 (ESV)

Jesus has taken upon himself the same 'emptiness' that characterised God's creation in the beginning: the world was without form and 'empty' (Genesis 1:2). Yes, he too was without form and empty (Isaiah 52:14, Philippians 2:7).

> God as it were takes the 'nothing' into himself in the destruction of his own son, which as it were frees us from the shadow of nothingness cast by creation. God, having rejected the nothing in creation, takes it into his own story in the act of redemption on the cross.[11]

Even in the darkest of all agony, as we sit in utter horror at what has happened to us or to our loved ones, even there the familiar old cross – that wooden and rugged cross – is present near for us to cling on to and weep. God comforts his people, not with abstract words, but with the Word fleshed out and made human (John 1:14).

Second, the suffering of God in the face of Jesus Christ also provides justification for all suffering. If God has taken the extreme step of pouring out his own life into the world he had created, then that rules out any other way of saving the world. God is justified in allowing all the pain and suffering in the world to continue because the cross of Jesus Christ demonstrates that the only way forward into the new creation is by passing through all the pain and suffering. Finally, the death of Jesus Christ provides redemption through suffering. If all our sufferings are written into his story of the cross and the resurrection, then our suffering can be redemptive. The sufferings we go through this life, says Paul, cannot be compared to the weight of glory that is to be revealed for us

(Romans 8:18). When we compare the totality of our sufferings with the glory that God has in store for us, it would be like comparing a speck of dust with the ocean!

But is Jesus really divine and was he really crucified and killed? Did he really resurrect from the dead on the third day following his death? We will now look at historical considerations of Jesus. Who was he *really*? A lot of secular people today just assume that Jesus was one among the founders of religion, a moral teacher and a social activist while a lot of religious people assume that he was merely one of the thousand manifestations of 'God' (whatever they mean by the word 'God'). But what do historical scholars who are specialised in looking at the ancient Greek manuscripts and archaeological evidences have to say about Jesus? They say that many of the ancient people who heard Jesus speak thought that he was a blasphemer, someone who insults God. Jesus had spoken to them of his unique relationship with God, elevating himself above all people and prophets who had gone before him (Mark 12:1-12), who alone knows God and reveals this God to people whom he chooses to reveal (Matthew 11:27), whose death alone can atone for human sin and open up a new and everlasting relationship with God (Mark 14:22-24) and who alone will come on the clouds in divine majesty to judge every people on earth and be seated right next to God in the divine throne of heaven (Mark 14:62). This naturally led the people of his day to say that he was mad because they assumed that his claims were all *false* (Mark 3:21). Even modern scholars have been forced to ask the inevitable question: Was Jesus mad?[12]

James Dunn, the historian who asked this question, is not a conservative Christian, but he writes that the question of madness has to be raised "in the light of the *distinctiveness,* even uniqueness Jesus sensed in his relation to God and to his kingdom, in his exercise of power and authority... Certainly we can hardly deny that Jesus was abnormal in some sense; but it is an abnormality which cannot really be explained in terms of insanity... Perhaps after all we are dealing not just with an abnormal person but with a unique abnormality which has no real parallel either in the history of religions or in the case history of modern psychiatry."[13]

The conclusion of James Dunn is that Jesus was *not* mad or insane; but he is uniquely different from every other religious figure in is high and lofty ideas about himself. Former atheist C.S. Lewis writes,

> I am trying here to prevent anyone saying the really foolish thing that people often say about Him: I'm ready to accept Jesus as a great moral teacher, but I don't accept his claim to be God. That is the one thing we must not say. A man who was merely a man and said the sort of things Jesus said would not be a great moral teacher. He would either be a lunatic — on the level with the man who says he is a poached egg — or else he would be the Devil of Hell. You must make your choice. Either this man was, and is, the Son of God, or else a madman or something worse. You can shut him up for a fool, you can spit at him and kill him as a demon or you can fall at his feet and call him Lord and God, but let us not come with any patronizing nonsense about his being a great human teacher. He has not left that open to us. He did not intend to.[14]

Theologian Georg Pöhlmann writes,

> With regard to Jesus there are only two possible modes of behaviour: either to believe that in him God encounters us or to nail him to the cross as a blasphemer...There is no third way.[15]

We therefore have two options concerning the identity of Jesus: he is either a false pretender or is really the unique and divine Son of God. Anybody can make claims. In the Bhagavad Gita, Arjuna's charioteer, Krishna, claimed to be the divine Lord of the universe and, as evidence, showed his unchanging and universal form to Arjuna. But did Krishna really reveal his eternal form? The Gita *says* he did. But did it *really* happen in historical reality? We have no way of knowing. Hence Krishna's claim to divinity is questionable from a historical point of view. But what about Jesus? We have some really radical self-claims of Jesus which scholars admit was what the historical Jesus thought of himself. But how do we know that his claims are true? The answer lies in his resurrection from the dead. Historians who have invested their lifetime in the study of the historical Jesus have universally concluded that Jesus was in fact killed by crucifixion in either A.D. 30 or 33.[16] Theologian John McIntyre writes,

> Even those scholars and critiques who have moved to depart from almost everything else within the historical content of Christ's presence on earth have found it impossible to think away the factuality of the death of Christ.[17]

But what happened after his death has surprised almost all contemporary historians. The tomb into which Jesus' body was buried was discovered to be empty on the third day following his death and many friends and foes subsequently reported to have seen Jesus alive, among whom were James, the brother of Jesus who had previously wanted Jesus dead,[18] and Paul, who had previously guarded the coats of the people who were stoning the followers of Jesus to death (Acts 22:20). It is also a fact that both James and Paul became leaders of the early Christian movement and in the end, James was stoned to death and Paul was probably beheaded for his fervent faith in Jesus Christ.[19]

This has led the majority of scholars to conclude that the early followers of Jesus really did see post-mortem appearances which convinced them that they were the appearances of the physically risen Jesus. Accordingly, critical scholar Paula Fredriksen writes,

> The disciples' conviction that they had seen the Risen Christ...[is part of] historical bedrock, facts known past doubting.[20]

Likewise the atheist scholar Gerd Lüdemann admits,

> It may be taken as historically certain that Peter and the disciples had experiences after Jesus's death in which Jesus appeared to them as the risen Christ.[21]

Non-Christian scholars may give naturalistic explanations as to the quality of the experiences which people had about Jesus (such as the hallucination hypothesis), but they admit that they had auditory, visionary and even tactile experiences of the risen Jesus which was of a quality that led them to develop a firm conviction that Jesus was bodily alive in a transformed state, even to the extent that they were willing to die for their belief. N.T. Wright has forcefully argued that the firm belief in the bodily resurrection of Jesus among the early Jewish people *necessitates* that Jesus be bodily resurrected.[22] Having examined all the evidences, he concludes,

> [A]s a historian, I cannot explain the rise of early Christianity unless Jesus rose again, leaving an empty tomb behind him.[23]

Now let's be sure of what I am saying. I am *not* saying that we have undeniable and absolute evidence for Jesus' resurrection.[24] Belief in the resurrection of Jesus certainly requires a leap of faith; but it is a leap of faith *in the direction of evidence.*

We now have to ask how the resurrection of Jesus validates the lofty claims of Jesus about himself. The German theologian Wolfhart Pannenberg explains,

> The resurrection of Jesus acquires such decisive meaning, not merely because someone or anyone has been raised from the dead, but because it is Jesus of Nazareth, whose execution was instigated. . . because he had blasphemed against God. If this man was raised from the dead, then that plainly means that the God whom he had supposedly blasphemed has committed Himself to him.[25]

The resurrection of Jesus, being a divine miracle, means that the God whom Jesus allegedly blasphemed has put his seal of approval on everything Jesus had said and did in his lifetime. Why? Because God would not have raised up someone who had lied about him. It is God announcing to a surprised world saying, "Yes! I approve everything he has said about me and about him. *This is really my beloved Son, listen to him.*"

We now return back to the story of the selfish Giant. When heavy snow had permeated the garden once again, the Giant looked out and, to his surprise, saw that in the farthest corner of the garden alone was a tree covered with blossoms and had golden and silver fruits hanging down from its branches. Underneath the tree stood the little boy he had loved. The child has caused one corner of the garden to blossom. Likewise, Jesus Christ, in his resurrection from the dead, has become the single green tree that has blossomed in the cold white garden of the earth.[26] Spring has come at last upon the barren earth in a small territory as a sign and hope for the entire earth to be filled with evergreen life and beauty. And the Christian proclamation of the Gospel – the good news – is an invitation to participate in that breathtaking world of new creation which God has *already* launched in the resurrection of Jesus.

God offers the invitation for non-believers in Jesus Christ to come to a saving faith in him. You might be an atheist, an agnostic, a Hindu, a Muslim, a Buddhist or anyone else. God doesn't want anyone to perish

(2 Peter 3:9). He wants all people to be saved and to come to the knowledge of the truth (1 Timothy 2:4). Indeed, there will be more joy in God's heavenly council over one person who repents and believe than over all those who already believe (Luke 15:7). God in Christ gently knocks the door of your heart and gives *you* the invitation to become his child. He invites you into the Garden. He may not guarantee a painless life; but he promises to be with you in your pain, and he will make your pain, his.

God himself will be our Shepherd in the Garden. He will make us lie down in green pastures. He will lead us beside the quite waters. He will refresh our souls. He will guide us along the right path for his own name's sake. Even though we may walk through the darkest valley in the Garden, we will fear no evil because he is with us. His rod and his staff, they will comfort us. And when he has made all things new, he will take us to the Father's House to live with him forever (Psalm 23).

Endnotes

[1] Oscar Wilde, "The Selfish Giant" in *The Happy Prince and Other Tales*; illustrated by Walter Crane and Jacomb Hood (London: David Nutt, 1888). Quotations will be from the e-book published by The Floating Press, 2008, under the original title.

[2] Oscar Wilde, *The Happy Prince and Other Tales* (The Floating Press, 2008), p 34.

[3] *Ibid.*, p 35.

[4] *Ibid.*, p 36.

[5] *Ibid.*, p 39.

[6] *Ibid.*

[7] *Ibid.*

[8] *Ibid.*, p 40.

[9] *Ibid.*

[10] Peter Kreeft, *God's Answer to Suffering*, (Ann Arbor, MI: *Servant Books*, 1986), Kindle location 2083-2197.

[11] Ross Thompson, *Wounded Wisdom: A Buddhist and Christian Response to Evil, Hurt and Harm*; Reprint edition (John Hunt Publishing, Alresford, Hampshire, 2011), p 142.

[12] James Dunn, *Jesus and the Spirit* (London: SCM, 1975) p 86.

[13] *Ibid.*, p 87. Emphasis original.

[14] C.S. Lewis, Mere Christianity, (New York: Macmillan, 1952), chap. 1.

[15] Horst Georg Pöhlmann, Abriss der Dogmatik, 3rd rev. ed. (Düsseldorf: Patmos Verlag, 1966), p 230, cited in William Lane Craig, Reasonable Faith, 3rd ed. (Westchester, Ill.: Crossway, 2008), p 327.

[16] Licona, The Resurrection of Jesus, p 318 (footnote).

[17] J. McIntyre, "The Uses of History in Theology" in Studies in World Christianity 7.1 (2001): 1-20, here p 8, cited in Licona, The Resurrection of Jesus, p 311.

[18] John 7:1-5 reports that Jesus was hesitant to go to Judea because the Jewish leaders over there wanted to kill him. But his brothers come to Jesus and insist that he go to Judea, implying that they wanted to get rid of Jesus because they themselves did not believe in whatever Jesus was saying.

[19] For the death of James, see Josephus' Antiquities of the Jews, Book XX, Ch. IX, Sec.1. For Paul's martyrdom, see 1 Clement 5:5-6 (as translated by J.B. Lightfoot). The beheading of Paul is mentioned in the Acts of Paul, which was written about a century after 1 Clement was written (1 Clement was written around A.D. 95 and Paul was killed in the early 60s).

[20] Paula Fredriksen, Jesus of Nazareth, King of the Jews: A Jewish Life and the Emergence of Christianity (New York: Knopf, 1999), p 264. Brackets mine.

[21] Gerd Lüdemann, What Really Happened to Jesus?, trans. John Bowden (Louisville, Kent.: Westminster John Knox Press, 1995), p 80.

[22] N.T. Wright, The Resurrection of the Son of God.

[23] N. T. Wright, "The New Unimproved Jesus," Christianity Today (September 13, 1993), p. 26.

[24] Some might say that absolute evidence requires that we be able to see, hear and touch the risen Jesus ourselves. But does visionary, auditory and tactile evidence count as undeniable evidence? Isn't it logically possible that we are just brains collected in separate tubes by a mad scientist and electrically stimulated to generate our everyday experiences? If it were so, then even if I see someone physically stand before me, in reality there wouldn't be anybody standing in front of me! Undeniable and absolute evidence requires that we be able to rule out all logically possible counterevidences, which clearly cannot be done. Hence, in our quest for truth, we should be content with reasonable evidence.

[25] Wolfhart Pannenberg, "Jesu Geschichte und unsere Geschichte," in Glaube und Wirklichkeit (München: Chr. Kaiser, 1975), p. 92, as cited in William Lane Craig, The Son Rises: The Historical Evidence for the Resurrection of Jesus (Eugene, OR: Wipf and Stock Publishers, 2000), p 141. The citation reference is in p 156.

[26] Jesus calls himself the green tree in Luke 23:31.

Conclusion

This book has been a quest for answers to the deepest question of life that man can ask: why is there suffering? We began by looking at the internal consistency of affirming both the existence of God and reality of suffering. We then explored whether or not the reality of suffering mounts a significant attack on the probability of the existence of God. Then we saw how there exists an interconnection between God and evil that makes denying the existence of God impossible while affirming the reality of evil. We then explored the inadequacies in religious responses to the problem of suffering, showing how Buddhism offered the way of escape, Hinduism the way of illusion and Islam the way of fate. Contrary to these religions, we saw how Christianity offered a realistic view of suffering by God in Christ taking upon himself the sorrow of the world, thereby liberating his creation from its fate of decay and offering us, not a way of escape from the world, but the energy for active engagement so that we may be agents that bring real transformation in this world.

The Christian response to the logical problem of evil lies in doctrine of God freshly rethought around Jesus Christ. Christianity agrees with premise 1 in affirming that God is omnipotent, omniscient and omnibenevolent. Premise 2 said that if God is omnipotent, then he can create a world without evil. Christianity responds by saying that "can" doesn't necessarily imply "will." Premise 3 stated that if God is omniscient, then he will know what evil will happen in the world and he will have the knowledge of how to eliminate them if they occurred. Christianity agrees; but argues that since God is committed to the progress of his creation, he will not

create a world without evil in the beginning, but will rather create a world
with evil and then work from within and through agents in order to make
it a world without evil. Premise 4 stated that if God is omnibenevolent,
then he will want to create a world without evil. Christianity argues that
the nature of divine love is to empty itself and give life to others at the
expense of oneself. If God is said to be the embodiment of *this* love,
then the world *requires* that it be empty and without life for it to overflow
with the powerful love of God revealed supremely in the crucified Christ.
Christianity, therefore, *disagrees* with premise 5 of the logical argument
which stated that God and evil cannot co-exist.

Christianity also offers a sharp critique to the evidential argument from
evil. It agrees with premise 1 which stated that gratuitous evils exist in
our world because God has made the world with several loose ends and
not like a tight machine; but it argues that, through the cross of Christ,
all pointless sufferings can be redeemed and aligned towards the overall
benefit for the sufferer (Romans 8:28). Christianity disagrees with premise
2 which stated that a good God would prevent gratuitous evils from
happening in our world by arguing for a revision of the word "good" in
relation to God by arguing for God as the Cosmic Artist with the messy
brush of creativity in his hand. In William Rowe's example of the fawn
being trapped inside a forest fire and suffocating to death, responding
philosophers have banged their heads in trying to find a specific reason
that would vindicate God's justice in allowing such seemingly pointless
suffering. Christianity offers a better and a more robust answer: the
fawn suffered because of the untamed nature of God's creation. God
has allowed fire to be itself, the air to be itself, the wood and the leaves
to be themselves, and is committed not to micromanage the world, like
an engineer, to make sure that everything works fine. This would entail
the occurrences of many gratuitous evils in our world that are consistent
with the biblical character of God that I have argued for.

Christianity agrees with Buddhism's first and second Noble Truths
in affirming that there is intense suffering in our world and that its cause
is primarily the self-centered attitude of human beings. But it differs in
offering the solution to the problem, not in the empty self of man, but

in the divine self of God. Christianity differs from Hinduism in arguing that the purpose of life is not union with Brahman, but *communion* with God. Christianity differs from Islam in arguing that God is not an ardent Examiner in the test of life, but a loving Father who will risk his own life for the sake of his children.

Suffering will continue to be a "problem." But I hope that this book has enlightened readers to see the problem of suffering in a new light. Although it might be said that God is the ultimate cause of suffering (since he is the creator of the world), paradoxically, he is man's only cure to the problem of suffering. The Bible says,

Come, let us return to the LORD. He has torn us to pieces but he will heal us; he has injured us but he will bind up our wounds.

Hosea 6:1 (NIV) (see also Job 5:18 and Deuteronomy 32:39)

Come! Come! Come, and take the free gift of the water of life (Revelation 22:7). Though the journey may scar your day, his grace shall guide your way! You will have nothing to fear; for he will be there, radiating the entire sphere! Even so, come Lord Jesus!